Scribe Publications
SUFFICIENT GRACE

Born in rural Wisconsin, Amy Espeseth immigrated to Australia in the late 1990s and lives in Melbourne. A writer, publisher and academic, she is the recipient of the 2007 Felix Meyer Scholarship in Literature, the 2010 QUT Postgraduate Creative Writing Prize, and the 2012 CAL Scribe Fiction Prize. *Sufficient Grace* won the 2009 Victorian Premier's Literary Award for an unpublished manuscript.

Sufficient Grace

Amy Espeseth

SCRIBE

Melbourne

Scribe Publications Pty Ltd

18–20 Edward St, Brunswick, Victoria, Australia 3056
50A Kingsway Place, Sans Walk, London, EC1R 0LU, UK

First published by Scribe 2012

Typeset in 11.5/15.5 pt Dante MT by the publishers
Printed and bound by CPI Group (UK) Ltd, Croydon, CR0 4YY

National Library of Australia
Cataloguing-in-Publication data

Espeseth, Amy.

Sufficient Grace.

9781922247162 (UK paperback)
9781921942891 (E-book)

Wisconsin–Fiction.

A823.4

scribepublications.com.au
scribepublications.co.uk

For my family.
We did the best we could.

We are hard pressed on every side, but not crushed;
perplexed, but not in despair; persecuted, but not
abandoned; struck down, but not destroyed.
2 Corinthians 4:8–9

AND THEN THEY STRING THEM UP. BRAIDED ROPES FLY UP through the high crotches of the old birch by the shed and slide back down the trunk like nightcrawler ghosts. Daddy starts pulling on one end of the rope, each pull pushing a moist cloud of breath out his mouth into the cold blue air. Higher and higher the deer rises until his hooves are hanging level with Daddy's head. That's my brother Reuben's buck — only a yearling — but his horns'll push three inches, and it will make him legal.

Another deer rises, cutting through the sharp air along with the sun that is sending heat toward our November morning. Reuben is pulling on the end of this rope. The deer is thicker around with well-muscled thighs and rump and will make good eating. Daddy took her because she kept standing there in the snow, stupid, just staring at him in his tree.

Mine's next, and I can feel my legs quaking even inside my thick layers and crusty mud boots. I'm a little embarrassed that, even with him high up in the tree, you can still see the white spots on his hindquarters and that he ain't even half the size of Daddy's deer. But when I heard the low swift whistle from Daddy's stand, I just pulled up quick and aimed and fired, my arms quaking hard even after I shot him. I know now that Daddy meant for me to take the big doe, but I still don't know why I chose the fawn. Reuben says that I got the tag so I shouldn't be worrying; it was a blessing to draw an antlerless permit, so he was mine to take, baby or not. I was glad when Daddy took his momma too; she almost looked relieved.

Sun's not full up and three carcasses are hanging in our tree. Daddy is so proud right now, he is grinning that crooked smile. His whiskers are hanging bits of ice and frozen blood that must've splashed up during the field dress of the deer, and his teeth are tobacco stained. We look the same except I am thirteen and I am a girl. I have blonde hair past my shoulders, even features and clean skin, and that is part of the problem. When I hunt, I braid my hair back and hide it under my cap so that nobody mistakes me for a whitetail. When my daddy smiles, I can't help but smile my version of his crooked smile too.

This old birch, with her peeling white and black strips waving against the blue sky, has shot out three brown and red furry buds this fall morning. Three slabs of venison cooling in the stillness, legs spread wide and swaying in the tree. I think it's probably sacrilegious to wonder which two are the thieves, so I keep that question private to myself. *At the cross, at the cross, where I first saw the light and the burden of my heart rolled away. It was there by faith I received my sight, and now I am happy all the day.*

Daddy says you can tell a lot about a man's heart from the way he kills a deer. First off, a body don't shoot if he ain't willing to take it all the way. A guy takes a bad shot and wounds something good, he best get himself ready for some long trails tracking. In the fading light, squinting at every broken twig and blood-smeared leaf on the path, he trudges along every step wishing he had shot her clean. Some folks around here won't track farther than the tips of their boots, but that's selfish and lazy, and in their hearts I know they know it. I'd rather crawl crackling through the leaves on the floor of the woods for eight miles, scrambling for slobber on berries and squeezing through the brambled patches where she fell, than leave one out there bleeding overnight.

So make sure you know what you are aiming to kill, shoot straight, and always finish what you started. A good shot will bring her down a few yards from your stand, and now that she's down she'll be wailing and kicking and making a ruckus like you won't believe. Most folks don't know that the thing sometimes screams a while once it's hit. They see a pretty doe nosing through their gardens and leaping like a gazelle over the ditches, but can't see that something with grace straight from heaven will fight for her life with all that she's got. And something she's got is a wailing like a sick nursing calf.

Now you got some choices. I've seen some fellas that they leave the thing kicking itself silly in a circle of leaves, bleeding to death and flailing like a child making a snow angel, while they slowly climb down out of their tree and then stand and look at it screaming. That sound pierces my heart and shocks the fear of God into me. I make doubly sure that I will be a good steward of this gift that has been given unto my body. I am thankful for both the meat and my life.

And my first deer is hanging silent in the tree now. Even early this morning, when I shot the fawn, I was not shocked at the sound coming from his mouth. I have heard that crying many times before, me waiting quiet beside my daddy shooting. When I finally got my own chance to shoot last year, I didn't see nothing, didn't even take a shot. But until I was holding the firing gun, I had never heard that death crying coming straight at me, and it scared me. I couldn't think of anything but to make the sound stop. I had heard my uncle preach about the wailing and gnashing of teeth in hell, but I had thought that that was the result of sinners' pain and was their punishment alone. I never knew that the hearing of some other's wailing and gnashing would be another punishment, yet another coal heaped upon our tongues. So, I kept shooting. I shot whatever moved: blew off the deer's front right leg at the knee, hit him again in the hips, and yet again in his baby back. I think that broke his spine, so he stopped hurting right then, and that made me happy.

Still, though, I had to wait for Daddy to come down out of his tree over the way and finish the fawn for me. Shame on me that I didn't do it myself. But I was shaking too hard to climb down the ladder of old boards nailed on the trunk of the tree that led to the ground beneath my stand. Daddy's a big believer in slitting throats; it don't waste a bullet and it's over right quick. As he walked across from his stand, though, he glanced up at me in the tree as I stood quaking. He saw that my face was wet, so he put the muzzle of his rifle to the fawn's tiny head and ended it with a bullet.

I came down from the tree and I lay the deer out on his back; the fawn's quiet face peered upwards through the tangle of tree branches that laced the sky. Even though he was barely past a year and I'm almost grown, he was about as heavy as me, so it was a bit of a struggle to manoeuvre him into a comfortable position. So little blood spilt out in the gutting. It might've looked to be more than it was as it stained the surrounding snow and soaked out through the white until, from above, me and him tangled together must've looked like the stamen of a heart-red flower. Daddy helped me with the parts I wasn't strong enough for, but he still let me guide my way through the carcass. He was mainly off to the side of me, anyway, beneath his stand carving up the fawn's momma.

Then Daddy looped ropes around the neck of the fawn so he could drag both deer together. I should've drug him myself, but I was still puffing from the excitement of shooting and the effort of cleaning him out, so I just gathered up and started carrying the rifles. That was when we heard the shots from Reuben's deer stand across the woods. We heard him fire then fire again. My brother yelled out that he'd filled his tag. Today was a good day for Rundhaugs, but maybe not so good a day for deer.

Before we headed off to find Reuben and start dragging the kill home, while Daddy was bent over his deer, I set down the guns and reached way in the pile of entrails and got my fawn's heart and liver. They were cooling down already; I could feel it. Still, they were hotter than my skin; they seemed to beat in rhythm with my pulse. I didn't have to hold them long, though; I had two square bags made of cheesecloth in my pocket, and I put each organ safely in its own little pouch. Tied with twine, they both would make it home safe and clean. I made the bags in the hope that I would get a deer, that I could give Daddy his favourite treat for supper. He'll be touched I went to the effort. Too bad that there's a hole in the heart where one of my bullets went through. There was enough left to eat, though, and I smiled a bit secretly to myself as we started to make our way home. I held and carried the organs close to my heart and pondered what small things please my father.

November

1

WHAT I KNOW OF WOMEN IS THIS: I CAN SMELL WHEN MY mother is happy. When I go hunting with my daddy and my older brother, I leave off dabbing my mom's perfume behind my ears. The scent the men make from doe glands and urine and such is better; it lets me get closer before killing.

What I know of men is this: when I disappoint, my daddy lets the trees slap my face. When we walk together in the woods, he breaks path, I walk second, and Reuben guards the rear. The trees have sharp, spindly branches to hinder us, and when he's mad, Daddy shoulders them and lets them fly back hard. Maybe we ain't seen any deer or maybe he's tired. Daddy tracking a big buck holds the branches longer and makes my way easy, only unless he's too set on tracking to pause. He and my brother got beards and don't know the sting. Reuben should: his beard is half cheek.

My family is my church, and my church — the Full Quarter Church of Failing — is my family. What I know of women and men I know from Full Quarter. There, folks have sore knees from hunting, farming and praying on concrete, crying out in the sanctuary and in the milking pen alike. Hands callused from axe handles, factory machines, and mixing spoons raise up in praise to the Lord. We sing *holy, holy, holy* and we welcome everybody, former drunks and wife beaters included. We don't drink poison and raise the dead, but we might.

Sometimes I know what they are talking about in church, sitting in the sanctuary in our pews or on folding metal chairs in a circle in the fellowship hall. They talk about the lost, the world, keeping a clean house, and standing before God to give account. But they don't question what I question. Like why we keep trout but leave suckers on riverbanks to die, and which caterpillars turn into butterflies and which to moths. How come cold rises up from the ground? Folks stay busy talking about flesh falling into sin, who and what's under the blood, and their prayer life and spiritual walk. All that is more about women and men, than God. But women and men is where God is.

Sunday means church, so we get up early in the dark. Daddy has warmed the pick-up truck; it's humming in the garage. My brother Reuben is yawning, and Mom's still braiding her hair as we pile into the truck and drive to town.

Before Uncle Ingwald's preaching starts, the worship service goes on for a half an hour, starting with the regular, old-timey hymns and usually finishing with a couple praise songs or choruses. Aunt Gloria, with her wavery, opera-lady voice and baby hands, is leading the singing. Sometimes, when the Spirit lays heavy in the air over the heads of the congregation, he will descend. It seems he descends quite regularly onto Grandma Esther.

My daddy's momma has the gift of tongues. Not that that is much unusual, as most folks in my church have been filled with the Holy Spirit and use heavenly languages to worship and pray in church most Sundays. But Grandma Esther's gift is more than a prayer language: she prophesies. Right when she was filled with the Holy Ghost, my grandma got some of her spiritual gifts, and she got some more as she grew stronger in her walk with the Lord. She grows more powerful daily with Jesus. We don't take up snakes like some churches we hear of in the South, but I bet Grandma could.

Grandma is stronger than a snake, and through Jesus she is stronger than death. Grandma is a discerner of spirits: she can tell the living from the dead, more like good from evil if I understand right. When the Spirit comes upon her and gives her a message for the church, she feels it in her bones whether it is the Lord or the Enemy speaking, trying to lead us astray. How she tells the voices apart, I don't know. But she knows, and the Lord knows, and that is enough.

Everybody is rocking slowly in the pews, standing or sitting as the Spirit leads them, singing their own song of love and joy or weeping out repentance to the Lord. Suddenly, it seems as if the air has been sucked out of the sanctuary, and my skin feels hot and tight. There is a stillness and a quiet like the middle of the woods. Grandma in her pale church dress bolts straight up in her pew. It's time.

'*Hebesheba nonna. Hebesheba nonna. Op it littlemoftastompka, hebesheba nonna. Keptilitforngorna keshnor link gup nonna fortuntintin. Jujkilop my organa rotyu. Jujkilop gorthu jus. Horphush young, most upostable ruk danke!*'

Grandma speaks out the words that the Holy Spirit puts in her heart; the Spirit of God indwells her body and gives the entire congregation a message. She speaks soft and slow, and she speaks harsh and fast. She always speaks the Word of the

Lord. Her rhythm matches the ancient drumming that plays on the reservation radio station, and her voice matches the tribe's low rumbling and pitched cries.

Aunt Gloria waits up at the podium on the stage. Keeping her head still and her eyes open, she waits silently with the congregation. She looks out on us; I see her eyes rest on her children, my cousin Samuel sitting next to his sister Naomi in the front pew. During this time, I'm meant to be praying to the Lord and waiting on one of his servants to bring forth a translation; instead, I'm holding my breath and looking round the room for tongues of fire to be resting on people's heads like the day of Pentecost. I haven't seen any fire yet, but maybe my eyes haven't yet been gifted for the seeing. I close my eyes and pretend I'm just not there, not alive in the Spirit, maybe closer to dead.

But my spirit leaps within me and I hear: *It is hard to tell the living from the dead.*

Then, I see.

In my mind's eye I can see what Grandma speaks: an opossum lies stock still, foam caking in the corners of its mouth and stank coming up from the hindquarters. The thing is laying on a dirt road, feigning death, telling a lie. Its fangy teeth glare up from the ground, daring me to move it, but even if I grab that bait by the tail and drag it off the road, the liar won't start. Possums blur the line between the quick and the dead.

Nasty pinched face with stinky white fur, that ain't attractive to me. Once, Grandma told me that she'd used an opossum fur sponge in the bathtub as a girl, and that nothing she'd used since had even come close to the clean she got with a possum. She also said that spring brides would sometimes eat possum tail before their wedding to attract a New Year baby. The only redeeming feature I can see in the opossum is that she carries her babies in a pouch or on her back; running or climbing, she keeps them close to her. And no snake can kill her; she is stronger than his bite.

The church waits. I play possum and hold my breath; I do not speak the vision. God's revelation to our church will have to be interpreted by someone else. I'm no prophet; I'm scared that Grandma's blood in my veins will call out to God and tell him that I'm ready. Then again, most everybody in our church is related already, so there is lots of Grandma's blood calling out. Besides my aunt and uncle, I've got cousins and second cousins and third cousins filling up the pews. Our whole family — except the dead and my prodigal Uncle Peter — sits inside this very sanctuary.

Usually, after waiting to give others an opportunity to walk in the gifts of faith, Aunt Gloria still ends up bringing forth the message anyway.

And Aunt Gloria speaks, clipping her words, almost quacking, 'The Lord sayeth unto us — do not be afraid of what is happening all around you. Do not look to the left and fear what tragedy is befalling your neighbour; do not look to the right and covet what joy is uplifting your enemy. For it is my will, sayeth the Lord, my will which shall determine the tragedy and joys, sorrow and smiles of my people. I will guide you. I will protect you. You are mine, I am yours, and you are safe in my arms!'

She did not see what I saw.

Everyone thanks God for the message of safety and love. Quickly, all the air comes back in the room and swells up folks into joy and thanksgiving. Most everybody starts calling out happy prayers to God, and little patches of singing erupt in different rows throughout the church. The breeze wafting through the church smells like grass right after the rain.

Daddy, though, stands with his hands folded and his eyes squeezed shut tight. Reuben and I lean together against the back wall of the church. My mom sways while she softly plays the church organ, and Grandma Esther sits down exhausted in her pew, next to my silent cousins. My uncle nods at them from the stage. Aunt Gloria leads the church in singing one of our favourite choruses.

As the deer panteth for the water, so my soul longeth after Thee.
You alone are my heart's desire, and I long to worship Thee. You
alone are my strength, my shield. To You alone may my spirit yield.
You alone are my heart's desire, and I long to worship Thee.

After morning service, we are having a special youth Sunday school class to talk about coming of age and meeting your intended. All of the teenagers in the church were whispering and joking during my mom's scripture study about courtship and marriage, but when Uncle Ingwald came into the fellowship hall, they stopped their kidding around. He's my dad's eldest brother — scrawny and bald — but he's stern Pastor Ingwald to most of them. Especially when my brother Reuben and our cousin Samuel sat up square on the couch and quit crossing their eyes at each other, everybody straightened out. Reuben's fourteen and big and quiet, but Samuel's sixteen and the one we watch. He's strong — maybe a bit wild — but he always knows what they want to see.

Uncle Ingwald starts sharing his testimony, pacing the carpet at the front of the hall.

Most of it ain't even a secret; I've heard Ingwald's testimony more than once. My Grampa Ole had always wanted him to take over the farm, but Grandma Esther says the Lord won out because Ingwald ran away to California and Strength Bible College just days after his high school graduation. When Uncle Ingwald returned to Wisconsin, he brought with him a Bible degree and a tiny, pretty girl. Gloria Goldstern's almost purple eyes looked straight into his chest; she was like a china doll with miniature hands but curly red hair and a California accent. They'd met at Strength in their final-year Old Testament Prophets class.

'I took my heart beating like it was about to pop out of my chest as a direct message from the prophets that this was my intended helpmeet.' Uncle Ingwald only smiles a little.

I don't know if he's kidding or not. I keep my hands folded in my lap.

But the private men and women part is a bit new, even to me. Uncle Ingwald tells us the story of how he and Aunt Gloria had been chosen by the Lord for each other, and how they were married in the holy chapel in California around six weeks after they met. Although they knew that the Lord had called them into full-time ministry, and that that could mean saving souls overseas in Africa or even India, they also knew that they had been called to come forth and multiply.

We believe children are just like pines: when they are seeded tight together, they grow up straight and tall. So, they set to building themselves a family, planting a forest. Cousin Samuel, 'our boy angel', was born seven months after their matrimony, and his survival — even after being borned before he was fully ready — was a testament to the grace of God.

Samuel is shifting and looking mighty uncomfortable in his seat. He must hate being compared to an angel on account that he looks so much like one with his curly golden halo and sweet pink cheeks. After birthing Samuel, though, Gloria had what medical doctors call complications, but that's not how Uncle Ingwald sees it.

'What she had were temptations, not complications.'

What she had was a temptation to complain and focus on her pain rather than thank the Lord for her son's survival. It ain't something we talk about much, but we all are family in the room — if not by blood, then by the Spirit — so we don't need to feel ashamed. We are old enough to know how we have been wonderfully made, and living on a farm helps figure it out a bit. Gloria's trial, her temptation, was that she was subject to bleeding just like the woman in the Gospel of Mark.

Gloria's issue of blood continued from the day of Samuel's birth through until three years and two miscarriages had passed. They tried hard to find her some help, but none of the doctors could help at all. Not that I'm surprised. We don't put much stead in medicine, but Gloria wasn't raised like us; she's got herself some worldly ideas. But the Lord had His way: neither the doctors in Milwaukee or Madison, nor the ones in Minneapolis and Saint Paul, could give them any answers either to stopping her bleeding or keeping her babies. They'd just scratch at their heads and say that they didn't even know how she kept getting in the family way. This complication, this trial, was just something that Gloria was going to have to live with; she'd have to live with it like the Apostle Paul's thorn in his side.

Uncle Ingwald and Aunt Gloria kept praying and searching the Lord for His will to be done in their family. Knowing in their hearts that God had intended for them to have more children, they eventually went to the state and asked for a child that didn't have people. They pledged to give that child love and care and a family; they pledged to give that child instruction in the Word of God. That is how we were gifted with our Naomi.

I'm glad Naomi isn't here to witness her father telling all and sundry that she was adopted. She is happily singing Bible songs in the sanctuary with her fancy momma and all the little kids of the Hope Prayer Group. Maybe such a personal issue should not be used as a sermon illustration, but, in my family, private things are used to further the work of the kingdom just like anything else. And Naomi is proof of Uncle Ingwald and Aunt Gloria's testing by the Lord.

It don't come as a surprise to me that Naomi is adopted. I've always known and not just because she has a second set of teeth pushing through the top of her gums right at the front of her smile. Well, not an entire extra set of teeth, but two more than a body has a right to, and they're setting right above her pointy dog teeth. I can see them every time she laughs. Anyway, Naomi has thick black hair and big brown eyes like a calf. All the Rundhaugs have blonde hair and bright blue eyes, like most everybody up here, well, outside of the Indian reservations anyways. But Naomi is a Rundhaug by love, if not by birth.

The moment Gloria took that squirming little baby in her arms, that Chippewa baby that was all big moon eyes and thrashing legs, her temptation stopped. Not just the wishing for and hoping about being healed and having more babies stopped, but the issue of blood also stopped completely, and that sweet lady has been healed ever since. Gloria reached out and touched the Lord; He felt her grab His cloak, pull at His sleeve, and she was released from her torment. That is the kind of God we serve. He gives us all that we need and exactly when we need it.

And that was the end of our learning about marriage.

2

DRIVE THE BACKWOODS WAY FROM CHURCH, AND WE CAN TELL plenty from that. It's only fifteen miles direct from town to the homeplace, but a good twenty if the aim is to watch on the way. Even sheep know where they live. Before the snows come, or in a small melt like we're in now, we can see the black paths a hundred hooves wore into the hills, snaking round trees and rocks toward water or shelter.

We are on our way home, and with a little extra driving we can catch up on our neighbours: a new plywood lean-to on the side of a trailer means someone's coming to stay; and an old fridge with gaping doors leaning next to the barn means someone's come into money or wishes they had. Seems nobody has all they need, but we have each other. And we can catch up on ourselves: Daddy's arm is slung across the back of the truck seat, hugging Mom around the shoulders; Mom's fingers trace the pattern of sun and shadow coming through the window onto his leg. Reuben pushes his dirty hair into his eyes then tucks his yellow bangs behind his ear; I sniff the air a bit and start back chewing my hangnails. My thumb is close to bleeding, but I believe it's near to fixed.

Our tyres crunch along the gravel while my parents talk

about smeary mimeographed newsletters, too-long wedding sermons, Chicago mission trips, and grape juice and saltine cracker communion. In Mishtogie, lightning near killed an organist: her hand was hovering above the instrument, ready to play, and lightning came through and struck her. She recovered, by the grace of God, and came back and played the piano that night for a wedding. Rain on a wedding day is a blessing, and Mom loves brave-organist stories. I'd like to play organ or sing, but I'm not made for either. Reuben says my voice sounds like a bleating lamb, and I know I haven't the patience to practise piano.

'I want to do something for God.' I say this while glancing out the window at the corn cut down and patches of snow melting in the fields, and Reuben mocks me with a sneering face and a big breath onto the window. He draws my name, Ruth, in the fog and makes the 't' big like a cross.

Before I even say 'Mom', Daddy is stomping on the brakes. He and Mom cut their eyes at us, and we know that we best get along or get walking. Five miles ain't worth it, so Reuben wipes the glass clear. I chew my lip and then go back to my hangnail.

But I whisper, just loud enough for my brother to hear. 'Are you a stranger to God?'

When he don't flinch at our Sunday school lesson, I squint my eyes and whisper, 'You smell bad, like rotten meat or a sore.'

That slices him to the quick, and he pushes against the truck door and away from my body. He stinks like fourteen does, but not that bad, so I am a bit repentant.

Mom's listing ways I could do something, if not for God directly, then for the church or to help Uncle Ingwald. There's the nursing home service, taken in turns amongst the churches of Failing; I could go help sing or read psalms to the old folks. We went once last year and my heart hurt for a white-haired man parked in a wheelchair near the window, squinting at too much sunlight but not having the gumption to move his head. Or I could help visit the sick, whether they were now trapped in the hospital or had stayed strong and remained homebound. I could bring prayer and soup. Mom says there's many ministries for a girl with too much time on her hands, so much time that that girl might be tempted to complain.

Daddy speaks low. 'Didn't hear no complaining.'

Mom's eyes close and she starts her humming.

'Ingwald still mowing the Turgeson place?' His asking is apology to Mom.

She nods.

'Stick with what you know, girl. Come summer, take the ride-on and go mow that big yard for the Turgesons.'

I know where he means. Not a quarter mile from our place live elders from the church. When grass is there, Uncle Ingwald comes and mows their yard, carefully guiding the lawn tractor around a river of orange-red Indian paintbrushes that sections the lawn. Turgeson ain't invalid, so I don't know why he don't mow. I want to know why.

'Girl, you can mow. You know that coyotes run with straight tails and that bears stink. That's what you need to know.' Daddy knows what I don't need to know.

Over the rickety bridge, past my Uncle Peter's farm, and we are near home. Compared to along the hayfields and the woods, it must be freezing, much worse in the shadows under the low-hanging bridge. It is a secret place, and secret places are cold. There are animals that can't survive in the secret places and there are beings that can live only there. I look at the marshy field and the river as we pass nearby, crusted here and there with muddy ice, and think of all that's waiting there to grow: wild rice, cranberries, rainbow trout and mud suckers. They are all sleeping, lingering, waiting for real winter to start and then to end. They are waiting for the sun to make the water move again.

After morning service on Sundays and midday dinner, my parents rest together. When I go into the bathroom after, I seek Mom's scent in the laundry pile. Her underclothes are more than I should touch, but I do. Against my face, the white smells of late flowers, dying purple roses that have sat on the church organ days too long. But when supper before evening service is short and cold — just eating chipped beef made from leftover venison and a boiled-milk gravy on toast, not even pickles on the table — I can smell they've missed their nap. The orange plastic saltshaker and butter dish pass back and forth without fingers touching. The laundry pile don't need to tell me nothing.

Mornings are for preaching and Bible school, but Sunday nights are more for prayer and praise. Evening services — both Sundays and Wednesdays — are always more relaxed with singing and sharing and such. With my family and friends around me, I can rest and feel covered and protected. But now, I wait in the fellowship hall alone, just peeping out between the coats, while the rest of them is inside the sanctuary praying. Not all of them, of course — Naomi and Aunt Gloria are busy cleaning in the kitchen — but most of them is in there together: Uncle Ingwald and Samuel, Mom and Daddy, and Reuben. As Uncle Ingwald was saying the prayer to send us out into the world and back again safely — 'without a hair on our heads gone astray' — he asked for prayer requests; not unusual, but Reuben raising a hand was.

Naomi's clanging the coffee cups together in the church kitchen, aiming at snapping off a couple white handles. If she's trying to pretend to be washing dishes and helping out of holiness, she ain't fooling no one. Aunt Gloria don't even look up from the long counter where she is reassembling the communion trays, slotting the small glasses back into their metal dishes; they've been waiting on the drying slat since this morning's service. After passing amongst us to distribute the Body and the Blood, the elders bring the trays back to the church kitchen, where one of the ladies rinses any leftovers away. Gloria just needs to put everything back together: the glasses slide into the round, silver platter without a clink, and she carefully nestles each tray atop the others. Before she slips out of the kitchen to return the stacked platters to their honoured place atop the oak communion table engraved *In Remembrance of Me*, my aunt puckers her lips together and makes a stern, moist sound. It is all that is necessary: without even exchanging glances, Naomi obeys her mother and quiets her work. Naomi is nothing if not well broken.

I'm watching from just outside their view, lingering back amongst the coat racks; I learn a lot this way. Sneaky, maybe, but I see and hear more than most. And I rarely repeat what I find out, so I believe it's something I'm willing to carry. Naomi ain't no saint, anyway; she can pretend holy all she likes, but I know she is being punished. I heard that too.

Aunt Gloria is after Naomi for all her haughtiness and vanity, for her attention-seeking ways. About time too,

I suppose, for it isn't a new thing this lip gloss and walking slow down the aisle, straight up the centre of the sanctuary. Even though the girl knew she was late tonight, she comes traipsing up the main aisle — thick black hair hanging down — wanting everyone to turn his head and look. I know Naomi is allowed the gloss — another mistake of her momma's — but she was putting it on during the service while we were singing hymns. Even if I was allowed to wear make-up — and I'm not until I'm sixteen — but even when I'm allowed, I won't be bringing out no purse mirror and smearing myself silly in front of the whole congregation. Naomi seems to think her face is the most important thing on her head, where I more admire my brain. She can be fool's gold, worried more about glinting and shining and less about her true value, but I love her anyway. Naomi is my best friend, and a blessing not a burden to me.

Carrying the communion trays, Gloria shoves open the sanctuary doors with her hip; they swing back and forth. Here in the racks littered with forgotten sweaters, mittens and even some Bibles stacked on the top, it is easy to miss me. I wouldn't forget my coat in winter, but I guess some folks have more than they need. And I wouldn't forget the Word either; my Bible is tucked safe in the purple quilted purse that Grandma made me. Naomi's matches mine exact, but I've stitched my name across the spine to keep it close to me. My family's jackets hang and wait, still damp to the touch, smelling of soap and mould and coffee. I twist in the woollen jackets and crook my neck, leaning as far as I dare toward the sanctuary.

My brother slumps in the last pew, hunched shoulders looking like a mountain, solid and unmoving. Mom, twisting her braid, and a solemn-faced Daddy flank him either side.

And Uncle Ingwald is kneeling toward them, his bony knees on the seat of the pew directly ahead of them; our pastor's arms reach across the divide and hold fast to Reuben's shoulders. I'm still surprised about the whole deal. My brother, he who don't budge for nothing, held up his big, callused hand and said 'unspoken' when the request for prayers was called. Now they're in there trying their hardest to make that need spoken; my parents and my uncle want to wring it out of him, make Reuben speak what's on his heart. They let us say 'unspoken' and pretend it is between you and the Lord, that they won't ask and you don't have to tell. But they'd rather track your path to salvation, checking for footprints and smudges, than leave you on your lonesome, struggling and bleeding alone.

I can hear snatches of Uncle Ingwald's prayer, but not much. Something about 'heavy heart' and 'right and pure direction, perfect will'.

Just now, I feel most sorry for Reuben; we fight, but I don't like to see him troubled and I really hate to see him pressed. He's carrying something, but that gentle push to tell everyone everything — to share your heart and sacrifice deepest desires and secrets — can feel more like a shove sometimes; it is relentless. Mom and Daddy just want to guard our hearts, keep us protected and clean. But now and then a body needs to keep its own secret space, maybe running down the middle of the soul like a candlewick.

Mom don't want any secrets; anything she knows she shares. She believes light always drives the dark away, but praying with Grandma and Gloria and the other ladies of the church shines the light even where it might shouldn't go. Daddy must feel useless, pushed aside, that even while he looks after Reuben's body — feeding, clothing and keeping him in every way — Uncle Ingwald's guiding Reuben's soul is held in higher value. Reuben should have thought twice about raising that hand, but he's got to learn it in his own time, I guess. It takes steady water to shape stone.

I feel a quick pull of my braid, and my head snaps back hard. My cousin Samuel is holding my hair and smirking. This boy should already be a man, but he plays too much and too rough. And he won't be broken. Held up by his own daddy, our pastor, as a man with a call on him, my cousin won't walk straight for nothing. Feigning like the angel his blonde curly halo makes them see, he'll act for the elders and the ladies, taking his turn at passing out communion or praying and laying on hands for the sick. Samuel will sit at the front of the church facing his own father and hold his face just right for them, downcast eyes and serious lips. But he only wants the praise, never the toil: he won't stack aluminum chairs after potluck supper and he won't shovel snow from the sidewalk. Samuel walks in the light of the Lord when it's warm but won't sweat in labour or freeze in the cold. Tonight, he won't even agree in prayer for Reuben. He's held up at church while they push him down at school; none of us kids stand up to none of them — not to our parents, not to the kids at school. Samuel stands crooked: he only lets them think he ain't strong.

'Why you hiding, Ruth?' Samuel crouches down and his face is below my waist. 'Reuben telling them something he shouldn't?' He's teasing but asking too.

I didn't even think of that. 'He don't know nothing to tell.' Now I'm wondering what my brother is saying, and if he does have something to say about me.

'Maybe he's guilty himself; that's what I think.' Samuel rocks back and forth on his haunches. The coats swing on their hangers. 'But I do believe, you've got some reason to be hiding here.'

How he knows, I never know. Maybe he can smell it. Whenever I've got something to hide, Samuel always seems to see. Maybe it's because when everyone else is moving and walking, Samuel watches and waits — like me.

I'm caught, so I've got to spread the blame. 'Eat this.' My stretched-out hand holds half a candy bar, the chocolate melted into my palm. 'Christmas candy; you can't tell.'

While everyone was praying, I stole into the storage cupboard and took one of the children's gifts; we each get a store-bought candy bar on Christmas Day. Not like we don't sometimes get candy, we do; but this is bought special and we're supposed to wait.

Samuel winks one shiny eye and smiles wide; he gets up and takes a piece and slips it into his mouth. As much as he is sneaky, he is kind; to hold up under what they want from him takes more than I have.

While I'm part disappointed for having to share and part enjoying the secret, Aunt Gloria's quick voice makes me straighten my back and swallow fast. She sees us; there aren't enough coats in the world to blind Gloria's eyes. Samuel is skinny, but he's too tall. Wiping her hands on a dishtowel, she is more than angry.

'And you wouldn't stay and pray?' she asks him. She's looking at Samuel, not me. 'Your father expects more than this.'

The boy knows better than to respond. He looks her almost square in the face, but lowers his eyes as she keeps scolding. In amongst the wool coats, I can feel Samuel's heart beating, hands trembling as he takes the rest of the candy from my hands. He wasn't praying, and I was hiding, not helping.

Aunt Gloria's looking at me, inside me. I am a worm.

'It ain't Ruth's fault.' Samuel puts his hands out flat for his mother to see; he's holding the candy bar wrapper and he's stained his palms. 'She was just waiting here, waiting quiet for her momma.'

Gloria's eyes move from his eyes to the chocolate on Samuel's hands. Now, she don't look at me, thinking I'm lazy; she don't ponder his lack of faith. He's spun her head to candy. But his parents punish: he could lose hockey practice or what little television he gets over this. If my parents get told, my momma will have me copying out verses about thievery and greed. And my daddy don't think I'm too big for a spanking either. Samuel's pulling her attention to the little hard knocks to try and slide by with the big bads. Risky, but he's ready to stand for me.

She looks at the creases in my worn dress and my messy braid. Gloria and Naomi always look like they're on their way to a party, clean and neat. Maybe I am too far gone to worry over. Samuel wipes his chocolate hands on his pants, and his mother clicks her tongue and shakes her head. But she doesn't have time for us tonight; there are cups to wash.

Gloria sighs and is still talking as she heads back to the kitchen. 'The more he hopes for, the more you take away.'

I don't know if she's talking to God or Samuel. And I don't know now what to do with my knowing, how to see or not see Samuel's shame.

Turning to face him, I stare at the flatness in his eyes. I look away as soon as I can, but he sees I saw. It's like staring at the sun and it burning spots on your eyes: those spots show even when glancing at something else. They aren't really there — those spots. There's nothing wrong with what you're looking at, but everything wrong with what you're looking with. I can't watch him and his humiliated face, so I turn my face to the side and wait. Soon enough — before I can thank him — Samuel shuffles away. I remain alone with all the forgotten things, the extra Bibles and the coats that have been left behind.

It's getting later than it should be, nearing almost nine and with school tomorrow. We have to be shivering in the snow at quarter to seven in the morning, waiting at the end of the driveway for the bus and the sun, so we'll have to sleep fast. That is what Mom will say when she checks on me before I sleep. It isn't that she still tucks me into bed, pulling up the quilts and such, but that she comes to see that all is well and if I want to pray with her or on my own. She'll say 'sleep fast' with her hand paused on the light switch, waiting for me to pretend to blow out the light.

3

WE ALWAYS SIT ALONE TOGETHER ON THE SCHOOL BUS.
Making believe I'm saving the seat, I'm lonesome all the way
to town. First picked up in the morning and last dropped off
at night, Reuben and me can choose wherever we want. But
nobody wants to sit with us or near; they'd rather just laugh
from behind, pointing and saying things. Reuben gets in his
own seat, saving a spot for Samuel the same. After picking
up some other town kids, the bus finally makes it to the
parsonage. I'm so happy to see Naomi's face. My cousin and I
are enough, anyway, and don't need others interfering.

Even though sometimes it seems that the Lord gave Naomi
to me to grow my patience — she don't care for hunting
and can be on the whiny side — I am thankful for this girl.
Sometimes our brothers spend the day helping our daddies
cut wood, and we have to ride to school alone; this is when
the trouble starts. Normal boys might pull our braids while
their girls whisper and smile mean; we do our best to ignore
them. Thankfully the boys are with us today, just across the
aisle. We ride side by side all the way.

Our bus rumbles from town past the broken-down dairy
farms and gleaming turkey barns. Rows and rows of metal

pole barns stripe Failing's fields now. About fifty or so years ago, a local boy's county fair project grew into our town's saving grace. Most folks don't own their own farms anymore, and many wives have to stand in bloody boots on the kill line slitting throats and plucking scalded birds, but at least it's work. Folks will do most anything when they're desperate, I guess.

The children of these turkey farmers tease us for our ways, and it shouldn't be allowed. We are more like them now than folks used to be. Our hair is long and we tie it back, but we can cut it or wear it loose if we want. We wear homemade but we also have store-bought. I like wearing dresses, but Naomi prefers pants. She can choose to wear pants on Fridays and she is; her parents let her pick. I can choose every day but don't have a big pile of clothes like Naomi. It was harder when our parents were young; we blend more now.

Finally at school, the bus sidles up to the sidewalk. Samuel and Reuben run off ahead toward the far entrance. We all share the same brick building: elementary, middle school and high school alike. But the high schoolers — especially the older boys, even our brothers — act like we younger kids aren't there. Naomi and I gather up our book bags and I make sure to remember the brown paper bag that carries my lunch. Naomi walks the bus aisle before me and I follow.

The bus with the reservation kids is spilling out too. These kids are here until the Indians can get their own school. Seems like half of Failing's students — us Pentecostals, the Baptists, the Mennonites, and the Indians — are only here temporarily, just until our families can find the money to keep us all apart.

It's only recent that these particular Chippewas have been given their land out there for real. Before a city judge went and made it right, the locals always said that the tribe was just squatting on land that wasn't truly its own. Legend had it that their old folks hundreds of years past had showed up at a meeting late, so they were a lost tribe without their names on the treaty. Even though the tribe was hunting, fishing and living in the same woods, lakes and fields that it had always hunted and fished and lived in, they didn't exist on paper. I wonder if they are still mad about it, or if they've forgotten the wrong folks have done to them. I wonder how long it takes to forget that you didn't exist.

Blood is important, and Wisconsin is making sure we know it. So far this week, we've made popsicle stick tepees, dyed cloth with sumac, and even beaded a rawhide leather rope. I knew enough to keep the necklace in my locker at school, but Naomi took hers home and her daddy took it away.

But today the Indians have come to our school to really give us heritage. In a rusted-out old Ford, six of them have driven thirty or so miles off the Ojibway reservation to teach us about their old customs and dances and such. One boy in my class saw them side-slide to a stop in the icy parking lot. He said they looked like too many clowns piling out of a squished car, only difference that the hood of this circus wagon had been on fire a time or two. He was the same kid who screeched through the hallway into the boys' bathroom, laughing and screaming, 'The Indians are coming! The Injuns are coming!'

Lots of kids started yelling and running around like they was scared too. Just a joke, but it made most of the teachers real mad. I could see the funny in it, but I could also see the rude. These Indians, with long black hair braided quiet down their backs and shining eyes that crinkle like Grandma's when they half smiled, are our guests. You don't scream at visitors, even if it is funny.

We are in the gym waiting for the program to start. Naomi is tracing a pattern on my back; I guess the letters she shapes. Everyone is very excited and nervous, giggling and not knowing what will come next. But all the Indian kids who are just plain there all the time don't seem to think what's coming will be funny or even special. They seem to sink down even lower in their bodies, barely speaking to each other.

And now the warriors dance. Do they ever dance! Dressed in tanned buckskin, beaver fur and eagle feather, the tall men who come out of the boys' bathrooms are somehow not the same lanky guys that went in covered up in faded jeans and Green Bay Packers t-shirts. My own eyes see the glory of a vest of porcupine quills, layered and twined shiny brown and white; I see soft, puckered moccasins studded with blue and red beads. When that armoured vest jumps and jostles past me and the shoe stomps the beat right next to my knee, my legs quiver and I know that they know by heart everything that I don't.

I tell myself to think of the dances and stories just as fables, not meant to be speaking of God and the like. I can enjoy them most that way without feeling like I am betraying my faith. Sitting cross-legged on the floor of the gym next to Naomi, I look up at these men and feel I must believe them. Whatever they show me, I will believe.

They sing their screaming songs and they dance. What sounds like wailing at the start, ends up echoing like a high wind twisting the very tops of the oldest pines. Creaking and groaning and moving with the breeze, stubborn trees push back against the wind while still bending its direction. That is what I am seeing as they whirl around our little gym. I am watching farmers force rivers to water fields, weavers plait baskets with twisted reeds, and carpenters bend wood to build shelter. But I learn that it is only the very strong who move themselves. I'll never know how the dancers avoid the lunch tables pushed up against the walls and ignore the hanging jump ropes and stacked dodge balls locked in their cages. Even the bigger boys acting bored and leaning against the walls — Samuel and Reuben included — don't distract them. Dancing Indians don't seem to need to look around to know where they are going. They sing their path before them.

The tallest man, wearing skunk and raccoon tails, speaks in his soft voice about the next coming dance. He explains that the dance tells the story of two brothers and a sister whose parents were real sick. The older brother and sister promised the dying parents never to forsake their little brother. After the parents died, though, the older brother tired and left, and then the sister got weary of doing right. In the middle of a hard winter, they both abandoned the little brother out in the woods. When he ran out of food, the boy had to pick berries and dig roots to survive. He even slept up in the crotch of a tree and ate scraps left by wolves.

After a while, that's all he ate: bloody meat gnawed by wolves. Soon, somewhere he got the courage to crouch next to the wolves while they ate, and the animals showed him pity by always leaving something for him.

'The sympathy of the wolves kept him alive until thaw. And when the lake was free from ice, the young boy sang, *My brother: I am now a wolf.*'

Except now, the little brother was howling because he had become a wolf. He ran into the woods with his new pack. The wolf boy's older brother and sister carried guilt and grieved and wept until their deaths. It was a sad dance, but it seemed right in the end.

After the beginning, God took wolves and men on different paths, and so they have to stay apart. To let a dog witness a sacred ceremony could kill somebody, the dog or man or maybe both. We can make friends with dogs, but I guess they can't make friends with God. It's about knowing the right order of things. It is about keeping things straight in your mind. Animals can walk alongside you, but you can't keep them; you can't really hold their hearts.

We walk hand-in-hand toward the buses after school, Naomi and me. To look at us, you'd never know that we are two sides of the same person: I am blonde, blue and skinny; she is black, brown and not. For we don't share blood; instead, we share a heart.

Naomi gnaws the corner of her lip.

'You didn't like the dancing?' I don't know what else to say.

She rolls her eyes at me and makes the same puckering noise Aunt Gloria makes. 'That wasn't dancing.'

'I liked it.' I did.

'You like anything.' She's sore about something. I wonder if it's about spending all day learning about things she's supposed to just know, just feel inside her bones. Poking at it won't help, so I start humming a chorus and she joins me. *Down at the cross where my Saviour died, down where for cleansing from sin I cried. There to my heart was the blood applied, glory to His name.*

We climb on the bus together and begin the long ride home.

After all the other children have been dropped off, we're finally to the end of the bus route and it is just me and Naomi, Reuben and Samuel. Whooping and hollering, we bounce up and down at the back of the bus, riding the bumps and dips in the gravel like what I imagine a rollercoaster would be like. The driver doesn't mind so much. She knows we have a hard time on the bus. And at the end of the ninety-minute drive, it's just Rundhaugs — us and our cousins if they're coming to stay — so nobody is going to make any trouble.

Samuel's talking about the Indian dancers and their stories. He didn't seem to pay much attention in the gym, but he sure is now. 'Now, can a guy just shoot a wolf in Wisconsin?'

He and his daddy hunt, but not like the men in my house do. Ingwald is always at church and Samuel is usually at hockey; they don't take it as serious. But Reuben and Daddy do little outside of bloodletting.

'No, you can't shoot them no more; can't even trap them. But it don't take a real brain to know that bringing timber wolves back the same time you're trying to build up the elk is a stupid idea.' Reuben just repeats what our daddy says about them real big wolves that the Department of Natural Resources is letting kill folks' calves.

Samuel just stares at his hands while my brother preaches. He hates that Reuben knows more about such things, but it's true. Memorising Bible verses is one thing, but taking and talking game is another.

'Up in Alaska, now up in Alaska, they got the right idea.' My brother loves repeating my daddy's stories about his hunting trip the year Reuben was born. 'Some guys up there, they'll take a roadkill deer. They'll auger a hole in a good lake, stick the deer leg in, and then let it freeze back up. They'll just sit back and let the wolves come to them.'

In my mind's eye, I can see shaggy wolves — grey, silver and some near to black — pawing the ice for that meat froze deep in the water. Hunters crouching in the scrub, sitting in a hide on the lakeshore, can fire on them without slipping on the ice or even being close enough to smell the damp fur. I don't so much like the idea of all that dark blood spread out on the ice and snow. But I do know I don't ever want to meet those yellow eyes out in the woods alone.

The bus finally winds down the long gravel road that ends at my driveway. The boys jump out and run toward the house. They've always got big plans that are so secret. Naomi's soft shape walks the bus aisle before me, and I follow like a dying-light shadow, longer and skinnier, pulled out of shape. The lady driver nods her grey head as she creaks open the bus door. Dusk has already come and gone when we step out into the cold air.

4

It took half of Saturday to convince Naomi to come up into the haymow with us. Reuben and Samuel go up all the time and are always building big forts from the hay bales stacked up there. It's a warm day for November, and we are out in the yard without even hats, so I wanted to go up and build me a fort too. Seems like Naomi ain't any fun anymore and always wants to be acting like she's sixteen or something. But she's more baby thirteen than I am, so I'm not buying her lady act. Soon she'll be pretending to ride her horse sidesaddle like the black-and-white pictures of a little girl Grandma on her way to church.

It's only the top of Grandma's barn, anyway, and usually there's swallows swooping in and out all the time, and it's fun. Through the old milking parlour door, we have to squeeze around a broken-down tractor, step by rusty pipes and cracked buckets, and pass through clingy spiderwebs to get to the ladder that leads to the haymow. We have to jump up a little from the floor to catch the first iron rung, pull up to the next rung, and then keep going until our heads pop through the floor of the barn's attic. The hole in the floor looks like it won't fit even me through, and I'm the runt of the litter. Even being two years younger than Samuel, Reuben's bigger by almost half. I can't believe either of them will fit. But, lo and behold, Reuben squeezes his way and Samuel shimmies through just fine. Part of the wood must be rotten, because slivers slough off the boards when Samuel's knees scrape against them.

I want to go up next, but Naomi is being a girl again, kinda whimpering over and over like it's a memory verse.

'I don't want to go up there. It's dark and dirty and scary. I don't want to go up there.'

This is annoying me to no end, so I decide that she's the next one up. I reach over and pull the hem on her thin, pink pants and use my stern momma voice. 'You shouldn't wore cotton pants, Naomi. You're going to get all scratched up. It'll look like you've wrestled a bobcat.'

She gets herself a good grip on the bottom rung and I give her a boost from behind. Grabbing her legs and bottom like this, I touch all over Naomi and think that I better have a talk with her once we build ourselves our own hay fort.

Samuel's yelling now. 'Get up here, you chickens! Reuben's killing himself a snake!'

I'm not missing that for nothing — the snake, anyway — so I give Naomi's hind end another sharp push and, with a whimper, she scrambles up through into the haymow.

Dust and chaff and old, old dirt has been falling into my eyes while I was shoving Naomi up. I run the bottom of my t-shirt across my face to kinda clear things up a bit. Outside, the clouds must have shifted: when I look up through the floor hole again, shafts of sunlight stream down at me. Dust mites and fine-sieved bird poop older than I am float in the air. As the particles turn and swirl, they are beautiful and glint in the light like tiny pieces of gold. Grandma says that swallows do nothing but make a mess with their mud nests hanging under the eaves of anything that don't keep moving, but I know now that they help make a beauty of this world too. I get a good grip on the iron rungs and pull myself up into the haymow.

Well, Naomi was right. It is dark and dirty, but it is a nice dark and dirty. The light is like when a thunderstorm pushes in on a sunny, summer day and shadows run together to form buckets of dark. Sunlight creeps in between the cracks of the boards of the wall and also through the window up at the peak of the barn. As my eyes adjust, I can see the bales of hay stacked up in three or four piles around the floor. Some of the piles are over thirty feet high and are mountains of preparation that Grampa left for the cows before he fell over and died. With only the couple of riding horses and few sheep we all got now, the bales have been waiting up here must be years. The hay smells warm and kinda tricks you into thinking that it might be a soft place to snuggle into; but as I lay back on one of the lower piles, I find out right quick that Grampa's old hay is as scratchy as any hay we got nowadays.

Samuel is pulling apart one of the bales, hoping for more snakes. This barn is a welcome place for any creature searching for some warm and dry to raise babies. I imagine that there are generations of field mouse and garter snake families living here, and with them are generations of swallow and barn owl families living on them. Bats swoop low round the barn at night too, and there might be creatures up here with names that I don't even know. Samuel's whooping loud and starting to throw the loose hay into the air; it scatters around Naomi's head and gets stuck in her tightly braided pigtails. She looks real pretty with her dark hair and tan skin and the pale, yellow stalks sticking to the sweat on her forehead and arms. I feel a twinge of jealousy and think that somebody looking in on this scene, God even, might not even see me or Reuben or Samuel because we just blend into the hay: blonde on blonde on blonde on blonde.

Naomi and I are in need of more sameness, so I run over and grab her arm and pull her toward what's going to be our hay fort. We just got to pile up the walls a bit and balance a good roof; then, we'll have a safe place to come and talk girl talk or whatever without the boys listening in and making fun. Reuben's yelling like Tarzan and swinging on a rope that is looped over the rafters. Hanging on for dear life, he swoops over the tops of our heads and his foot nearly scrapes my hair.

Not really, because it wasn't that close, but boy it makes me mad. 'Reuben! You bring your bottom down from there! I'm going to tell Daddy you kicked me in the head!'

This scares him a bit, so it settles him down some. Naomi and I are left to work on our fort while the boys try to build a second storey onto theirs.

I've been wondering since that boost at the ladder, so I decide that I'm just going to come straight out and ask her. While Naomi helps me move one of the hay bales that's soon to be part of the wall, I talk low. 'You've started, haven't you? Why didn't you tell me? Why didn't your momma tell Grandma?' I'm sure that if something that important happened, Grandma would know; the whole family would know.

Naomi looks at me with her big eyes all wide like a deer caught in the headlights and flat out lies to me. 'No, Ruth, I haven't started. No, honest.'

Well, her lie smacks me like if she'd slapped me, and I get mad enough where I could hit her myself. 'Yes, you have!

And now you're lying about it, which is even worse than not telling. I felt something in your underpants when I was shoving you up into the haymow, you little baby.'

Now I feel bad, because Naomi starts to cry and I know that I've hurt her feelings again. She keeps crying until her shoulders heave, and I can see snot slip down across her mouth and slide off her chin. She slinks over into a corner of the fort and slumps onto the floor. She's crying so hard that I lose some of my anger, righteous though it may be, and come over and settle beside her with my arm around her shoulders.

'I'm sorry, Naomi. I was just mad that you didn't tell me, and that you're a woman and I'm not. I was just jealous. It's not so bad, is it?'

Naomi snuffles and heaves and tries to talk, but she needs to just catch her breath a bit before she can. I wait patiently, and I don't think that she'll gloat, but I did make her cry.

Finally, she can talk. 'I'm not a woman, Ruth, I'm just a big stupid baby. I've started to pee my bed again. Mom says it's alright and she helps me change the sheets every morning, but I'm scared now that I'll wet myself during the day too. I've got paper towels from the kitchen in my panties because I couldn't bear for you and Reuben to know. Samuel knows, but he's promised not to tell. He's promised.'

I feel really bad now and rock Naomi until she stops crying so hard. 'Well, girl, we got to get on and build this fort.' I talk soft to her. 'I can't do it without your help. Get on up and help me move these bales.'

She gets up and gets to work, only small hiccups break into the sound of us dragging bales. Naomi's got streaks of dirt down her face where her tears caught on some dust, and she looks like a baby raccoon. I don't tease her, though; seems like she's got enough on her heart right now.

Reuben's running around with another garter snake stuck on the end of a rusty pitchfork. He's pierced it on three of the four tines, and the snake is writhing with its eyes all bugged out in pain. My brother meets its gaze with a mean and hungry glint in his eye, and he grins like a barn cat ripping the wings off a bat.

'You ain't no Moses, Reuben,' I tell him quick. There is no need for the bronze snake; we haven't been bitten. We seek no cure.

He sees the seriousness in my eyes and moves as if to fling the limp creature up over a low barn rafter. I call out and he stops. He's leaning on the pitchfork, relaxing with half-lidded eyes.

Naomi is still sitting on the bales, braiding twine into her hair and humming a chorus.

'You're hurting that snake just to hurt it.' I hate to see a creature suffer.

And Reuben sticks the fork hard into the floor. The sharp tines are through the snake and stab the wood, but it doesn't take. The pitchfork bounces and hits the ground. I'm looking where it landed — feeling the slice of the tines through my body — when Samuel comes up behind me and tickles my back where my hair touches my waist. I jump and turn around and he smiles. I was scared, but there wasn't no harm done; I smile back at him.

Samuel reaches down and pulls the snake off the end of the pitchfork. He passes it over and I hold it limp in my hands.

'What a girl.' Reuben smirks at me and goes into his fort. My brother's peeing in there now. I can hear it and smell it strong and sharp in the still air.

5

SO MANY THINGS CAN COME BETWEEN NEIGHBOURS, EVEN good neighbours. Friendships formed through generations of raising barns, crops and babies together seem to weather like uncut grass when some unexpected sun shines too hot and too many days in a row. Some grasses will cure standing; heat just makes them all the better for cattle. But then, some grasses will steam in humid sun or plain wither in dry heat; after that, they ain't good for nothing. That's the way it is with friendships in Failing.

Grandma is my family's main neighbour: our house squats on an acre carved off the side of her nearest cornfield. We don't even need a fence. Grandma owns all the woods around here and more land here and there. Uncle Peter owns the adjoining Magnusson place, and most of the folks around here have farms with many acres. Grandma can keep track of all of us from her porch. Uncle Ingwald lives in town in the parsonage, but the Lord watches over him, so Grandma can have a break.

But we count them all neighbours, up and down the river that winds through the tangle of branches in the woods we all share. We are connected by these woods and the river. We are connected by land and history.

Near the river, along the path that leads from our house to Grandma's house, there stretches a battered old fence. Years ago, we had a horse that needed penning in the spring. He ain't there anymore, but the straggly wires still string along one side of the path, with the other side hemmed in spring and summer by chokecherry bushes, plum trees and wild strawberries scattered on the ground.

There was a cold rain last night and the temperature dipped back below freezing this morning. I take myself for a walk down the wire-lined path to check on some of my most special trees and see how they fared. I haven't walked that way for weeks; after snowfall, I usually stick to the road. But a sneaky wet like that with a sharp freeze can hurt the trees; they can lose a limb to ice or worse even. Near to the biggest plum tree — the one with the sharpest thorns in springtime but juiciest fruit in summer, plums that will just bleed down your arm from the first bite of flesh to the last suck of the pit — near to that tree I find a fawn.

But it isn't a white-spotted tan beauty curled up quiet in a nest of swirled grass. My fawn is a bleached white skeleton hooked in-between the fence wires; she is stuck tight, left behind. Rabbit fencing traces that part of the path, and when the momma jumped the fence, the baby must have tried to jump and instead ploughed straight through. Not exactly through, though; more like in, into the fence. I cry. All the way down over the hill, I cry. Seeing those white ribs tangled in the fence with only ribbons of hide and sinew still clinging to the bones, seeing that was too much for me.

I wonder on whose pain was greater, the momma who left or the baby who stayed behind. Was it hunger or wolves that ended it? And why? I most wonder why. I can barely walk for crying.

My face streaked with tears, I finally make it to Grandma's warm kitchen. I tell her I twisted my ankle in a snow-packed gopher hole, but she gets the story out of me soon enough. Out it comes with choking and heavy breathing, and at the end with hiccups. All mixed up in my mind is whether or not they were chased into the fence and how long the momma waited and if the baby kept making noises or shut its eyes or so many things that hurt to even think. Like stillness or quivering, like cold in the snow or wet in the rain? So many things I just can't know.

Grandma doesn't know neither. She pats my back and rubs my leg. I cry into her apron that smells of apples baking and vinegar too. Grandma pulls her soft hands through my hair and sings a soft hymn.

'Take it to the Lord, my Ruthie. Take it to the Lord in prayer.'

And I do. I pray and sing a little with her when I can quiet my crying.

'There are a many great losses in this world,' Grandma says. 'Great losses all up and down that fence, all up and down that river. But we do our best. And when we can't do our best, we leave them to the Lord.'

Grandma's making a crazy quilt from worn-out clothes stacked in brown-paper grocery bags. She settles me down next to her in the wooden rockers near the cast-iron fire. A crocheted blanket warms my legs. As I thread needles and pile squares by colour, she sews together patches of summer dresses and unmendable coats. As we work, Grandma's hands are always moving, pulling fabric and touching my arm; like hummingbirds, they rarely settle against her soft belly.

There is a noise on the screen porch and we hear the door open and slam shut. My daddy walks straight in through the kitchen without taking off his boots or even knocking the snow clear.

His eyes are on fire. 'What did you tell Reuben about hunting?' He stands there dripping in his work clothes, quilted flannel and worn pants.

'Good morning, Eric.' Grandma slowly lowers her sewing and raises her gaze to meet her son's. 'Can I give you something warm to drink?'

'Momma, Reuben has his heart set on shooting a coyote. And trapping — the boy wanted to try for a bobcat this year, maybe a wolverine. He'll take care of the beavers so you'll get your river back.' His wheaty hair is all stuck up crossways on his head, and he is wiping grease or dirt from his thick hands.

'I've made up my mind, son. I don't aim to harm you or Reuben. And I'm letting the boy trap this winter; Lord willing, he just might get his bobcat. But hunting on my land is over for this year. And next year, no hunting or trapping neither.'

I've never seen my daddy so angry. Looking at Grandma with almost a sneer, he is trying to find words to say.

Grandma talks before he can. 'Not even tracking anymore. Not in my woods, no sir, not in my woods. And they are mine, until the Lord calls me home.' They are hers, the woods: the trees and the river and the animals that abide in them.

'That's downright cruel,' Daddy says. 'To let a wounded deer struggle through the woods and not let folks come and finish it off?' His voice is rising.

'But I know now — I didn't always know, but I know now — that those bleeding deer are mine and my woods are mine, and it is my decision. So, no.' Grandma is set in her mind; she won't let them track no deer, wounded or otherwise, in her woods. 'If the Lord decides to take a life, animal or otherwise, the Lord decides. And the wolves and coyotes and the other will take care of the struggling.'

Daddy laughs a mean laugh, looking in her eyes. 'They'll take care of it alright. There ain't no blood on my hands.' And he turns on his heel to go, throwing up his arms in exasperation. 'You know, this don't hurt the others — Ingwald and Samuel, especially not Peter — like it's going to pain me. Hell, it's going to almost kill Reuben.'

Her son has cursed to her face. Grandma lowers her eyes back to her quilt. She will say no more. Daddy stomps out of the house. The wind takes the door and slams it twice.

And so they'll talk, the neighbours and my daddy and my uncles. I say as much to Grandma without trying to stoke her anger. She isn't angry. She's too old for that.

'They can talk all they like.'

But she came to the conclusion that she had to provide a sanctuary for the hurt and the wounded when she found that pile as Ingwald drove her home from church last Sunday. Right next to the old swimming hole where the bridge crosses the river, right where Grampa and Grandma used to swim when their boys were little, she found the pile. Heads and hooves, and some ribs with meat still sticking to them were spilling out of torn plastic bags. One head had a horn — a young spike buck, must have been — still attached with the other side torn straight off. The rest of them were does, fawns, or were missing horns: bloody holes sat burrowed in the meat and soft fur between their eyes and ears. Curled-up hooves spilt out on the riverbank and some picked-over bones lay right where she was fixing to relax and remember and look at the water. This bag of bones and skin and fur had been thrown from a passing pick-up; I can see it in my mind's eye. And now they were dumped and spilt out and picked through by scavengers, rat and vulture and coyote.

'I made up my mind — swaying there amongst the blood and the fur and the dirt — I made up my mind.' Grandma knows what she knows.

The sins are on both sides. They are on both sides. For every buck deer that breaks a trail through the corn and eats half an ear off of each stalk, there is one of our neighbours crouching in a stand, high up in a tree, aiming at shooting it dead. For every weasel stealing silage or coon chewing crops, there is my brother setting up grip traps with steel teeth that will pinch that rodent through and through. Or worse, even worse than a beaver chewing and twisting its own foot around and around until it breaks free from a foothold trap, even worse are the drown traps. Damming up our river with sticks and mud, that beaver is just building himself a home. But when he takes the bait of a drown trap, he can't just break off his foot. It holds him deep in the water, with the green plants swaying and the fish swimming by, down deep in the water. And he can't take no breath and he can't swim up to the top. He is held beneath the water with no breath until he don't move no more. The poor muskrats, with their tiny feet and hands, they die the same.

Up and down this river, by these broken-down barns, peeling houses and crooked silos, up and down this river the sins are on both sides. Our Lord Himself is a neighbour to Himself, the Trinity holding Itself together in community: Father, Son and Holy Ghost. The everlasting Trinity shows friendship and responsibility within Itself, amongst Its neighbours.

'Ruthie, girl, are you a good neighbour not just to the beaver and the deer and your brother and your cousins, but are you a good neighbour to yourself? Are you a friend to yourself?'

It is hard. Grandma tells me these things so that I can be a good friend, a good neighbour. Many things can get in the way of being good neighbours. It might be that you weren't there in someone's time of need. Or, it might be that you were there, and now they can't hold their head up to look you in the face. Either can get in the way: shame or need. One or the other or both, it can get in the way.

There is another scraping noise on the screen porch, and I turn my head. Daddy must be back for another round. Heavy boots are clomping inside from the wind and weather into the slightly protected cold just outside the kitchen door. I crane my neck to see who is out there. Grandma does not move her eyes; they stay on the patches she is matching, each swipe of her needle pulling together the pattern.

'Expecting company, Grandma?'

Still, she does not lift her eyes.

'Should I go to the door and see who's there?' I hope I'm not being impertinent. My daddy would have something to say to me if Grandma gave a bad report. He can say what he wants to her, I guess, but my place is to help, not to hinder.

Grandma sighs and puts down her needle. She takes her glasses off her face and rubs them with a tissue she keeps up her sleeve. She seems to know what's waiting outside. 'Ruth, we'll just leave that man on the porch.'

And I hear the sound of heavy things being piled on the bench outside the kitchen door. The wind sweeps a little through the house each time a new load is brought near — but not inside.

'There you go, Momma.' And the door to the outside world swings open and stays open for a second. I hear my daddy's younger brother, my Uncle Peter, call quiet from the threshold. 'Some nice pork there, if you like.'

With a clatter and catch in the wind, the door shuts and Grandma puts her glasses back on her face. For some time, she doesn't speak a word. She will not ask Uncle Peter inside.

Instead, we sing a little while. We sing: *What a Friend we have in Jesus, all our sins and griefs to bear! What a privilege to carry everything to God in prayer! Oh, what peace we often forfeit; oh, what needless pain we bear. All because we do not carry everything to God in prayer!*

Grandma rocks a bit, back and forth, and I can hear the wood beneath her chair squeak and shuffle. She touches the thread to her tongue before threading her needle, and she tucks stray hairs into her tight grey bun. 'You know your Uncle Peter didn't come to the Lord until he was a grown man, don't you?'

I didn't know nothing of the sort. Uncle Peter don't talk much to me; Reuben has always been his favourite. Grandma tells me that Peter didn't meet Jesus until after he came back from the navy. He had been to church with all the boys, but Peter didn't know the Lord.

He'd never made that decision. Peter — always getting attention for being the tallest and the strongest around Failing — was too busy putting up hay in the summer, playing football in the fall, and courting pretty girls year round to draw close to the Lord.

'That was a thorn in my side from the time he was in high school, especially after, when he was out in the world. Many's the night I brought his name to the Lord in tears and in prayer.'

Uncle Ingwald had been out at Bible college for a couple years, and they hadn't seen hide nor hair of him, or even met Gloria or baby Samuel. He couldn't even afford to come home for his father's funeral, but made it home by deer season the year the church called him to pastor.

'There was so much to do that season: we had to come to know this pale girl with blackberry eyes and tiny hands. We needed to learn to call Samuel our own, this angel child crawling across the yellow linoleum.'

Grandma was shut up in the house with Gloria while the men hunted, and they had to find their own way. My mom was homebound with chicken pox, so Grandma had to watch baby Reuben, only a few weeks old. Grandma had Reuben so long that he wouldn't even take his momma's breast when he finally came home. Our women hold each other together. And before the men even saw their first deer, Grandma and Gloria were joyfully baking and minding the babies, and lifting each other up in prayer.

'Since my sons were born, I had fretted over their salvation and the helpmeet the Lord had chosen for each. That week in the kitchen, aprons dusted with flour, Gloria became my daughter, Samuel bloomed in my heart, and Reuben made room.'

Ingwald and my daddy hunted and brought back nothing. The disappointment and worry for winter meat was felt by all, but seemed to dig deep at Peter. 'He wouldn't join the men hunting. Shame was what he was carrying, and it was past anything I had seen in him.'

I ask my grandma why Peter didn't hunt with the men. Why he doesn't hunt now.

'You ask your daddy about that or — better still — you ask the man himself. Since Peter left our family, he's never really come back.'

But back then, after evening chores, Peter would leave the house and walk the fields until dark. No one knew where he went. He didn't speak in the house and refused to even touch the babies. Through this dark mood, the family held Peter up to the Lord, and slowly they began to think the cloud had passed. One night after supper, he kissed Gloria solemnly on the forehead and shook Ingwald's hand with his giant fist. He didn't say nothing to my daddy. Then, Peter walked over to Grandma where she was rocking the babies, cradled them both in those big arms, and walked straight out of the house.

Ingwald found his brother behind the milking shed, weeping so hard that his square shoulders were shaking, speaking of grave failure. Samuel was squirming, and Reuben lay screaming in the cold shade of the wall, both now wearing only cloth diapers. Peter knelt against the stone foundation, his skinning knife unsheathed and stuck into the snow. He'd sawed branches off of the spindly birch and, in the midst of the patchy snow, had a green wood fire smouldering in a scraped dirt circle.

'We never spoke of it, so I don't know what brought Peter to his despair, and I'll leave that to Jesus. What I know is this: Peter didn't believe when he took those baby boys behind the shed, but as Ingwald held his trembling hands and they cried out to the Lord, he believed.'

I know Grandma wants it to be true, that unwrapping a toddler and an infant and making a fire brought Peter to the Lord. She holds on to once saved, always saved; she believes he'll leave behind his sin and come back to the Lord. But for most, that's not enough; you got to walk the walk, and that just ain't my Uncle Peter's way. He just knew something we don't; maybe he still knows. He saw deep into those boys: something about where they were going or where they were from.

Uncle Peter is a black sheep; for all his coming-to-the-Lord story Grandma told me, he's still got a ways to come. I guess I always thought my uncle was unsaved and that all he did and said was still waiting to be swept away by the blood of Jesus. Now that I know he's been saved and is backslid, I worry more about his soul and I understand why Grandma don't want him in her house. Peter's been found once; I hope he finds his way again before the Lord returns. Reuben's seen him with beer, and Mom says he can't seem to settle down with one woman. Grandma says that he'll come back to the Lord. When she was but a young girl, the Lord spoke to her: *All your boys will return home before I call you home.*

Grandma asks me to put another split log on the fire, so I go to the basement to get the wood.

When my grandma was a little girl, Wisconsin was a frontier. Her daddy traded pelts with the Indians and her momma minded the store. Grandma, blonde pigtails tied in ribbons, tidied paper sacks and swept the plank floor with a straw broom. 'Be still.' That's all she remembers of when the Indians would come through the door. 'Be still.'

She still knows those words in German because that's how

her momma talked. Little Grandma was let loose on the candy under the counter and could cut brown bags into paper dolls as much she liked as long as she kept quiet. I can hear those snip, snips while she slices long lines of girls holding hands all in a row. She liked to eat striped candy while the tall shadows leaned over the counter and her momma guarded her beneath her skirts. Grandma still claims a fear of Indians, but I believe she just wants candy.

It makes her laugh, my reckoning about her sweet tooth. She smiles wide and shows me her rows of perfect teeth. They aren't stained with coffee and wine like those in the world, but she does misuse them to bite off stray threads. I've seen her do it. She claims she tries not to be afraid of good Indians, Christian Indians, just the ones that still do the worshipping of the trees and such. But I've seen her fearful in the grocery store, too scared to walk an aisle with an Indian in it. I guess she can't forget her momma's legs trembling beneath her skirt when the men, smelling of campfire and horses, stood in the store. Grandma's blonde hair would have been a prize scalp, so her momma said.

'Once I peeked out, low by Momma's foot, and I saw a buckskin moccasin.' That's all she knows. Naomi's an Indian, and that ain't nothing she's got to be ashamed of, not her or us. Grandma says it and it is true. Naomi is part of us now. 'She's no more Indian than we are.' Snip, snip, she cuts the stray threads of a patch with her teeth; snip, snip, she cuts the stray threads with scissors. 'Liquor's another story. Only the blood of Jesus can cover that.' And she believes that for any man.

Naomi ain't no Indian to Grandma; Grandma can't get enough of that girl. But, for once, Naomi ain't here; it's just Grandma and me rocking and working, staying warm by the fire. I thread needles and pile the patches by colour: blue with blues, stripe with stripes. The wooden chair creaks across the floor while Grandma's hands stay busy with the quilt.

Sometimes I wonder if I'm one of the righteous or the wicked. Would the Lord spare this place and this people for my sake? Or will He sweep it all away, all of us together, sinners and saints alike? He will not do it; I believe it in my soul. The Judge of heaven and earth will do right. But it is not my place to know the mind of God, or the timing of His return.

6

YESTERDAY AFTER SCHOOL, DADDY WANTED TO WORK ON THE old tractor that he's reassembling. Someday he'll have his own shed — maybe we'll even own our own woods — but until then, his projects are piled up in the dust and grease of Grandma's barn. I stayed inside with Grandma for an hour, but once she started talking about making lefse, I made my escape. Peeling potatoes makes my hands go red and itchy.

When I left Grandma in the kitchen, she was pressing a white kitchen towel against her forehead. Sometimes I look at Grandma and see the Haralson apple tree we have in the orchard in the yard. This August, it had so many little green apples pulling it down, its branches were fit to break. Straining to hold its arms up to allow its fruit to ripen in the sun, the tree was slowly losing its fight as it drooped closer and closer to the ground. Deer eating off it at night were like dark, silent ghosts surrounding a weeping willow. Grandma holds all of us up to the Lord in prayer, trusting God for our safety and salvation. As she leaned against the kitchen sink, Grandma looked bone weary, and it don't seem fair that she didn't have anyone anymore to help hold up her arms.

It ain't really fair, neither, to call the abandoned little patch of fruit trees we got an orchard. The pines surrounding it have grown too close and are shadowing what apple and cherry trees have survived ice storms and lawnmower crashes. Daddy planted most of them for an agriculture project his senior year of high school, so I guess we are all still hoping they'll become a success. I thought on all of these things while walking out to the barn, dragging my feet in my hand-me-down pink, puffy moon boots.

Sliding the barn door across to squeeze into the shelter, I thought I heard a coon or a skunk or something scratching around the back of the lawnmower. Already covered in grime, the mower was sitting idle as it had since the end of September, so leaning against it to peer over into the corner was my first mistake. Nothing living was in the corner anyways, and my second mistake happened right quick. An old Gustafson's ice-cream-pail handle, twisted up and tangled by the mower, had been kicked out the side of the blower and was there waiting for me to plonk my foot down hard. The wire ripped right through the bottom of my boot and screwed up into my foot. At first, I only felt wet soak into my boot, like I was barefoot on the cold, concrete floor of the barn. The metal must have clanked my bone inside my foot, though, because I felt that hit right up to my teeth.

Daddy was there quicker than I thought he could move. He'd been wiping his hands on an oily rag, cleaning up, getting ready to come back inside when he heard me cry out. Kneeling over me, down on the floor with the swallow droppings and the dust sticking to my boots and jacket, he shook my shoulder to get me to stop crying, look up at him and tell him what was causing the racket. When I pointed to the wire tangled around and through my boot and he saw the thin trickle of blood staining the sole, he caught the hair hanging in my face and tucked it behind my ear.

'What you over here crouching around for?'

I explained about the possibility of coon or even skunk.

He just grabbed me up in his arms and carried me out of the barn. 'You let them skunks look after themselves.' His arms were shaking, but he was smiling the comfort smile he gave the ewes when they were lambing: knowing they was hurting, but loving them the same. He carried me to the house like I was still little and light.

Daddy showed my wired boot to Grandma. She put down her potatoes and told him to set me on the couch.

I was wailing — I balled my hands and bit my lip, but I couldn't keep the sound down — and he said, 'I got to take her in.' Even his hands were trembling.

Grandma shook her head no; her mouth was set firm and she pointed him to the kitchen. They went in and there were some words, but I couldn't hear them rightly over my own noise. But I didn't need to hear; I knew. Grandma's momma seemed to fall into whatever faith was passing through Failing on any given day. We're blessed that that woman came to know the truth of Jesus Christ when she did, but still, our family hangs on to some of Great-Grandma's beliefs picked up from travelling Jehovah's Witnesses, Latter-day Saints, and even questionable revivalist preachers. Grandma wants always to pray for healing and to believe for the touch of the Lord. I guess we still have to suffer now even though we have insurance through Daddy's construction job.

When they came out of the kitchen, the time for words was over.

And then they took it out. Grandma ran a bath and Daddy

sat me, clothes and all, in the warm tub. He cut my boot off, real careful around where the wire went through, with his skinning blade. Grandma held my leg up and Daddy looked to the problem; in one quick pull, he untwisted the twisted metal from me.

'They would have cut it out,' he told me when I asked why he didn't let me pick doctor or home. I used to always get to pick doctor or home.

They would have cut it out. So I was glad he made my choice for me.

Today, I am waiting just inside the door of the county courthouse. The bus dropped me off after school because I had to get a tetanus shot at public health. Mom said Grandma didn't have to know about the needle. So Mom didn't have to drive into town so early, Uncle Ingwald is going to collect me from county health; he's willing to keep our secret. Afterwards, he'll drive me to church for the annual spaghetti supper before youth group. Winter coats amongst some of the larger families in the congregation have been kind of scarce this year, so we are raising some money with spaghetti.

Picking me up, Uncle Ingwald leans across the church van to open the door and make my way easy.

'This year, the spaghetti supper will keep some warm inside and out.' He chuckles, and he is so corny I laugh at him.

It is only a couple streets' drive to the church, but with my injury it would have taken me all night to walk. As we drive, Uncle Ingwald sings with the gospel radio. *I've got peace like a river; I've got peace like a river; I've got peace like a river in my soul.* He taps out the beat with his hands on the wheel and gives me a grin. An older and balder version of my dad's, his face carries scars from childhood. His calm voice and smile always make me feel happy and safe. It's a bit early for the supper, so bunches of kids are running around in the vacant field next to the church playing touch football. They run and scream and crash into the piles of leaves and snow, laughing.

We are singing *peace like a river, joy like a mountain* when we roll past the clump of trees all us kids call Babylon. A collection of twelve or thirteen pines in various stages of health, the ground beneath is littered with the long, auburn needles of the giant red pines and cedars and the sharp, short, green prickles of the ponderosas.

In the darkness there, under the canopy of sweeping branches, Samuel is hunched on the ground. He is wrestling with Zachariah Oleson, one of the boys my age. Samuel is on top of him like the bull in the yard. They're both wearing pants — it's too freezing for skin — but there's no mistaking what would be happening without the cloth, without the cold. Zach's pale face is pushed deep into the needles with only his wild eyes staring out of the dark like a startled sparrow. I see Samuel, and Uncle Ingwald sees Samuel too.

'That damn boy.'

I have never heard him curse.

'Not again. I'll kill that damn boy.'

The kingdom of heaven is sowed with good seeds and weeds both; it's not until the wheat sprouts, raising heads higher than the rest, that the weeds show themselves low down, close to the soil. With my own eyes, I see.

Uncle Ingwald parks the car crooked next to the trees we call Babylon. The lacy white-ridged scars that crisscross his cheeks are raised up and quivering. He tells me to go inside now and get Glory, and he runs toward the shadows of the trees.

Samuel spots him. Samuel stops.

I don't see my uncle all during the special coat supper. Throughout the fellowship hall, people are laughing and enjoying each other's company. All of us are thankful for food and friends and family. Aunt Gloria, with puffy eyes, comes inside after one of the elders says grace. Working in the kitchen, serving steaming spaghetti and garlic bread, she leans shaky against the high countertop and sighs with each scoop. Her arms must be so tired.

Mixed in with the overflow barn coats and snow-wet coats and new coats, Samuel has to stay in the nursery and wait for the spaghetti supper to end. When he sees me peering in through the door crack, he grabs my hand.

'We were just playing, just wrestling.' His face is sad and covered in pimples; where a beard could be are just infected bumps. I don't want to look at him, his slumpy shoulders, skinny arms and that tight curly hair, but he is talking close to my ear now. He wants me to stay in here with him, smelling garlic and milk, crouching on shrunken chairs and playing with baby toys. He wants me in here with him so he ain't alone.

I wish I'd stayed out front with Naomi and Reuben, clearing tables and scraping plates. I point at my hurt foot and make a show of my hobbling, so he grabs a little chair for me to sit on and then pushes puzzles off the table for me to rest my leg.

He is digging in his pants pocket for something to offer. 'I've got a peach pit to suck.'

'Where'd you find a peach in autumn?' I ask him. It is a

hard crumpled stone hung with bits of pink-orange flesh. Looking at the sticky lint, pine needles and dirt, I can see it's been in his pocket awhile.

He barely pauses to think. 'I got it in your daddy's orchard.' He is lying, but it don't change his face. Samuel holds his mouth in a smile, tight over his yellow teeth the same when praising or cursing.

There is a green felt board on the wall waiting to hold a floppy Moses in the bulrushes or Jesus on the cross. Aunt Gloria has always taught the nursery class, and I remember learning Bible stories and the Fruit of the Spirit on that board: apples of love, something or the other for goodness, and the like. Aunt Glory's red curly hair is now shot through with wiry grey, but she's kept the same short crop my whole life. Rows and rows of braided blonde can judge her all they like; she knows her way. My aunt wears her hair like a man. The nursery is tight, barely four steps long and three across from the far blue wall to the stacked cribs with wooden bars to mind the babies. Thirty teething toddlers must've gnawed the plastic rainbow I hold in my hands.

Samuel tries to get my attention by hanging his tongue out the side of his mouth like a dead deer. He ignores me at school or on the bus, but now he wants my undivided.

'Aren't you supposed to be at hockey camp?' I ask him. Samuel loves to skate hard, breathlessly skidding to a shredded-ice stop, wearing heavy padding and the blue-and-white Failing jersey.

'Not until December, after deer season.' Samuel thinks he's got friends on the hockey team, but he don't. He can sharpen his skates all he likes, but they call him Smell-ule both behind his back and to his face. Samuel is held down in the world as firm as he is held up here. And it is hard being us at school. Most of the worldly kids won't waste their time on us except for teasing, so we are friends amongst ourselves and with the Bible-believing Baptist kids and other Fundies. They sit out the dances and sex talks with us Pentecostals, so we all know each other from the school library. But we aren't many.

Samuel is spread out on the carpet, arching his back and stretching his bowed legs. He smiles and shines his eyes soft.

'Are you in season, Ruth?' This is how this boy is, trying to joke like a man. 'You sure are real pretty.'

And I can see how he will be then, taller but still not much thicker round; he'll be the pastor of this church and the father of children. He will lead. They'll all think they've drowned him, but he'll still have a secret fire buried. Amongst all the pale ghosts that sit in this church — baby-weary mommas and work-broken men — hardly anyone holds that spark inside. Samuel does, but I don't know how he keeps it safe. Maybe he could guard mine too.

I shouldn't think such things and he sure shouldn't say them: cousins are too close. But it ain't the first time. Whenever Samuel is near — especially if we are alone — he holds his eyes too low on me and leans closer than he should. Even in church, he'll press my hand hard during prayer. But all the boys do it: sitting thigh-to-thigh in the pews with the girls, they breathe in our smell. Reuben always makes sure he's next to somebody who's not blood, but it seems like Samuel aims to claim me. And sometimes, even I like feeling a bit special, maybe chosen.

Samuel's eyes shine blue in the light from the Noah's Ark lamp. Holding each other's tails, the elephants and all the handpicked animals march two-by-two, male and female, around the shade. Animals' histories can be traced in their bones, whether they had a leg break or a too-heavy load. Diseases, too, can show themselves on the inside of a carcass, old wounds or whatever brought the thing to finally give up and lay down. Whether you're slaughtering goats or killing weasels, the inside will show the creatures' lives. Samuel has spaghetti sauce caked in the corner of his mouth. His heart knows that he can take without paying, at least for a little while.

I stare at the chewed Noah's rainbow in my hands; he don't need to tell me what I already know.

After church, Mom and I are squashed together in the truck, our sweaters and jackets making us wider than we should be, as we wait for the windshield to thaw and fog to clear from the glass. Outside, Daddy is struggling with the ice and I feel the sound of his scraping down deep in my teeth. My tongue prods a hollow place inside my molar while the noise rasps our ears. Reuben is kicking frozen slush away from the tyres; it is finally time to head home. I tilt my head to rest on Mom's shoulder and I hold my mittens over my nose to keep it warm. The day is done.

'Why on earth would that woman be walking?' Mom rubs on her side window to melt a way through the frost to double-check. 'In this weather?' Freezing cold air whips into the truck as she opens the door to call out. 'Glory? Something wrong with the van?'

Gloria's head doesn't so much turn as twist hard on its stalk. I didn't see her and my cousins bundled up and crunching across the parking lot, but now with my aunt's eyes raging all afire, I wonder how she hasn't melted a way through; her hat is pulled low across her forehead, but it can't tamp down her heat. They walk over to the truck.

'Van's fine, Marie.' As she stands at the gaping vehicle door, Gloria's breath puffs like smoke, and her hollow eyes are still red-rimmed and burning like coals. 'Pastor's staying in prayer, so we'll walk.' Her lips are straight and tight; she don't let her thoughts betray her none, even if she's got some betrayal in her.

When my mom suggests a ride, taking it in turns since we all won't fit at once, Gloria shakes her head and keeps that rigid mouth.

And Naomi starts in, whining and complaining about her good shoes and the snow and wind whipping up her dress. 'The ride is here, Momma. Can't we take it?' Naomi stamps her feet, trying to thaw through her legs, and wraps her purple scarf higher around her face. 'It's not my fault.' Naomi's eyes are always so brown and wide and warm, but tonight they are blinking and squinting against the cold. She is moaning and carrying on, but Samuel stands still, hands holding on to his elbows. He doesn't open his mouth to speak. He is without a hat, and his hair catches in the wind; he isn't wearing a jacket, just his Sunday button-down shirt and a sweater. His sister keeps on going. She makes the whimpering of a turned-aside calf.

There is no moving her, Gloria; she chooses the hard way for its own sake. She silences Naomi with a fierce look and points her chin at Samuel, slumping silent and head down. 'Thank you, family, but we'll live.' And she pushes Samuel in the back, forcing him to walk ahead of her while she holds Naomi to her side.

Mom shuts the truck door and then reopens it and yanks it fast again; it never catches the first time closed. The rubber inside the door has cracked and come away, but it will seal eventually given enough firm direction. As they walk away, Samuel dragging his feet one step ahead of Naomi and Gloria huddled together against the wind, the night seems to get darker with stars burning millions of miles away moving even farther from us. Maybe the moon has gone behind a cloud.

Mom's fingers kneading her sore leg lets me know she is troubled, that none of it sits right with her neither. 'He's on his knees,' is all she says, and she starts her humming, her heart reaching out to the Lord.

Whether she means Ingwald or Samuel, I'm unaware, but she does not speak against the anointed. We don't always know another way. Daddy and Reuben clamber into the truck, snow clumping off their arms and melting onto our warmer bodies.

As he clunks the truck into reverse, Daddy takes one look at Mom and holds up his other hand. 'Don't start, Marie. I can't tell my brother what to do. They'll survive the walk.'

And Mom keeps on humming, looking straight out the window. Then she pauses her song. 'Who will Ingwald pray for when there's no one left?'

The engine churns under the hood.

It is a dark, cold night, and we are all tired and in need of rest. The truck has warmed long enough; we begin our journey home.

7

GRANDMA'S BARN NEEDS RE-SHINGLING. MOSTLY IN TATTERS, the shingles left hanging on the roof through this past summer's storms are starting to slip under the weight of wind and wet. Every now and then, you can see them dropping to the dirt, caught on a blowing gust like crumpled maple leaves leftover from fall. Where the shingles land, they smudge the snow, and Grandma says that from her kitchen the roof looks like a patchy cur dog with mange. That can't be good. Seems like most the barns in our area burn down before they fall down; we've had three go just this last year. But Grandma don't want to lose that barn no matter what.

We women are clearing the table after Thanksgiving dinner. Even though my foot hurts, I have to help. We scrape and stack the plates near the sink where Grandma is running the faucet. The hot water steams up the window that looks across the farmyard; each of the four panes of glass is clouding over, and the barn is now out of sight. The shingles aren't out of Grandma's mind, though.

'Boys.'

I think it's fun when she speaks to my daddy and Uncle Ingwald like children.

'Boys. You know it wasn't long between when the Svensens'

roof went patchy to when the whole heap fell down altogether.'

The men grunt in agreement, look up and nod slowly. They are both stuffed full and stretched out in the living room: Uncle Ingwald's on the worn green couch and my daddy's on the orange davenport with his stocking feet hanging over the armrests. The boys are outside somewhere. Usually Daddy and Reuben would be out hunting on Thanksgiving, but with Grandma's new killing ban, we're all homebound. We got enough venison to fill our freezer this year anyway, but what we'll do next year, I don't know. I guess we'll have to hunt up at the cabin.

'Am I just talking to the wind?' Grandma slaps the towel on her skirt.

'Repairs take money, Momma.' Daddy knows the dollars and cents of every farm building in Failing. There's plenty he would do around our house and the homeplace if he had the means; he spends most of each Sunday pencilling plans on the bulletin. Nobody's proud of the state of Grandma's barn. 'You got some put by we need to know about?'

And I know right away he don't try to be mean — just seems he gets tired. He works and works and got nothing to show for it but rough hands. A man can hardly feed his family. And he's still sore at Grandma.

'Maybe you should talk to Peter about it.' Daddy's picking at her scab. 'He's got no end of time and money, and he sure don't have no sense.'

Grandma makes a sound like a hurt pup. She shakes her head and moves slow back into the kitchen.

Ingwald opens his eyes and gives my daddy a harsh look. He don't even say a word, but the matter is closed for now. It will rest.

She really shouldn't be hassling them right after they've eaten like that. We've fed so much today, we're all feeling a bit sluggish and weighted down. We ate cheese soup and wild rice soup; cranberries straight out of the can; fresh rolls hot from the oven with butter sliding down their sides; boiled potatoes, carrots and rutabagas; and turkey, ham and venison. I ate a lot of both dill and bread-and-butter pickles and green and black olives too, because I do love pickles and olives.

Daddy ate a lot of pickled pork hocks, salted herring and slimy lutefisk, because Daddy loves things that look and smell foul. Reuben and I teased him after the big dinner, and he pretended to be all offended. He said we were lucky that he was full and sleepy like a wintering bear, too slow and dumb to catch us kids and give us a good swipe. He might now need to consider some hibernating, as he looks like he's having some trouble breathing easy even when he's laid out flat on his back.

Grandma is right about Svensen's barn. Down across the rows of corn stubble in the fields that separate our homeplace from theirs, you used to could see Svensen's red barn barely standing like a worn-out, swayback cow. Her main ridge was all slumped and broken, and her side timbers let through the sunlight until it seemed you could see right through her ribs to the other side. Late last winter, we woke to a different view of scraggly jack pines behind a pile of red scrap dusted with white; she'd collapsed under the gentle weight of a new snow. Come summer, even her remnants had caught fire and burnt. But our barn can't be that bad, even though it is as old as Svensen's. Even if the roof looks a little mangy, our family wouldn't ever let it all just fall apart. And anyway, most of the barns around here burn before they fall.

Wafting across the kitchen, the smell of hot coffee and cinnamon-spiced apple cider wakes the slumbering gluttons.

Grandma looks itchy and seems ready to get the roof settled. 'Keeping up the homestead is the same as keeping up the family. Just think of Thanksgiving without pumpkin pie or lefse. Letting that barn die would be like letting go of our name or letting go of our faith. Boys, what would your daddy be thinking right about now?'

My own daddy's busy eating lefse right now, so I believe that he couldn't imagine Thanksgiving without it even if he tried. Uncle Ingwald is slowly stirring cream into his coffee. Grandma's not getting the reaction she wants.

'Peter may have forgotten who he is and where he's from and where he's going, but I thought both you boys knew better than that.' She lets loose the same little cry-sounding sigh from before. Seems she's got to almost bleed to get their attention.

Of course, Uncle Peter couldn't — or wouldn't — make over for Thanksgiving again, even though we can almost see his house from Grandma's porch. Mom told me that Grandma misses Uncle Peter for he is still her middle baby. So when she is mad or ornery, it is really because she is sad over her son.

Uncle Ingwald puts down his coffee spoon. 'Momma, there isn't anybody here forgetting who they are or what they owe. We'll get that barn fixed up come summer.' He takes another sip of coffee and then breathes out real slow. 'And Peter's bound to come back soon enough.' It is hard to tell whether he means back to the homeplace or back to the Lord. 'Peter's sins will be far from the mind of God, just as far as the east is from the west. The Lord does not forget the ones He loves.'

Ingwald makes plans without keeping promises: lumber

and nails he won't buy, hauling and hammering that my daddy and Reuben will have to do. My uncle will be minding souls with his soft hands, and we'll owe more to the farmers' co-op. Ingwald keeps talking. Daddy just nods his head.

The boys are back inside, and Grandma wants to settle with us kids and look at the few pictures from when our daddies were little. Reuben, Samuel and Naomi scrunch in real close around her big chair by the fire. I need another piece of lefse, so first I scoot back into the kitchen. Mom, her hands still soaking in suds, and Aunt Gloria, swishing a drying towel across the heavy pots, together have their backs to me. They don't pause their talking while I creep toward the lefse, so I disappear under the table real quick. I almost let out a yelp when my arm touches fur, but it's just the barn cat hiding under the table too.

'She shouldn't be one to talk of forgetting names,' Aunt Gloria says under her breath.

My mom reaches out and stills Aunt Gloria's drying hand. 'Glory, she's got enough on her heart right now, worrying over Peter like she does.' The cat keeps busy washing her pelt, each scrape of the tongue revealing maple-coloured fur underneath its regular orange coat. 'Esther came up in an old time, that's all; she can't be held accountable for all the wrongdoings of the past.'

'Marie, please let me hold some grudges.' Aunt Gloria laughs. 'A preacher's wife can't be too perfect, you know.'

Crouched under the table, pressing the warm cat against my tummy, I learn a lot about Grandma and our name. How Grandma's name wasn't always Esther. How Grandma had a part-Indian momma who gave her an Indian name before the momma died. How Grandma's daddy got her a new, German momma who gave her a new, German name. And how Grandma won't ever talk about being no Chippewa, Cherokee or Sioux; she won't allow being no mixed-breed squaw at all.

Mom is putting away the big cooking pots now. 'Glory, if it wasn't for Esther and her mommas, whichever one she cares to claim, this family wouldn't know the Lord. Your Ingwald wouldn't have become a preacher, and you pair never would have met. So your Ingwald wouldn't even be your Ingwald, and you wouldn't ever have become my Glory.'

They're both laughing their quiet lady laughs, and Aunt Gloria puts her arm gently around Mom's waist. At the sink together, Mom's soft hips and Gloria's narrow bones lean on the counter, aprons wicking up splashed dishwater. They just rest together silently and still for a little while.

'I wish we had what you share,' Gloria says and starts wiping the dishes again.

My momma tilts her head but don't say a word. She reaches for a plate.

Gloria speaks quiet. 'Just watching him look at you — love you, want to touch your arm — makes me lonesome. That was so long ago for me, but I remember what that's like.'

Mom bites her lip and looks at her hands.

The cat leaps from my arms and scuttles away from the table. Gloria straightens quick, like being woke from a dream. They stack the plates in the sideboard.

I can imagine forgetting the names of the states or even forgetting part of the Lord's Prayer, but I can't imagine forgetting the name my momma gave me. Aunt Gloria and Mom are finished washing up, and they brush by the table on their way through the kitchen.

I can see my mom's right knee, its purple scars running down the front and sides, like runs in stockings you can't ever fix. Right after Reuben was born and she was learning to drive, she was hit by a milk truck that ran a stop sign; she never did walk quite straight again. I guess it all just goes to show, don't it, that you don't always know what's there until you look underneath. And, sometimes, you've got to look real close.

The dishes are washed, dried and put away. The men are snoring on the couches and the women are now talking with Grandma by the fire. Since no one has thought to give us kids something to do, we've found some things ourselves.

Naomi and I are in the haymow at the top of Grandma's barn. We scratch away at old straw and pigeon droppings to get down to the wooden rafters. Peeking through the cracks below us, we can see long lines of Samuel and Reuben tinkering with a snowmobile deep in the stone foundation of the barn. Hushed, their voices are barely separate; they're making some sort of plan — I can feel it in the lean of their bodies — but I couldn't say what's coming.

The haymow has a door that slides open into nothing. Swing through that gate, and I'd step out into air; only swallows would swoop around my flailing arms as I fell like a stone for fifty feet down. I reckon that the hay chute used to butt up against that door, and bales would ride up or down the slide in style. Snakes, rats, toads and whatever else got itself wrapped up in the hay would worm out of the itchy bales and discover that they had themselves a whole new life high up in the barn. Sure, they might have lost a leg or tail in the transport, but I believe that didn't slow them down none in discovering their new world above the trees. Whatever they suffered on the way, thanks to the ride, they were born again.

Being trapped in a hay bale after having my leg ripped off by the baler seems to me a pretty horrible way to travel. It seems as if much of nature gets about trapped. Look at seeds: a winged maple seed floating on a breeze has a hard core weighing down one end, and inside that weight is the seed. He's squished up inside nothing bigger than the end of my pinky, a big maple waiting to spread his branches. Trees look to me like they have faces etched in the ridges and scars along their bark. Walking in the woods, I came across a white birch tree with a pin-oak twisted through its branches. Maybe they once were sisters who couldn't abide being apart, or maybe they were brothers who couldn't bear being together.

'Ruth.' Naomi is crouched near a green tarp.

Shoving aside the rocks at the front corners of the old cloth, I smell oil and dust. When we've pulled it halfway back, we see two oil cans. Stacked in the rusty cans are rocks; Naomi reaches into the nearest to grab one. The rock looks like a glob of concrete, but as she lifts it, it separates into two: inside there are dark, maroon ridges with creamy swirls. These are agates, Grampa's agates that Grandma said he found down by the river. He cracked them for her, hauled them up the ladder, and they've been safe and waiting in the haymow all along.

Each one is different: some, swirls of maroon and cream; some are castles of pink and green ice. Even though they're all cracked, we can't tell from the outside what's going on in there until it's pulled apart. Naomi's wearing mittens, but my hands are cold and rough. Rocks carry with them something of their family and home, but they also seem to leave behind sandy pieces of themselves wherever they travel.

Naomi takes the first agate she touched and slips it into her coat pocket. Those rocks have stayed hid up here for longer than we've lived. On the back of my coat, she wipes her hands clean of grit.

'Grandma will let me.'

I suppose she will.

I make sure Naomi climbs down the ladder first, pretending it's because I'm still half-lame. Soon, I'll tell her, but I want to decide when. She doesn't wait at the bottom.

As I haul myself lower — rung by rung, trying to tread gentle on my sole — I think about the smallish creatures that keep changing and I wonder about the trees and the rocks that never seem to change. Like a hurry-up tadpole frog, I used to pray to become a woman. Now that I have bled brown for three days, I pray that God will make it stop. I pray for the peace I hold when I am walking in the woods under my trees. I want to be as silent and still as a stone, as hard as a rock. *Rock of ages, cleft for me, let me hide myself in Thee. Let the water and the blood, from Thy wounded side which flowed, be of sin the double cure, save from wrath and make me pure.*

8

RIGHT AFTER SUNRISE, AND UNCLE PETER'S MUSCLY BACK IS to the door when I slide into his shed. A pale axe handle is pinched in a steel vice bolted onto the shop bench. His big hands are shaping the wood, rasping away whatever can't fit his grip. A decent hickory handle allows the guiding hand to slide free, up and down without hitching; he could afford them store-bought, but a good man shapes his own. I'm thinking he just might not see me. Crinkly wood shavings pile near his boots on the concrete floor.

'What can I do you for, Ruth?' He doesn't even turn around, just keeps pulling the rasp along the handle, drawing the metal through the wood.

'I won't be in your way.' I really won't; I'll sit on a bucket and pick my scabs or any old thing. 'Mom's cleaning.' I bite my lip and wait. The wood shudders, almost trying to twist away.

Uncle Peter keeps working and then hunches his shoulders. I can stay. He still hasn't turned around. There's two ways here: keep still until he forgets me, or get him talking and wanting me to stay. I'll try quiet first, just sit here and watch the man work.

Seems like I never get to see him: never at church, not at Grandma's, not nothing. That shiny truck of his only shadows our driveway if he's helping Reuben run the trap line or if he happens to need to ask Mom about something. He missed Thanksgiving and he wasn't even out hunting his own land. Uncle Peter sat alone in his house or maybe in a broken-down trailer with some lipsticked woman eating microwaved turkey-meat dinner. And me, I was stuck inside mashing potatoes and washing dishes. Even before she banned hunting, Grandma didn't care much for me shooting. Thanksgiving is a day for hunting, and Uncle Peter could go if he wanted; he just won't.

Uncle Peter don't hunt, not since he was sixteen. He don't talk about it much. No surprise as he don't say much of anything unless asked; usually he just sets there smiling — hair combed tidy, shaved face shiny and clean — but always with those eyes on him like a beat dog.

'Can't sleep, can't hunt.' That's all the explanation I've ever heard him give. Other folks say the law won't let him hunt. My daddy says Peter hears it again almost every night: the shot rings out; the bullet smacks the body; the man crumples to the ground with a scream. And those who saw do not speak: there is a silence that hurts his ears. For a while there are no voices. There is no sound. It is a frightful, still blackness.

'Uncle Peter.' My bucket creaks, and I stare at the floor. 'Can you tell me — not if you don't want to — but will you tell me why you don't hunt?'

The rasp stills for a moment, and the man sighs. Silence hangs heavy in the shed, and I regret my question. I don't mean to cause him pain. Pushing up from the bucket, I start stammering about leaving. He looks straight at me and halts me by raising his hand. I hush. I settle again.

His voice is strained. 'Ruth, I'll tell you once.' And he does. And in my mind's eye I see.

They rumble at night so we can't sleep, harvester machines in the close cornfield: stripping ears from arms, kernels from ears, trampling and breaking the now brittle stalks. The fields are stripped almost bare. Only a few rows remain, a couple three sacrificed to lure in the hungry and plump up the deer before hunting season. The red, purple and yellow leaves have left. Naked and plain, the trees stretch branches like antlers against the sky.

When crossing a fence — even just a barbwire fence crossed a hundred times before — a guy's got to have a plan. Rifles are a heavy load, so crossing a fence has rules. One man relieves himself of his gun: his friend holds it for him while the man goes beneath and between the wires. The next fellow does the same: his friend holds his rifle while the fellow scales the fence. If there is a third man, all the better: he can hold all the weapons while the others cross and then hand them through before he makes his own way. Along with setting your rifle on safety — or, for some, walking unloaded — sharing the burden don't make it easy, but makes it near enough to safe.

They are hunting. My daddy is only fourteen, but farmer-strong with callused hands and a long-looking squint. Peter is sixteen and taller still, but thick with the hay-throwing muscles that hurtle the football like a college-bound boy. The neighbour boy, John Magnusson, is sixteen too. Known for his lanky legs and meanness, he is the only son of an unhappy man. There are rows and rows of broken cornstalks with a few sections standing strange and alone. What snow has come has melted in patches, but this has already been a light year. Mostly frozen mud makes their way hard, pulling at their tripping boots and scraping their shins, and it has been a long, cold day.

John scratches his nose with red, gloveless hands; he wants to make the most of the weak light and make a final push through the woods his family and mine share. Daddy and Peter agree: they might as well try and not come home empty-handed. Toward the trees they walk, across the field that joins Grandma's land with Magnusson's. Up over their left shoulders they can see Magnusson's barn. The silo is painted with an American flag. There is no smoke coming from the house's chimney. Toward the woods, they are walking without talking. John walks fast with those long legs and leads the way, while Peter and my daddy bring up the rear.

John hits the fence first and scrambles through easy, even with his gun strapped across him. He pauses to lift up the top wire for Daddy as Peter reaches out to take his brother's gun. Daddy is already crouched to go through but — reminded — he straightens and turns to hand Peter his gun. Daddy bends and starts to clamber through again, and his jacket back snags on a barb. He is caught, but only by fabric, and with a rip he keeps moving. But Peter has already moved forward to hand John Daddy's gun; John holds out those cold hands, touches the wooden stock and the gun drops onto the frozen ground. Knocked off safety, the gun discharges and the bullet sings past Daddy's ear and into John's stomach.

And there is blood on the snow. John screams once only and there is blood melting the frost on the dirt. John is struggling to get up and Daddy is holding him down, flat on his back. They hear their friend holler and watch the entrails bulge. There is so much blood.

Folks say that Peter don't hunt because he killed that Magnusson boy. People talk and reckon he is a felon and the law won't let him hunt. Now he killed him, but he didn't do wrong and he wasn't charged. All the boys were guilty of being in a hurry for the hunt. Uncle Peter quit the day John Magnusson died. No more football, so no more waiting on maybe-someday college. No more killing, so no more waiting on hunting seasons. He didn't even graduate high school; instead, Peter joined the navy so he wouldn't have to handle a gun daily. When he came back from the navy — even with farm prices falling through the floor — he bought the farm off old Magnusson. The man didn't have no heir. Peter still plants corn in that field. Around and around, he rides that rusty tractor: tilling the soil, planting the seed, and cutting down the crop. He don't leave no corn for nobody.

My daddy still hunts. Maybe he can because the boy wasn't his friend or maybe because the bullet took a chance but didn't cut him. Daddy says a guy's got to learn to carry his burden and let others carry their own. Uncle Peter carries a too-heavy load. But Jesus himself will take up our infirmities; He'll carry our sorrows. That ain't something God makes His boy do, strikes Him or smites Him with our afflictions. Instead, that is Christ's own nature: *He was pierced for our transgressions, He was crushed for our iniquities; the punishment that brought us peace was upon Him, and by His wounds we are healed.*

Peter can't sleep for the echoes that keep him awake at night: the sound of the shot and the sound of the fallen.

And, mostly, the stillness after. Being tired is an awful thing. In autumn, we all just want to get some rest, lay down and drift off, not scared as children are. We will sleep only a little while, won't be leaves afraid to let go, won't be pumpkins fighting decay. Harvest ain't death, just means little sleep. And harvest is over; now we rest.

Hot and wet is what I feel, not pain. My palms are slippery. I am shook from Uncle Peter's story and look down at blood smeared across my hands. I was smoothing my fingers across the biting edge of the axe and almost sliced the tips. No cuts, but when I drew back my hands fast I dropped the axe and somehow sliced something. My hand is bleeding like a headless chicken, but I sure ain't running around none. I just sit on the bucket, stunned by the hard pain beating in time with my heart and the blood running down my hand. I'm still not making a sound. But he knows.

'Damn it, girl.' Uncle Peter is wrapping a greasy rag tight around my hand quick. His voice is still low but sharper than usual. 'Can't even keep body and soul together.' But it ain't a rebuke on me; he tries to smile while he's talking and wrapping. I know we both hear Grandma's voice echoing in our heads.

Pulled to my feet and over to the workbench, and my hand is stretched beneath the light Uncle Peter uses to tie trout lures. He unwraps the towel to see what I have done to myself. He spits on my hand and wipes gentle: the skin is sliced clean off beneath my knuckle and a big flap of meat and fat is hanging off the side of my finger. The hurt starts pounding real hard.

Uncle Peter holds his face an inch from my hand. 'Should get some stitches, Ruthie. We got to take you to town.' He looks straight in my face. 'You know them stitches hurt worse than the cut. I got to take you in, but you'll wish we hadn't.' He ain't been scared until just now.

I shake my head. 'No hospital.' I don't know what stitches feel like, but I know I don't want no more metal in me. And I don't want Grandma to find out I went to town.

He nods. 'You sure?' He angles his head at me like he's trying to gauge my pain. 'This is your choice, girl. I'm not about to make it for you.'

And I look at my hand and I think of the blood. 'No hospital.'

Uncle Peter reaches beneath the bench and gets a shoebox holding aspirin, little scissors, needles, fishing line and duct tape. I hold my breath and look at the ceiling, the spiderwebs and nests and dark. He doesn't use the needles though, just wraps it tight with gauze, putting it all back in place.

Grandma was a stickler about not needing no doctors interfering with her boys' salvation. Growing up on a dirt farm, the boys had their share of knocks and bumps, but none was ever brought to — or born in, for that matter — a hospital. Grandma says Uncle Ingwald survived to be a man of God only by the grace of God. He had been scalded with boiling potato water as a baby, torn away half his ear lobe, and caught an exploding canning jar with his face all before the age of sixteen. Even being the youngest, Daddy barely made it, being sickly since birth and coming down hard with scarlet fever as a baby. When he was six, my daddy's belly button swelled up and seemed like it wanted to pop right out of him, but Grandma and Grampa just wrapped cheesecloth around Daddy's middle and prayed and fasted every day for a week until the infection passed. Uncle Peter had more of a safe passage through life. He came off the farm to enlist in the navy without a single scar and the Lord continues to watch his way for him whether Peter likes it or not. Grandma remembers everyone's trials.

The scarless man works almost silently, just making a soothing sound now and again. Near my hand, Peter's face is soft and almost clean; a few wood shavings cling to the sweat in the crinkles by his eyes. I can hear him breathe, slow and deep.

When he finishes the final wrap with duct tape, he breaks the quiet. 'There. And it will heal flat.' He winks and smiles his own crooked smile.

And I know that scar won't bother me none neither. It will lie flat beneath my wedding ring. On the day of my marriage, I'll be doubly glad to be a bride.

December

9

A WORN MAP OF ALASKA, EDGES TATTERED AND CREASES WORN, hangs on the cement wall behind the canning jars in our basement. Amongst the dusty put-up tomatoes and the pickled beans and cucumbers, I can trace the path my daddy took when he went to the frontier. Daddy says he was hunting moose and tracking caribou. Grandma says he was shirking duty, making his family care for his abandoned wife while he was off avoiding God and his child. Mom won't say nothing except that Daddy was the first to hold Reuben in his arms. He didn't go right away: he lost a month of hunting to make sure Mom could manage on her own; some men wouldn't have had that patience. Even though Daddy was gone in Alaska for over three months, at least he waited for the boy to be born. With my finger, I can almost reach to trace the path he walked so long ago with a heavy pack and heart. Mountains of tall trees and snow, giant grizzlies and salmon, Daddy's Alaska was a free place, undiscovered and lawless.

Swinging the maul hard and fast, that grown baby is splitting wood outside. Through the high basement window, Reuben's steel-capped boots are level with Daddy's head. I can hear the rhythm of his work: wrestle the log onto the stump, raise the maul and hit and split, kick aside the pieces that fall right and left to the ground. The snow is covered with bark and wood. After Reuben gets so far ahead he runs out of space to split, he knocks on the window and Daddy pulls the glass away. I back out of the wood room fashioned from the plywood sectioning the basement, and in comes the wood. Reuben pitches it down the window chute in front of the neat woodpile, and Daddy starts to stack.

I want to wait until Reuben is done throwing the wood; I don't need a log to the head. Lingering over by the canning jars, I swing open the door to the meat freezer. Heaped inside the freezer are square and other angled packages wrapped in butcher's paper. Some are labelled with my daddy's crimped writing: *Polish sausage, venison steak, ground venison*. But most packages bear Uncle Peter's hand; they say *ground beef, blade steak, prime rib* and the like. Uncle Peter gave us almost half a cow this year. Daddy's mouth turned down and he wiped his head with his hand like he didn't want charity, so Uncle Peter said it was to pay Reuben for keeping the varmints down with his trap line. Frozen strawberries and freezer-jam berries are piled in flat plastic bags along the top shelf of the freezer. I like them even before they thaw.

'Ruth, you down here to stack or watch?' Daddy's voice is a bit of a growl, and he is holding his back right where his jeans hitch up at his belt.

He knows I don't like to stack wood: it is dusty and dirty and the bark tears at my hands. Most of all, I don't want to be not looking — bending over concentrating on piling wood neat and tight in the corners — and take a flying lump of birch in the face. He ain't joking, so I push out my breath in a bit of a huff and start my way toward the wood. I climb across boxes of broken toys and worn clothes, Christmas decorations and tinsel, and photographs sketching our family from black-and-white to Polaroid. Next to a smushed cardboard box of deer antlers, a broken bike that should be in the shed is tangled across a collection of *National Geographic* and some westerns that Daddy bought at a garage sale. He knows the story behind each of the antlers, but I doubt he's gotten through the stories in the magazines and books. Neither science nor adventure would be the type of reading material he'd want the family to know about, so he must read them down here on the sly.

Daddy hides down here. But he don't waste time: there is an oil stain on the floor where he reconditioned a carburettor, and he used to butcher deer on the table before Mom made him move the whole operation to Grandma's barn. The basement is his, from the stacked ten-gallon buckets to the orange or camouflage hunting clothes hanging on the rack. There are new and old feed hats dangling off nails, machinery calendars featuring tractors and combines on the walls, and canning lids screwed to boards with the glass jars beneath hanging full of spare nuts and bolts.

In summer he hides more behind the barn, over by the rhubarb pile where his coon dogs lived before I was born. He chews tobacco out there — resting on an upturned bucket unsnarling fishing line and the like — and he thinks we don't see. But in winter, the house needs the heat and he needs to keep that wood boiler fed, so he hides most in the basement.

'Ruth? You got something better to do?'

Now I'm at the end of his patience. That's how it is with my daddy. Something can sit there for a month — maybe a book on a chair in the kitchen — and not make him mad. Then he'll tell you to move it, and if you don't jump before the words have left his mouth, no youth group for you. Reuben is splitting again, so I'm alright to stack and I start bending and grabbing. Gathering up the wood into my arms makes my sweater dirty. The basement is musty and I reckon there is mould down here in the dark corners, probably growing under the stairway that's missing all the backs of the stairs. There must be mould in that dark and dank place, mould in amongst the eyes that glow when I imagine the basement at night.

Thinking about those eyes, I find the nest: a tangle of dog hair, mattress stuffing and must-have-been newspaper. There is a round mess made in the wood we stacked in the late summer. My favourite part of laying in wood has always been finding the mice: snuggled together in a mess of grass and fur, the tiny pink babies have needle claws and bulgy eyes. Since I was little, my daddy would let me pick through the nest to see the pink, hairless babies and stroke them light with my finger. After I was done petting them, he'd walk me up along the path to Grandma's house to where the gopher lives. Since their momma abandoned them — and because we tore up their home — we'd drop the baby mice into the gopher hole so that he could adopt them. A couple years ago, it hurt my heart when I realised that those babies were chewed rather than loved. But remembering that walk with Daddy — him stopping to pick the wild strawberries that grow along the path, holding out the best for me, still warm from the sun — touches my heart too.

Putting aside the wood, I hold up the empty nest with both my hands. 'Daddy, guess we missed the adoption.'

'Don't be silly. Grow up, girl.' His mouth is drooping, hanging open a bit, and he looks at me like I'm crazy.

But I was just pretending, being the baby girl he used to set on his knee or take by hand up the path. Daddy goes back to stacking, but I stand there stupid and staring; I'm wounded. He don't hurt Reuben like he does me, not looking me in the eyes when he says mean things — 'good luck keeping a husband, Ruth' or 'that face won't make a man forget a burnt supper' — always pretending after it's a joke when it's not. He must think I'm proud, too big for my boots. He needs to squash me, but Reuben don't need squashing. I put down the mouse nest and go back to stacking wood, but the tears come and I keep wiping my snot on the arm of my sweater.

'Go help your mother, Ruth.'

Daddy hears my sniffing. He can't bear watching a woman cry.

'Mom ain't doing nothing, though.'

'Well, go and help her with that. Do nothing, just don't do it here.'

I throw down my wood and stomp toward the stairs. Even though he don't hold me no more, I know my daddy still loves me. Daddy didn't have any sisters, so he didn't learn nothing about girls. His insides are hard like the inside of a stone. Maybe my daddy's meanness is like when I loved those baby mice so much that I held them tight, tighter, until I crushed them soft and pink in my hands. Next time I find a mouse nest, I'll step on it; that'll show him what a girl I am then.

So I hunker down in my room for a couple hours, squished between pillows stacked high on the carpet like walls. I'm reading my devotions when Reuben knocks soft on the door. I act like I don't hear him, like I'm more interested in the Philistines — reading the scripture and checking my Bible guide — than my brother standing at the door. I wait until he calls my name to look up, with my eyes startled open, feigning surprise.

'You want it?' Still covered in sawdust and grimy from sweating while splitting wood outside in the snow, Reuben holds out one of our last oranges.

Fruit in winter is a luxury we usually do without, our parents neither willing nor able to pay for food that's travelled up from Florida or California or some other sunshiny place. Outside of Grandma's dried apples and frozen strawberries, what few shrivelled oranges we have left now will have to do until summer. Store-bought canned peaches will sometimes make their way to our home; Daddy's got a sweet tooth and both Mom and Grandma try to keep him happy. But for Reuben to break into our dwindling rations means he must feel there's something he owes.

I love eating the white membrane of an orange, stripping back the peel to chew the soft fuzzy casing covering the flesh and dividing the centre like a wick. Reuben likes eating the orange's heart, especially any strange middle slices, stunted misshapen pieces holding the inside together. Your taste is special, what you like or what you don't. Like Naomi with crusts, I don't like to eat corn kernels but I will eat apples without any forcing. Eating corn — even fresh sweet corn and not mealy field corn meant for cows and folks up from Chicago — feels like I'm eating seed. Corn kernels are too inside out for me. Apples have cores and seeds, but I don't mind them. Oranges have seeds that folks spit out or chew. Fruit without seeds is something I don't aim to try.

Leaning on the door, Reuben holds out the orange, waving his arm up and down like a flag, like I don't see. I turn my head so he knows I'm looking, but that fruit ain't going to fix my hurt. My brother can't help his feelings, but neither can I. I look Reuben straight in the eye. He's angry himself now, having gone to the effort but getting skunked. But he's still going to try.

'Ruth, if I never split the logs I'd never learn.'

It doesn't mean much coming from him, but I see his heart. I soften my eyes and walk to the doorway. When I take the orange, our fingers barely touch.

'I can't always change it, but I believe I'll always try.' And he leaves my room, his boots clomping on the stairs.

I'm not able to see it, but I'm sure there are crushed lines of ice and sawdust marking his path out the door: melting piles of water and wood, boot prints tracing his way outside.

I'll save this orange for later, maybe give Reuben half after supper. It isn't that Daddy loves my brother more, maybe just better. I know that is what Reuben meant. But it isn't anybody's fault. Sometimes you have to split your own wood. I know that is what Reuben said. The orange's skin is dry and puckered; it was picked a long time ago.

'Anything on your heart, Ruthie?' Getting ready for bed, Mom's babying me tonight, worried I'm still mad at Daddy.

She is combing out my wet hair, ready to braid it tight. Overnight it will almost dry, and in the morning I'll unwind it and wear it down and wavy like a mare's tail. She used to wash my hair in the bathroom sink: I'd lay along the counter and let my head fall back while she put shampoo and creme rinse through the tangles. I'm too long and old for that now, but those framed needlepoint black bears on the wall still tell me every day to: *Remember to brush your teeth. Remember to comb your hair. Remember to say your prayers.*

This upstairs bathroom has locks on both doors. Other than opening them from the inside, only a nail will get you in from the outside. If Reuben gives chase when mad, I'll lock the doors and secret myself away amongst the towels in the closet. I don't need to hide when the doors are locked, but I do anyway, just to be safe. I rest for hours in the tub, soaking. Sometimes I sing and pray. A couple years ago I realised that I was meant to get clean in the water, not merely lay and ponder. Mostly it relieves my achy knees and my head full of worries. It soothes me, body and soul, to let the water wash over me.

'If you're coming down with something, I'd rather know so we can head it off.'

She's done braiding, so I lean back into my mom's soft legs and chest and look up at her face. She gave me my straight nose and heart-shaped face. Her eyelids are drooping now, like mine will soon enough, and she's got little creases in the corners of her eyes. But she is still lovely, even with the worry that's worn her beauty away. When I was just born, Mom decided to get both me and Reuben vaccinated. Her bout with whooping cough didn't bring her or anybody closer to Jesus, so she reckoned the needles couldn't take us farther away. Daddy agreed in faith but I don't believe Grandma knows. Mom still frets, though; she lost a couple brothers in childhood.

'Are you under the weather?'

There ain't nothing wrong with me. 'I guess I'm just quiet.'

I look at the mirror. If you devote your heart to Jesus and stretch out your hands to the Lord, if you reject sin and strike it from your land and give no quarter to evil, then you can lift up your face. Hold your eyes high and straight, for shame is not on your shoulders, weighing you down. Stand tall and solid and strong.

When she left her family to make my family, Mom's picture was turned to the wall — not taken down and forgotten, but left hanging to be remembered. Above the fireplace in my grandparents' house, where I have never been, are the portraits of their family: my grandparents, my uncles and my aunts, and my many cousins. My mother's photo hangs backwards, the brown-paper backing and stapled twine showing instead of her small, square teeth. Reuben and I do not exist on that wall. Beneath that backwards photo, I don't know if there are even spaces waiting for children.

My mom is back-slid Holiness. Her Grandma Wyse was back-slid Amish. Generation by generation, we are a family of women who are slowly slipping away from heaven and toward the world. We don't ever see those Yoder grandparents. My grandma on that side says that we'll meet in heaven, or she'll watch us being sent to hell. But she won't cry, for there will be no weeping in heaven. She says that in the letter she sends every year on Mom's birthday to try and bring us back into the fold.

I don't know how the woman can judge; if it weren't for her own momma running away from the Cherokee River Amish down in the south of the state, she herself wouldn't know electricity or even motor vehicles. She can't see the sameness in her daughter and her momma. All she sees is that her daughter don't wear no prairie dress, and that she cut her hair to her shoulders and even wears fingernail polish now and again. You won't ever catch Mom in make-up or even persuade her an inch on ear-piercing, her own lobes or anyone else's, but Grandma Yoder can't touch my mom for fear of … for fear of something I don't know how to fear.

Of course my mom's parents didn't approve of the union. Even though my daddy came from clean farming stock, he wasn't Holiness and he wasn't ever going be. Grandma Yoder tried to scare her daughter off of the boy by telling her gossip about dancing and shrieking at the Pentecostal church. Grandma Wyse told Mom that we didn't know the way of salvation and that we were lost along with the world. But ever since my mom saw my daddy showing cattle at the county fair, she was smitten. She was all long blonde braids and strawberry cheeks, and he was dirty overalls and bucktooth shy. To hear Daddy tell, it was my Uncle Peter who spoke bold first and fell for her a bit as well. But it was my daddy and his shiny black bull that won her heart and the reserve champion ribbon too.

At first, their courting was done normal: Uncle Peter would drive and Daddy would buy Mom a malted milkshake at the Dairy Queen. But after Peter left for the navy, and Mom's parents forbid contact, my parents had to sneak. After her chores, Mom would take long walks through the field corn and Daddy would do just the same. Daddy says that's why Reuben's hair feels like cornsilk. Mom says she was afraid they'd be mistaken for deer and be shot dead in the field. Accident or not, gunshot from a .30-30 ain't a pretty way to travel. It's been said that deer hunting sorts out a lot of family problems in Failing. It's hard to believe how many fathers of bruised and black-eyed daughters accidentally wing their sons-in-law during the hunt. So gunshot wasn't far from my parents' mind all through their courtship. Mom said Daddy seemed to be all she needed then and forevermore; he was the one to both keep her safe and cure her lonely. Ingwald was in California, but Peter made it home special to be best man at the wedding. Mom's family wouldn't witness the union, so the wedding was small. Mom wore a plain church dress.

No matter what, even when she is lonesome for her family, my mom won't lay any fault in the whole thing, the shunning. She only says we all struggle against our sinful nature and that she knows Grandma Yoder is praying daily for our salvation, which can't be a bad thing. After Mom's car accident, she thought for a while that maybe she was being punished by God for walking away from the Holiness and her own grandma's walking away from the Amish. She was even angry at Daddy for him being gone in Alaska, and her needing to drive herself. She was thankful, though, that baby Reuben wasn't hurt — not a cornsilk hair on his head was harmed. He was proof that the Lord had protected them. Even though a car accident scares a body away from cars, it don't have to scare a soul away from God.

When they let her loose from the hospital, she didn't want to ride in a vehicle again. But she couldn't yet walk, and it was the only way home, so ride she did. Uncle Peter handed her a swaddled, sleeping Reuben, and she held him and prayed in the truck all the way home. And while Daddy hitchhiked from Alaska, desperately trying to make it home, Uncle Peter helped her learn to walk again. Mom says that you have to keep walking, just keep on walking. And when you can't walk no more, there ain't no shame in riding. Maybe she was outside the will of her momma, but I know she wasn't never outside the will of the Lord.

Troubles will be forgotten, remembered only like leaves on the current in the river, flowing by quick and tinkling. Even darkness will look bright enough to you. You stay safe standing or at rest; even laying down, you won't be afraid because no one will want to hurt you. With the Lord on your side, the righteous won't ever be lonely. *But the eyes of the wicked will fail, and escape will elude them; their hope will become a dying gasp.*

Without noticing, I sometimes stare at my face.

Mom's peering at me in the bathroom mirror, everything backwards from our usual way of looking. I'm in my nightgown, and she traces me with her eyes: I'm filling out, too much so and too fast. My hips are spreading more than I'd like, with faint white lines squiggling across my skin. At night, my pushing breasts sag and hurt too much to sleep.

'It's a burden, Ruthie.' Mom puts her hands on my shoulders and measures my reflection.

I feel my face flush and drop my eyes to my feet.

'Beauty's a hard gift to bear.'

10

Naomi's hair is long and black and when she dreams, she dreams of trees. Even all the times I sleep over, Gloria comes to tuck her daughter in; they ain't embarrassed. Before bed, her momma brushes Naomi's hair with a hard bristle brush, and with each stroke it gleams until it crackles and sticks staticky away from her head like a coal halo. When she visits her sleep trees, Gloria has already braided Naomi's hair into a long rope down her back, swishing past her middle. Depending on the season, her trees are different.

If I can wake her while she is still sleepy, Naomi will tell me about the long dreams of her trees. When she speaks, she says little, but I can see them in my mind's eye: in the springtime, white, paperbark birch with crisscrossing black ridges like slowly knitting scars. And in the summer, sweeping willows, sun shining through the lacy leaves, making shadow patterns on her arms. But in the autumn, her tree is a sticky sugar maple dribbling sap out of a gash in its skin. The drips have gone hard down the side of her bark, and winged ants are stuck in the syrup; the seeping hole makes her ooze with insects.

Naomi just couldn't sleep sound nor well this fall. She is more restful, now that we are deep in winter. When the cold wind whips through the tops of the trees and howls across the stubby cornfields, I also find myself sleepy and safe inside near the fire. But seems like all Naomi does now is sleep.

I'm here at the parsonage for the laying on of hands. Naomi's here, sort of: her eyes are shut and she is sleeping sound, laying in the bed again. It's been over a week that she's been on the prayer chain, and I can't say that she seems to be getting any better. Gloria thought Naomi was just going on with her sleeping all the time, and that her achy bones were just telling of the coming of freezing rain. We all can feel the weather creeping near or changing in our bones, and complaining don't make any hurt go away. But now, Naomi's holding water: her long yellow legs are thick and soft; her ankles are overstuffed bratwurst ready to burst. But faithfulness means that we continue to lift her up in prayer. We pray, in this family, without ceasing.

And yet there she lays: on Ingwald's big bed, stretched out in the middle with her palms flat down hard on the outside of the patchwork quilt. It looks like Naomi's holding on even when she's sound asleep. The elders of the church have gathered round, brought by a tearful phone call from Gloria to Uncle Ingwald.

When told she was interrupting the Men's Supper, Gloria wasn't swayed. 'Interrupt it. The girl still won't wake.'

And so they did. But it seems like Ingwald came home for the Lord, not Naomi. She's been sleeping now for three days, hasn't stirred since after potluck on Sunday afternoon. Only now, with the elders on watch, has the man come home to pray.

The parsonage ain't that far from church anyway. The house is like a cardboard cereal box, sitting tall, brown and tan within a row of squat yellow and white-shuttered neighbours. Of course, it is too big of a home for the current pastor's family: just Ingwald, Gloria, Samuel and Naomi roam through the long hallways and empty rooms. But before Uncle Ingwald came home from Strength Bible College, the old pastor had plenty of family to fill it up. The evidence of his and his wife's blessing is etched in the kitchen pantry, where they measured the heights of their six children at the start of every school year. The biggest boys grew past the top of the cupboard door before they left for their new church in Michigan.

Standing in a circle around the bed with arms raised, the elders are tall, old pines swaying with the wind. Outside the circle, Gloria is teary; her pale hand rests like snow on Ingwald's shoulder. Voices in prayer and praise convert from low murmurs to high music; I feel this change too like weather in my bones. From below, Naomi's little voice joins the noise. At first I strain to hear it through the tangle of men's voices, but as it starts to trickle into their ears, the elders hush and listen too. Her voice is like the taste of snowmelt in the water.

Naomi is speaking in tongues. It is a scramble of Grandma's voice and Naomi's sighs.

'*Hebesheba nonna. Hebesheba nonna. Op it littlemoftastompka, hebesheba nonna.*'

She starts off low, but swells loud; her voice begins to crash against the room, straining at the walls and ceiling.

'*Hebesheba nonna! Hebesheba nonna!*'

With words swirling around her, Aunt Gloria is labouring to make sense of the rushing noise; her tiny hands are fluttering about her collarbones, and her eyes are shut tight. No matter

how hard she struggles — how too long the sound continues —
her mother can't make sense of the words. With all the words
piling up on my head, I feel like I am swimming underwater,
straining for the surface.

'*Hebesheba nonna!*'

My ears and eyes might burst, but I will not open my mouth.

'*Hebesheba nonna. Hebesheba nonna. Op it littlemoftastompka,
hebesheba nonna!*'

Naomi suddenly stops, and I am beyond out of breath. The
room is silent; no one brings forth the message.

It is over now, and Naomi's eyes remain shut and her
breathing has returned to the deep, slow rhythm of a breastfed
baby. The elders are nodding in prayer, taking Naomi's
sounds as words straight from the mind of God; the men are
looking at her still, sleeping lips as if they are holy. Ingwald is
looking at Gloria, who is looking at Naomi as if she is trying
to decide whether a demon or an angel lies upon the bed.

I stay in the shadowed corner of the room, just looking.
I don't know if what I heard was blasphemy or prophecy; all
I know is that Naomi remains asleep. Maybe my belief would
help her wake. Jesus rebuked evil spirits and commanded them
to leave the afflicted. Their bodies would shake and shriek
violent and then lay still like the dead. Even the disciples were
amazed, for they could not exorcise every demon. But Jesus
could and did and does still today. *This kind can come out only by
prayer.* So here we are, again, still praying.

After the elders left, each touching her head with a sweaty
palm, Uncle Ingwald cradled Naomi like a baby and carried
her into her own room. I sit with her there on her fluffy bed,

tucked up close with a cup of hot water and lemon that Aunt Gloria brought me. Naomi's hair is sweaty and tangled, and it is all I can do to keep from pulling it away from her face. For all the sleeping, her face is tired with dark circles and pulled-down lips. I don't want to wake her by stirring her hair. Her eyelashes flicker as she breathes, her chest moving up and down, and the sound of her breath beating regular.

Why didn't her real momma want her? I don't know why she wouldn't. Naomi is most precious, and we can all see that. Maybe that was the problem: the momma didn't want to fade back next to Naomi; maybe no one could see her anymore. Most likely it was like those berries that the birds eat: good for their bodies but poison to me. They taste sweet to all creatures but can't benefit us all. Beyond Naomi's purple curtains, snow blows white and hard against the window. It is drifting over the streets in peaks with barely any dips; the ditches along the roadsides are full of deep snow. I do not know what God said, or if it was even God speaking. But Naomi spoke clear to me, most clear to me in my heart: *There is a seed.*

11

HE IS JUST BONES AND COAT, LIKE THE JESUS PICTURE HANGING
at the front of the sanctuary: Christ's eyes are lonely, slinking
out of a bony face framed by lanky hair and a mangy beard.
This dead coyote resembles a sad Jesus. It's a real nice one with
thick yellow-grey fur like an overcast sky and a drooping-down
heavy tail, tip dipped in ink. Nearly as high as a wolf, he sure is
skinny, though; he might have himself a tapeworm or maybe
he's been away from his family a good while. If he's been on
his lonesome, he couldn't knock down a deer on his own so
would have stayed fed on rabbits, rats, corn and whatever he
could scavenge in the way of carcass. A guy wouldn't want
to ever leave the pack if it meant the only venison he sunk
his teeth into was going to be flyblown and rotten. Folks have
their reasons, I guess.

Reuben, stocking hat pulled low over his ears, is all excited
and rushing his words. My brother do love coyotes. 'He come
running straight at me like you wouldn't believe. I'd been
calling for a while, hunkered still for just over an hour. Sun
come up, here the 'yote come running straight at me. I'm
yipping a bit and trying to do a woodpecker call, because them
rabbit calls weren't doing me no good. And, sure enough,

here he comes loping 'cross the field straight at me.'

Coyotes move to the sound of other coyotes or the rustling and wailing of a wounded animal. Reuben takes himself up from our house in the dark; because of Grandma's new ban on hunting, he now has to trek all the way over the hill to Uncle Peter's place. Following the fence line, walking quiet as can be through the brush and bramble, he moves silent like a bobcat until he sets himself down and waits. Wearing camouflage of white, tan and black, he crouches ahead of a tangle of brush with the wind blowing in his face. He sits real quiet; he sits real quiet a long while. Then he starts to call. He don't make no howling, though that's what folks hear when they think coyote. Reuben calls more like a bark, even sometimes like a dying fawn.

Folks still do a lot of coyote trapping with a dirthole set; you just find an old den with tracks scratched in the dust at the front of the hole. They'll dunk those sharp metal teeth in anti-freeze and store-bought coyote urine or skunk scent, use god-awful smelling bait, and do all sorts of other tricks to out-trick the coyotes. Coyotes are always about. They stay downwind of whatever herd you got, don't matter if you are running cattle or sheep or deer. Coyotes are born hungry, and they stay that way until they die. It could be a winter feedlot, froze cows squashed in amongst the snow and grain — or a spring calving barn, birthing cows moaning and babies sucking. Either way, a farmer's got coyotes. I've heard of 'yotes sleeping cosy in field haystacks or inside with the livestock on hay bales, steam rising off their sleeping bodies when the barn door is opened for morning. To watch one in a stubble field, circling around before bedding down, stretching skinny legs before folding ears and shutting yellow eyes to sleep, it's like spying on the neighbour's dog. But keep in mind that forever-empty belly crouching alongside the new lambs in the pasture; he's no lapdog.

So Reuben sets up his hunting blind just the same as the dry trappers set their traps: along the worn dirt path that leads right to the beaver dam on the river, between the tall stands of jack pine, just up over the hill. Behind where Uncle Peter dumped his old tractor, atop generations of rusty Magnusson scrap, he's got a bone yard to drag dead cows and the like. Each and every coyote in the county can smell that bone yard all year round — and sometimes in a stinking-hot summer, all the neighbours can smell it too. Death-bloat Holsteins will be covered with black crows so you can't see any white of their hide. Coyotes know good eating, and Reuben sure knows his coyotes. Reuben is a soldier who stalks antler rub on trees, bear tracks in the mud, and coon scat on the path. Reuben will catch you. He knows all your hiding places and all your secret names: prairie wolf, kyute, *mush-quo-de-ma-in-gon*. Be sure, he will find you out.

Reuben is almost panting. 'I thought something was up when the jays started to chatter in the pines. Then a black squirrel ran up a trunk real close by. He come running. He come running straight at me, and then he sat down and just stared me plain in the face. Stupid, like. I tried not to blink. I didn't nearly breathe. Then he picks up and keeps running straight at me.'

Meat in the belly of a coyote don't always stay there. Folks say he's got a double stomach. The very same 'yote that'll push a new calf away from the herd takes the care to vomit a stomach-full of meat out to feed its pups. Reuben's even seen a coyote struggling along, dragging the backbone and hindquarters of a fawn with its teeth. I can't decide whether that's just plain evil or just plain nature. Baby cow, baby coyote, baby deer; everybody just wants to eat. In times of plenty, there's no excuse to cause so much pain. But hunger excuses plenty, it seems. I haven't seen yet what makes a body just plain mean.

So we load the coyote up in the back of Daddy's rusty hunting truck and drive together all the way over to the parsonage. We are riding in the back, pulling a woodheap tarp over the top of us to keep the cold wind and blowing snow off. Starting out, I didn't want the thing even touching my leg. But by the time we get to town, Reuben and I both are snuggling into the coyote's scratchy pelt for warmth. Traced around his mouth and all along his throat, his fur is creamy white, just like the inside of his floppy ears and all of his underside. I even lay my head down on the coyote's back, but just for a minute. It is real cold. He has a sore or something, full of pus and blood, eating into the black, rubbery gum of his mouth. There is a scab, white and mushy, forming like ice on the river. The wound is trying to close. My hand knocks against the muzzle as we corner a sharp curve. I think I got blood on my hands, so I wipe them deep in the fur.

Because we called ahead, as we pull into the driveway Uncle Ingwald is waiting, stamping his boots outside the door of the garage attached to the house. As Daddy drives up to him, Ingwald hinges open the green metal door with a creak. After he parks the truck inside the garage, Daddy climbs out of the cab and steam rises off his barn coat. The door from the house is stirring; Aunt Gloria is half carrying Naomi down the stairs. Squinting in the garage light with matted sleep in the corners of her black lashes, Naomi is wearing her pyjamas, Ingwald's flannel robe, and a patchwork quilt wrapped around her body. We are here to show our family Reuben's coyote. Samuel will miss it because he's at hockey practice. Reuben don't play hockey seeing he can't afford the gear, and it cuts into his hunting time. Seems like for once, Reuben's the big man today.

But the talk turns to the fever dreams again. Next to the freezers, Aunt Gloria is telling my daddy all about it. Gloria's been sleeping next to Naomi while she's been nursing her back to health. Before Naomi opened her eyes this morning, she told her momma — in a high, sorrowful voice — that she had wandered inside a great cave which was the gaping mouth of a giant. Inside his stomach, Naomi fed starving people and animals with meat and fat cut from the giant's belly. His heart was a volcano and his blood was lava. She used her hunting knife to stab the giant in his volcano heart. The people and animals inside his stomach flowed out his mouth and were freed. As the big mouth clamped shut in death, Naomi pulled a wood tick out between the giant's clenched teeth. The tick was pulled out alive, but it was flat as a tack. We don't know at all what to make of these feverish dreams.

I don't think Naomi should touch the coyote, as sick as she's been and all. I can't keep her from him, though. Bending over in her coat of many colours, Naomi looks into the mouth of the cold, still animal. Her brown thumb pushes up, hard, onto the sharp, pointy tooth jutting out the side of his mouth. The tooth is the same colour as a hen's egg, white-like with shadowy bruises. The muzzle is starting to freeze solid; no steaming cloud escapes from his mouth. When she takes her hand away, a purple-red imprint remains on her thumb. She moves so slow but gives me a shy smile, and I can almost see her secret dog teeth.

Rubbing the dent on the inside of her bottom lip, she looks up. 'I do believe I'm better now.'

Reuben puts his arm low around Naomi's waist and she lays her head on his wide shoulder. Loose and wild, her hair spills across her chest. I feel the beating of their hearts. He is so proud.

'Boy? Watch your hands.' Uncle Ingwald's breath puffs white even inside the garage.

Reuben and Naomi break apart, but the girl's daddy ain't having it. Ingwald grabs his daughter and pulls her to his side.

'I was only showing her the coyote.' Ain't much use in protesting, but Reuben can't just stand there dumb.

Naomi shivers and looks down at her feet; she is barefoot on the cold concrete. No one thought to make her wear shoes. She should say something — maybe Reuben was helping her stand — but she doesn't say nothing at all. Uncle Ingwald wraps the quilt tighter around her and glares at Reuben.

Daddy and Aunt Gloria walk over from the freezers. They both look at all of us waiting there silent. We hear breath and the wind blowing outside. There is nothing to say.

On the way home, I'm scratching at a bump in my hair. It sure ain't a scab. I got a wood tick stuck deep in my head: something more to remember this coyote by. And it comes to me unbidden: the tick is a messenger of the Most High. What Naomi's dream says, I don't rightly know. But I know that God has come upon me. He is speaking through Grandma's blood.

Reuben and I are singing, yelling loud with the wind in our ears.

Would you be free from your burden of sin? There's pow'r in the blood, pow'r in the blood. Would you o'er evil a victory win? There's wonderful pow'r in the blood.

Reuben digs it out for me: he scrapes his dirty fingernails close down by my scalp and pinches the body tight.

Would you be whiter, much whiter than snow? There's pow'r in the blood, pow'r in the blood. Sin stains are lost in its life-giving flow. There's wonderful pow'r in the blood.

One quick pull, and the nasty thing is scrambling all over my brother's shivering, gloveless hands. Later, we'll roast the tick on a match. Angel or not, its dark brown body will shrivel up as the flame burns through him. The big grey ticks that hang on the dogs are all bloated with blood, but this one is still flat, hard and little like a seed. He will stay hungry. Lucky we got him off me early.

12

ACROSS THE BLACK SKY, GREEN STREAKS SHRED THE CLOUDS.
Scratches of white vein a yellow cone; it is a tornado of light
pulsing in and out, worming its way higher and higher. The
heavens are slit: ripped, split, gashed. Fire is splashing; it is
dancing faster. It hisses and crackles and spits; it hoarsely
murmurs, *Armageddon*. It is more than unusual to see the
northern lights in December; they stripe the sky with colour a
couple times a year, but usually in autumn and spring.

After the Sunday evening praise service — once everyone
had finished treating Naomi like she was new and shiny,
holding her hand, blessing her, and blessing God for her
healing and for her gift — we all left the church expecting
pinpoints of stars shining through the night. But what we got
was colour: aurora borealis. Side by side, the congregation
huddles together whispering in the parking lot, heads lifted,
eyes fixed at the sky. In the dark, the voices don't belong to
anyone in particular.

'Beautiful. Just beautiful. Our God is an awesome God.'

'Ain't the right season, though. Can't say I've seen them
without sitting on a tractor, either harvesting or planting, eh?'

'Right. Makes a guy wonder.'

It is a wonder, so we stand and watch, breathing and shivering together awhile. Families start to drift away, and I can hear their car engines struggling to turn over in the cold. Naomi's sleeping at our house tonight, and she walks with her hand tucked inside my jacket pocket. I see folks whispering about her to her father — some about miracle recoveries and others telling of other unknown prophecies — but we walk away and pile into the pick-up. Naomi don't even look behind her as people watch her with their eyes. Daddy's driving with Mom snuggled in beside him. Reuben and I balance Naomi half on our laps. Usually those two would snuggle together, but tonight he's treating the girl like she's spoiled meat. Our coats rub together, smelling moist as they dry in the loud blowing heat of the truck. As we drive, I press my nose on the window frost and ponder the lights.

The prophet Ezekiel speaks of a fearsome, northern windstorm made of light, its middle all glowing metal forming four living creatures. They were men, but men with four faces and four wings and straight legs capped with glinting cloven hooves. Hands hung beneath their wings; their wings flashed and the feather tips touched, but each creature forged directly ahead. There was no turning with them. Each creature possessed four faces: a man, a lion, an ox, and an eagle. Their wings were mighty: for each, two wings spread out touching another creature and two wings covered its own body. They flew straight, following the Spirit, never turning astray. To look at the creatures burnt the eyes of men like coals. The touching wings flashed fire back and forth; they were lightning as they sped across the sky.

At school we studied the aurora borealis, and it is all about cycles and what it says in your own mind to mean. Vikings believed the lights were maidens mirrored on the sky; I like to imagine being in a ship out on the water, gazing up at a girl made all of colour and cloud. The Indian tribes around here seemed to disagree as to what the lights meant. Some thought that the lights spoke of war and disease or that they were rising ghosts, enemies looking for revenge. Some thought giants used torches of fire to shine light enough to spearfish on a dark night, just like they fished from birch bark canoes with torches tied to the ends. To those Indians, the northern lights were just that big fire shining off the water into our eyes, the reflection of a lake of flames. If I've got to pick a story to stick to, I pick the lake of flames. Lac du Flambeau ain't too far from Cranberry Lake, so I know it must be near enough to true.

'Deer!'

Daddy slams on the brakes and the pick-up skids on the ice. But Reuben was wrong: it's a fisher. Almost a wolf but stragglier and closer to the ground, I barely see the thing as it skedaddles away from the road. It is all hunchback fur and yellow-green eyes, with a weasel face and fangs. Animals walk this road at night; roadkill brings them in and roadkill they become. Barn owls swoop for bats while bats swoop for mosquitoes, and they all avoid people the best they can. We're parked crooked in the road, engine still running, all watching the shadow of the creature sidle through the cornfield. Daddy straightens the wheels toward home.

'Naomi's lucky she didn't go through the glass,' Reuben says low.

Why the boy needs to open his mouth, I don't know. True, the maps and caps stored up the front of the dashboard did fly when the tyres slipped, but Reuben and me both held tight to Naomi. There's no seatbelts in the hunting truck anyway.

'The Lord probably told her to hold on, though; she knew it was coming.' Reuben says it loud enough for only Naomi and me to hear.

I can't see much of her face in the dark, but I know how the hurt would look. Naomi slides off of Reuben's lap and sits on me alone. Her weight is enough for me to settle back into the vinyl, and her hair is covering most of my face.

'Daddy don't believe neither,' he whispers.

I want to tell Reuben to shut his mouth. I want to tell Naomi that he is just jealous and don't doubt her being sick nor getting well neither.

But he don't even believe in Grandma when she talks to Jesus, so it don't matter he don't believe Jesus is talking to Naomi. I can't see Reuben's face, but I know how even his hard eyes shine when he's hurting because he's wounded something good.

I want to make it better and tell Naomi that I believe, but I don't want to lie.

As we pass Uncle Peter's land, Mom and Daddy are both looking out the driver's window at an abandoned house. That house was there when he bought the Magnusson place, and there it still stands. The four-pane glass windows are all broken and the porch has started to sag. Lilac bushes bloom around it in spring, but they're only thorny branches all winter. My uncle talks about tearing it down every year.

Once we're home, Naomi takes a bath before bed. We've got plenty of pictures showing us as toddlers laughing together in the tub, but now that we're grown, sharing a bath might feel a bit too close. Even though our growing seems unnoticeable to our family, both Naomi and I are most aware of our changes. Standing bare and goosepimpled before my bath, I glimpse myself in the bathroom mirror and see my mother's body pushing through my little-girl hips and legs. Naomi's not so lucky, though, as she don't have the memory of her blood mother's thighs to reassure her that she is forming to plan. But Naomi is thicker than me, with my arms and legs like birch sticks; she is soft and round where I am sharp and straight, even with my too-proud hips.

I've got to use her bathwater after she's done because we don't want to run out of hot. The floor is slick, and the mirror is steamy. She's left her clothes and wet towel rumpled together in the laundry basket. I hold her clothes close to my face and breathe in her smell: it's a mingle of me, and my mother, and the doe scent the men wear in the woods. Naomi's underwear is white. No sad brownish smears, her panties are clean. Even someday, someday when they are stained, I believe she will bleed perfect: red-pink cranberries frozen on the snow.

Naomi and I snuggle together under the quilts and blankets, sharing warmth in one bed rather than split between the bunks. My nose is freezing, but my nose is always freezing; seems like the blood never makes it to the tip. My body doesn't always know its own way. We've finished reading our devotions, trying to memorise the ABCs of an excellent woman. Now with our flashlights off, we speak these things in God's name.

Even though we are probably getting some wrong — and Naomi keeps making me laugh — we will become Proverbs 31 women: attentive, busy, compassionate; dignified, early riser, frugal; good, homemaker, ingenious; just, kind, laughs; meek, not lazy, opens her home; praiseworthy, quiet, righteous; smiling, trustworthy, understanding; virtuous, wise, excellent; yielding and zealous. We will be wives of noble character. Together we say: *Charm is deceptive, and beauty is fleeting; but a woman who fears the Lord is to be praised.* Naomi memorises quick, but she doesn't always remember long.

Even calling out our ABCs makes me feel like I'm lying, for my chances of being noble are low. I'm not alone in my failings, in what I find when I search my heart. When Grandma prays for me, she prays against rebellion. She's seen it in me since I was little, my wilful and stubborn spirit: refusing the breast too early, spitting food, and my steady stare. And now with my talking back and such. For Naomi, her thorn is vanity; Grandma saw that in the moment they touched. Grandma held that tiny baby in her arms, kissing Naomi's shiny black hair, smelling her scalp. And modesty was lacking: pride sat deep in the dark. I believe Grandma is right; she gives us a word of wisdom and she intercedes with the Lord. But even in bed, Naomi is holding her head again in that tilted way, looking out the sides of her eyes to make sure I see her praying before she sleeps. It's dark in my room, but I see her checking that I watch her walk in her gifts. And in church, I see her believe she's chosen, and I watch her blush and bloom.

Naomi's mumbling under her breath, still praying while I'm trying to sleep. Vanity is its name. She needs to shut those dark eyes and quit looking. I'm waiting for her to fall asleep; I won't be able to rest until I know I'm alone. When the dark and the cold sit heavy on my chest and I worry for my sleep, I tell myself stories of peace. God brings me peace from both my praying and my remembering. When I was little, before bed, my mom would run me a deep bath. She'd slip her hand inside the tub and check that the water wasn't too hot, and then she'd pull off my shirt. 'Skin the bunny.' And my shirt would fold inside out and skim up over my head. 'Skin the bunny.' I'd sink into the tub, letting the warm water cover my body, sliding like a cased rabbit into the pot.

13

NOW I THINK IT IS TOO EARLY TO BE OUT ON THE ICE, BEING barely a couple weeks past Thanksgiving. But Reuben and Samuel say that it is December, and December is winter, so they are going ice fishing up at the cabin whether I like it or not. Naomi and I are invited if we have to be. We've gotten a pretty good winter so far, I suppose, with plenty of cold nights and not too much snow since deer hunting closed, so the ice ought to be thick enough. It didn't have no cosy cover of snow to keep it from freezing thick through and through. Strange how we hope for barrels of snow for blood tracking come November hunting, and we pray for God to hold it back a bit for the ice to firm up and get us out on Cranberry Lake fishing in December. I like snow anytime, I guess, but I understand feeling the call to fish, low and deep in my belly, too.

Reuben's been running tip-ups with shiners and sucker minnows as bait since late November, seeing he knows the ice up north is at least three inches thick. Up at the cabin, the lake freezes much earlier than the lakes around Failing. It might be that the water is left alone way up in the northwoods, left to switch its heart to winter, while the town lake and its ice are distracted providing light entertainment to Failing people.

Come the end of football season, the boys from the wrecking yard put a banged-up truck or such way out in the grand centre of the lake. Talking about when the truck will go out on the ice come winter freeze and when the truck will go through the ice come spring thaw keeps a majority of folks in our town occupied for a good four or five months each and every year. I've even heard talk that some of the bars in town have a board up where the drinkers can place a bet with money depending on when they figure the ice'll break. I can't say that it is true that they're gambling on nature in the dark corners of Failing's bars, but I can't deny it neither.

But the ice up at our cabin's Cranberry Lake is left alone to her own devices. She's out there in the midst of the tall, white pine and scrubby jack, freezing hard and meaning to ignore the wild turkeys and straggling deer coming down off of the hill looking for a mouthful of water. Meanwhile, there are schools of fish — bluegill, perch, sunfish, walleye and pike — swimming under the forming crust, their slimy hides slowing down for winter, their dawdling breathing becoming shallow, each gulp bringing in freezing water to chill along their skinny bones and flesh. That ice up at Cranberry ain't thin and honeycombed like in Failing; no, she's a clear blue ice — a bit slushy in parts but nice and new, and you can trust her. It ain't crispy river ice, but you still got to take a good look for soft pockets of water that prove a current is running underneath. Sliding through a fissure will get you good and wet and cold as you've ever been. So you got to always keep an eye out, especially when she's still freezing, like she's still freezing in December.

But the boys won't pay me no nevermind and have decided that we are all going out — here at Little Failing Lake barely outside town — and we are all going out today. We are crunching through the snow single file like Indians. Each carrying a bit of the gear — an ice auger, the rusty old bait bucket, lures and hooks and jigs, tip-ups and jigging rods, and a shiny new skimmer — we are packed down heavy. Reuben leads the way, tapping the ice with a stick before he guides us over; his ear can tell by the sound that comes back to him what the ice will hold and what it won't. The shack is already out on the lake near a good spot for walleye, thanks to Reuben begging Daddy for a week solid. We aren't allowed to keep the gear inside, though, as Daddy and Uncle Ingwald still think she might thaw in the night, and we'll lose the shack. Reuben begged like a dog, saying last time he was at the cabin, he listened close to Cranberry; he couldn't sleep for the sound of her making ice: cracking and freezing and cracking and freezing. Daddy said Little Failing ain't Cranberry, and that nobody's listening to the ice in town. Finally, Reuben had to promise that he and Samuel would rebuild the fishing shack, stick by stick, if she went through. I guess the men had no choice but to let them fish.

I don't have trouble sleeping for listening to ice. In my head instead, tangling ropes swim, twisting and pulling tight, hard against me. Sometimes I dream that I am floating around the ceiling, sticking close to the tops of the walls, flying but afraid that I'll come crashing down hard to the floor. At night at the cabin, if the bed and couch downstairs are full of men and boys, the girls got to go up the ladder into the attic and sleep with the squeaking bats and scratching mice. Sleeping at the cabin under my grandma's patchwork quilts, I still fall into the shifting and sliding dark dreams, but at least I've got Naomi lying there beside me. When dreaming, she tends to suck her thumb, and I tend to call out in a fright, but we keep each other company, close enough.

Right near to the shack, a split in the ice races out from where Reuben is walking and cracks loud and rippling across the lake. Echoing off the wall of pines, the sound grows and gives me a shiver probably worse than it ought. Reuben is pretending he wasn't ever scared, that he hasn't already been picturing himself slipping through the ice: sinking down, down, down into the freezing deep, his eyes peering up through the frosted water, trying to find the hole out that was his hole in.

Throwing down his jacket and the jig poles he is carrying, Samuel is scrambling to get on his hockey skates and clear a circle for a bit of practice. I know, though, that those boys can already feel the water filling and freezing their lungs and choking out their breath. I know they can because I can, and it wasn't me that broke the ice.

I guess it is my fault because I am watching Reuben unpacking and Samuel skating and not really keeping an eye on my feet. All of a sudden, the ice beneath me is swirling slush, and I feel my right leg slip deep into the water. Filled up with freezing water and chunks of ice, my boot starts to drag heavy and means to pull the rest of me into the lake and under the ice. Flailing my arms and screeching, I fight the pull downward and grab the edge of the hole to keep my left side, leg and arm and body and head, up above the water. I can't say that I am praying, but I don't know who else I am begging to let me live. I guess you don't need to speak the name of God for Him to know that He is needed, because just as I feel that I will split right in two, Naomi and Reuben and Samuel pull me up and walk me away from the hole quicker than I even remember falling in.

Sopping wet, water dripping from my hip down to my toes,

I can feel the rest of my body going numb and tingly. Looking back over my shoulder, I see there wasn't ever any risk of me slipping through the hole, as it is only about twice the width of my thigh; my arms alone would've kept me up above with the living. That slushy hole I stepped into was made by a school of white fish swimming round and round together, whether to get air into the lake or to get revenge on ice fishermen, I don't know. But at this moment, shivering head to toe and teeth rattling in my head, I am sure those plotting, scaly fish were out for retribution. I have a hard time catching my breath at the thought of sinking into the deep mud at the bottom of Little Failing, and my folks waiting until spring thaw to fish me out and bury me. Although the fear of drowning will soon pass, the risk of freezing out here in the sharp wind is mighty real. Wet from my splashing, the hair inside my nose is freezing hard and crisp, and I can see ice forming on the tips of my eyelashes, so I let my brother and cousins bundle me into the shack.

Over his knee, Reuben breaks branches piled next to the shack to make a fire to get my blood moving again. I figure he is awful worried that he will get the blame for my frostbite death and that Daddy might never let him out on the lake again. They pile the wood into the hole in the steel bucket that serves as our stove and get the fire roaring quick. Embarrassed, I stand there soaking, waiting for the boys to leave so I can strip down to my bare skin and wrap up in the wool blanket on the bunk. Naomi catches my darting eye and hustles the boys out for more wood so that I can hold on to at least a semblance of my pride. As she helps me pull off the many wet layers of snow pants, jeans, long underwear and tights, my body twitches and flicks like a muddy cow's tail, and I think I will never again get warm. Naomi wraps me up in the green army blanket, and I lay down on the top bunk, still shivering hard but breathing better.

A hand comes round the door, holding more sticks for the fire. Naomi grabs them up and thanks Reuben for bringing them. At least they are working together and aren't fighting anymore.

Sheepishly, he peeks his head through and barely whispers to ask if I am alright. Reuben's scared, wrinkled-up face looks so worried, I laugh out loud and tell him to go on ahead and get fishing.

'Watch out for those whitefish, they're gunning for you now!' I tell him, still laughing.

His smile tells me that he is relieved, and with him stopping his worrying, I stop my worrying too. I can see that I will well and truly live through a bit of a wet, cold leg.

The plywood door bangs shut after Reuben, and Naomi plops down on the bottom bunk and pulls out a secret roll of chocolate caramels from her coat pocket. We are shoving them into our mouths, and she is rubbing my wet foot hanging off the side of the top bunk when Samuel comes in out of the cold.

'You get out there and skate a bit, Naomi.' Samuel always talks in that low voice. 'You didn't walk all the way out to the middle of the lake to stuff your face full of candy. I'll watch her.'

Naomi gets up and paces the room. She offers the caramels to Samuel, but he shakes his head. She stokes up the fire, but Samuel says it is burning high and right.

'Go find Reuben, Naomi,' he says with a sneer. 'I'm sure he's making another fire somewhere.'

She finally laces up her skates, throws a look over her shoulder at me, and slides out the door.

'Ahhh, it's getting hot in here, ain't it?' Samuel takes off his jacket and snow pants. 'My jeans are a bit wet, don't you think?' He slides them off too.

By the time he climbs up into the top bunk, Samuel is wearing just his tight long underwear. He has to warm up now, and he has to help me warm up too. His breath is hot and his hands are cold, and I can see the slit of his thing sticking out the top of his underwear. It ain't an accident this time, and I can't even pretend anymore that it is. I know now that the other times — through the woods when we accidentally saw him skinny-dipping, in my tent when he didn't mean to come in when I was changing, at the swimming hole when he sort of rubbed against us in the water, at church during worship when his arm brushed against my chest — none of those times was accidental neither. *Even a child is known by his actions, by whether his conduct is pure and right.*

During, I hear Naomi come to the door, press her face against it and ask Samuel if she could warm up now. He tells her no, and she shuffles away. She comes back; he says no; she goes away. Samuel has laid on me and wriggled around before, earlier in the summer when Naomi was at Bible camp. But it was August and hot then, and because I am wet and cold, he has to really warm me now. He tugs at my nipples and rubs my chest with his rough hands. My heart is beating fast and I can't breathe. He rolls on top of me. It hurts, though, and I push him away a bit, and then I pull him to me, and then I push him away hard.

He says, low and slow like he always talks, 'You don't have to. I might just go to Naomi.'

Naomi still wets the bed. I have to protect her. 'Naomi's only a little girl.' An anger rises up in me, and I hit him hard on the arm. 'You keep away from her.'

Samuel jerks back from me. 'She might be a little girl, but she don't have to stay that way. And she's more woman than you'll ever be, skinny.'

Now jealousy burns through me, down to my core, like a hot splash of urine melting through snow. My face is wet with tears. But I pull him down to me again and let him stay there until he is done.

Seems like I don't know nothing, don't know what to believe. Pictures twist through my head: a snarling badger hunting a snowshoe hare; Samuel towing Naomi round the ice, her skates slipping in the slush and gleaming in the glare; Reuben stabbing a northern pike through the eye with a maple stick; Samuel, leaning against the side of the shack, pissing a high yellow arc steaming into the snow.

But my spirit sees a spring empty of water, like snowflakes driven by a blizzard. Blackest darkness is just as dry. If a man knows the Lord — escaping the sin slavery of the depraved world — then entangles himself again and is overcome, he ends worse than he began. He should wish he never knew righteousness rather than reject the sacred commands. You don't live long in Failing without knowing what is true: *A dog returns to its vomit. A sow that is washed goes back to her wallowing in the mud.*

14

SOME BAD KID HAS BURNT A CIRCLE INTO THE GREEN VINYL OF the bus seat in front of me. The edges of the hole are brown and smell like leaves on fire; a cigarette has left its mark. I'm sitting alone on the school bus. Naomi decided to share a seat with Reuben, and they are giggling under his big jacket. Samuel's clear in the rear with the rough crowd. High school kids sit back there, swearing and throwing paper out the windows. I can't help but hope they eat him alive.

After school today, Reuben and I are riding the bus to the parsonage. Naomi and I have to make the boys supper, and then Aunt Gloria will take us all home after she and Mom are done with their ladies' prayer meeting. We got to rely on the church van because Daddy's got the truck; he's helping rebuild a burnt-down milking parlour out near the county line. Through the window, I see the too-tall box of the parsonage looming over its neighbours and I change my mind: I will not. The bus slows and stops and the door opens. Carrying all their books, Reuben follows Naomi's swinging, chubby hips toward the exit. I make myself small and still as Samuel slinks from the back of the bus to the front. But I will not get off the bus; I can't follow that boy down that aisle. Nobody notices, and the door closes. When I turn my head again to look out the smeary window, Samuel has already started walking toward his house. Reuben and Naomi, though, are standing looking stunned as I wave slow from inside the bus. Her mouth open, my cousin just gawks at me. My brother starts running, chasing the bus like a dog. We leave him behind in no time; our lady bus driver ain't known for keeping an eye on the rear-view.

I stay hunkered down in my seat and most of the normal kids don't even notice I'm there. All the way home, I listen to them talk of fancy vacations and television, rock music and movies. They are rich and don't even know it; I am poor and I do. But I ride content in myself and happy — for the first time in a long time — on my lonesome. The children get dropped off house by house until only I remain, like an unhatched egg in a nest. I climb down from the bus and walk our long driveway. Truck tyres have splashed this morning's fresh snow muddy. My shadow weaves amongst the scraggly pines that line the road; somehow, that darkness seems more real than my own body. Near the house, I see that Uncle Peter's big truck is parked next to the garage. Strange, because nobody's home — at least, nobody is supposed to be home.

I think he must be in our little garden shed, so I decide to go in there first. The footsteps to the shed are too far apart to follow; the men have big strides. The snow is deep to my knees, and there is no one to make a way for me, so I break my path myself. Because it is stuck with cold and ice, I have to push open the side door of the shed with my hip. The light ain't on inside the shed, but I can hear something moving. My eyes adjust to the dim light, and I can see to the back of the shed.

There is a wire cage with a raccoon shivering in the corner. Even now, as cold as it's been, it appears Reuben's kept himself a coon — freezing and near to starving by the state of it — in this draughty, crooked shed. Me, I couldn't sleep for thinking of that coon's black-rimmed eyes all scared and her stripy fur shivering with the wind that breezes through the cracks.

But the boys don't lose no sleep and the boys break all the rules. Like Samuel don't have no self-control, but he do have selfishness plenty. He cares only for him; him and his pretty curls are all he thinks of day and night. To look at a broken windmill, its arms stretched crooked against the sky, most folks would feel sorry. Not Samuel, though; he looks at a crippled windmill and decides to clip the wings of birds. It is never enough to just look; boys need to keep. And they always need to touch.

There are rules for a reason. If a poor man has only one little ewe lamb, he'll treat it like a daughter: share food with her, press his cup to her lips, and sleep with her in his arms. A rich man would have so many sheep and cattle, he wouldn't even know their names. But if a traveller came and the rich man killed the poor man's ewe lamb — instead of sacrificing one of his many, one of his own — it would be the wrong thing to do. It seems like folks with lots don't care about those of us making do, always having little, always choosing the cheapest kind.

And in my heart of hearts, I believe Reuben knows what happened in the ice shack. When he looks at me — even tonight through the foggy bus window — I can see it in his eyes. He knows something special was taken away; he looks at me like I'm broken. I don't know why he ain't telling somebody, why he ain't protecting me. Folks have their reasons, I guess.

Day is quickly dying, but I'm determined to let this raccoon go. I start toward the cage but lose my balance and almost hit the deck. There is a red gasoline can and a box of rags sitting in the middle of the floor. The box spilt when I tripped over it: beneath the rags are dirty magazines, women of all shapes and sizes, but always naked. I hold one of the magazines up to try and see what is appealing about ladies, what is so worth looking at.

The door behind me opens and brings in the light. I drop the magazine to my feet and feel my face flush.

'Ruth?' Uncle Peter is calling my name.

Breathing quick, I turn around.

'Girl, aren't you supposed to be in town?'

They always catch me. Others get away; I don't.

But he ain't got no reason to be here neither. 'What are you looking for, Uncle Peter?'

And it's his turn for a red face. 'Your mother was feeling too poorly to go to meeting.' He is speaking quick. 'I came by to check on her. You should go inside and see if you can help.'

I nod my head yes, and he turns to go. His truck starts, and I listen to it pull down the driveway. And I hear that animal rattle her cage. She is straining against the wire. Before I go to my mother — make her chicken noodle soup and stoke the fire, whatever she needs — I'll help here first.

The raccoon is squatting in filth; she's got no way to stay clean but she sure as heck has somewhere to go. As I lean down to unlatch the cage, I wonder for a minute if she will fight me. She don't. She just lays there. She's learnt, I guess, that they can squeeze the life out of you. I open the cage and she stays put. She's too dumb to know how to escape; too dumb or too scared or just too plain tired, I suppose.

By morning she'll run and hide. What a funny word: hide. It is the skin of an animal. Hide is where the hunters sit. And hide is what we do to escape. Hide from harm, little coon. You run and hide quick.

15

REUBEN AND DADDY ARE ICE-FISHING UP AT THE CABIN TODAY. I didn't want to go anyway. The old shack at Cranberry Lake is rickety and wheezes in the wind. They'll fish sunnies all day, try for the northern pike during their feeding run at noon, and then expect crappies and walleye from sundown before supper until midnight. That is a long, cold day: Reuben struggling out of the shack to bait tip-ups, watching for flags flying up, faraway on the ice. Inside the shack, they'll hook grubs, waxies and mousies and lower them into the ice hole. Daddy will take a mousie — meal-worm larvae — and warm her up in his mouth before lacing a hook through her. Whether it makes the bait or the fish awaken, I don't know. I do know for sure I don't want a soft baby worm in my mouth. Drinking out of the hole in the ice makes me cold, so I'd have that taste on my lips awhile. And when a pick-up drives by, we know where we are: the ice cracks and water gushes up the hole and overflows on the floor. The ice talks with cracks as it expands and grows. We can't forget we're fishing on ice on water; it is a thin and temporary truce.

But I wasn't awake when Daddy and Reuben left, and they didn't bother waking me. So I'm not sitting on ice; instead,

I am hiding in the cold basement, pawing through a box of photographs. Some are black-and-white and cracking down the middle; yellow tape tries to hold them together. Coloured photos from when my brother and me were little have thick white edges. Some battered Polaroids are coming apart at the seams.

My favourite picture of me is this: a skinny man with mutton-chop sideburns cradles a rifle while balancing a four-month-old baby. The baby is riding a deer sprawled across a knife-marked table. The deer's tongue lags quiet and his antlers are a modest spreading four point, but the man is more than happy. *We'll eat from the garden all winter.* The man's cheeks stretch in a big smile. Stacked behind him are shelves of glass jars holding green beans and tomatoes; before him, laid out, is the buck he shot amongst the leftover corn. He got it all from his garden, animal and vegetable. The basement is bare concrete; its ceiling studs stick out like wooden ribs. But we've got meat and more to get by during the coming cold, and the man's eyes are relieved. He is smiling, showing his teeth to the blonde woman on crutches leaning half in and half out of the photo.

But it's not really a picture of me. Mom's stomach isn't in the picture, and she didn't even know she was pregnant yet. I was so little, my arms couldn't reach my hands. I was dancing and swimming and gulping my mother's water; I was closest to her then. I was living, though. I'm still living beneath cobwebs down here in the basement; spiders prowl above my head. It is my brother riding the deer; he was gulping mother's milk. The basement has stayed a warm place for me: it is near and safe. Down here, I am away from them but most close to what they leave behind: outgrown snow pants, broken snowshoes and fading photographs. Near me, a pony on rusty springs sits in a wet corner; he wears a red wool stocking cap.

'Ruth?'

I hear Mom limping — left leg always first, her hurt knee always behind — down the wooden stairs. She knows I hide in the basement. I go low in the house when I need to be alone, when I need to be away from their together. Sorting through pictures helps me sort my heart. Mom's hair is wet, snaking long and unbraided down her back. She is fresh from a bath, wrapped in a terrycloth bathrobe. Her breasts sway soft with her moving and that little pouch of a tummy pushes beneath the faded blue belt that ties around her middle. My mom was a beauty, slim and gentle; even when she's tired and dripping, it shows itself still. She comes toward me and my blanket on the worn couch.

'Still feeling left behind?' Her eyes are tender.

I shake my head, but she sees my heart.

'You remind me of him, your daddy.'

She pushes aside the pillow next to my knees and settles near. Her hands start to trace my eyebrows, but just as they touch they move away; she turns my head to unbraid my messy hair.

'He has a mouth like yours, crooked all along.'

Without his beard, I wouldn't know my daddy. I never saw his mouth in mine. Looking at Daddy, I see bowed legs, thick forearms, and stained teeth: cows stamped his thighs, horses pushed his wrists, and tobacco burnt his mouth. I don't see him in me.

'He's got plenty to be forgiven for, Ruthie, but it ain't not loving you.'

I don't know who took the photo in the basement. We are

all together in the picture. Someone stood a little bit away and watched my daddy hold my brother proud while my mom held me. Still broken from her accident, Mom carried me deep inside and stood only half in the picture. Fresh home from Alaska, Daddy held the gun and balanced Reuben on the deer. And I half remember being unborn, safe in the womb, sinking like a fish waiting to be pulled from the ice. We have stayed this way. Mom and I each sit alone, together in the dark, watching the snow fall outside the high basement window.

We don't know when the snow will fall or when it will melt. All these things are hidden from our sight: broken toys scattered on the lawn, bare branches stripped of their leaves, and whatever else is buried under the snow. Mom and I are looking up at the sky with snowflakes in our eyes, eyelashes not catching this time. Even from inside the window, the snow melts into my eyes and I think it will freeze my sight. Nothing will change: the world will remain white and still. Even photographs alter, crumpling at the edges and growing yellow crackles across their skins. But I will always see like this: black naked trees, clear ice hanging in sharp points, and hard-packed snow in the crooks of the branches.

It is not for us to know the times or the dates the Father has set for the return of the Lord. The disciples had John to baptise them in water but had to wait upon the Holy Spirit to come and baptise them with fire. And when the Holy Spirit came — and when He comes now, and when He comes again — we all receive power, power to witness to the ends of the earth. Jesus was taken up before their very eyes; He was hidden in a cloud and the apostles stood dumb and wondering, staring at the sky. Angels came to tell them the good news: Christ will return the same way. He will come down for us, riding on the clouds.

Grandma's bird feeders brought us to Field-n-Farm: she is out of seed. Well, not completely out of all birdseed, but she didn't have any more of the little oily black seeds that some of her winter birds like so much. The best time to feed birds is winter: snow covers tiny seeds and dangling, dry berries, while insects are even harder to find. It is then that they need the feeder the most. Heavy snowfalls and ice storms make it necessary to look beyond nature, to hold on to someone who can set out those trays and hang the seeds even when the sleet rains down. Once the birds rely on a feeder, especially during winter, they hold that commitment in their hearts at least until spring. Midwinter is no time to change your mind. If you stop feeding the birds in the middle of the cold, suffering and death are sure to follow. Hurting and dead little creatures aren't an accident or a gentle mistake; those frozen bodies are your choice.

The weather outside ain't the only enemy: at night the opossums and raccoons seek to steal and destroy. The dark prowlers will take the seed and break the feeder. Squirrels too will work against the birds, and not even suspending the seed on a wire between two trees will keep it safe. Metal guards and higher wires will convince some of the enemy to stay away, but sacrificing some seed is the only way to save the rest. Scatter some food at the base of the trees. Spread some seed on the ground. Some seed is lost, but the birds are saved. Morning and evening, they'll come and feed. There are kinds of birds — even knowing the risk — who choose to eat the seed straight from the ground. Sparrows and juncos are that way; it is just the way of their kind.

Grandma hates to disappoint the birds — imagining their orange beaks curving down and fluffy black feathers tamping flat — so she called Mom to help her spare them. Grandma was out of birdseed and we were out of things to do at home, but we didn't have a vehicle. Mom's hair was still damp, freshly braided down her back, when she told me we were done waiting for the boys to finish fishing. She made a phone call. When Uncle Peter roared up the driveway in his shiny truck, she was in the bedroom putting on something decent. We weren't going to sit around all night in an empty house. Uncle Peter was taking us to town.

And so here we are, freezing in front of the glass doors of Field-n-Farm, waiting for them to swing open automatically. I am hopping back and forth in my new moon boots, and Mom is stamping her tiny leather shoes; we're trying to keep warm and awaken the doors both. We can see through the glass to the tables piled with Christmas decorations and the line of folks waiting to buy items, but the doors just can't see us. Uncle Peter waves his thick arms and then he shouts. We are laughing when a red-vested man presses a button inside the doors and they swing open. Uncle Peter steers Mom and me beneath the warm, buzzing lights. He holds my mom light by her elbow, and he holds me firm by my hand.

Uncle Peter and Mom head toward the seed and I go to the salt. I watch them walk away, my uncle's boots leaving light tracks of slush on that gleaming floor. The path seems to dry behind him beneath those bright lights. I don't know how Field-n-Farm keeps these white floors shiny; I've never seen a red-vested gal mopping the aisles and I've sure seen folks tramping through in muck boots. Whether you change your boots for town or not shows whether or not you care.

Way back with the camouflage jackets and cracked-udder cream and duck decoys, I'm chipping away at the salt blocks in the rear of the supply store. After scratching the square,

I use my tongue to scrape the salt from beneath my fingernails onto my tongue. I let it dissolve slowly in my mouth. I have to watch my raw hangnails: rubbing salt in a wound is more than just words. This salt section is meant for folks buying salt for their horses and maybe cows, and we always buy a block to set in Grandma's field. All summer, deer mince up and lick; they don't even mind us watching them. They stretch out their long necks and bend gentle toward the salt block. Their velvet ears swivel at the slightest sound. They are brown and beautiful in their mildness. They even run calm.

The sharp edge of the salt block crumbles: it is no longer a perfect square. I have been picking at this corner for a few minutes, wetting my fingers for the taste and using the wet to work against the solid salt. Used to be, I would just pick up the broken parts of the salt, crouching low beneath the piled blocks to scrounge the chips off the floor. But now that I'm older, I'm not content to eat off the floor, so I work the edges myself. It ain't that the floors aren't clean, they are. They are spotless.

Sin lives in me, so I went to the salt-lick section to crumble the corners and suck it. Sin lives in me, and I chew my hangnails until they are ragged. Now I am standing next to the pile of salt blocks; they are balanced one atop the other like bricks with spaces for spying. I lean into the salt wall with my hips while my hand picks the edges. The store buzzes: the bright lights pulse with heat and electricity. I feel the buzz in my bones, seeping through me like stray voltage. It's no wonder the cows dry up.

I am walking past the ice-fishing gear because I'm dizzy and my mouth is salty and I'm hot and I need a drink of water; orange tip-ups and rainbow bobbers and shiny ice skimmers are waiting to go outside. As I lean over the drinking fountain,

I read the sign written in blue ballpoint: *Please don't spit tobacco into the fountain.* There is a rusty stain around the metal drain. If I were small, little like a not-born baby, I could slip down that spigot drain. I could slip down, sliding into the pipes. And the buzzing and the bright don't stop, and I think of the raping wasps, and the giant bees that will come after the rapture. Those left behind will be punished beyond my mind: men with black hoods and long knives will hurt women and babies. They will hurt us all.

I will be left behind. Sin lives in me, in what Samuel did to me and that I let him. I know I am ruined; I will be used up by him before the Lord's return. Maybe I will never marry. Worse, maybe Samuel will marry someone else, even Naomi; they ain't blood related. And I know that Reuben knows. Reuben knows that Samuel has ruined me and he doesn't care. All anyone cares about is Naomi; seems like she's all I care about too. She will be kept pure, safe from the demons.

The floor is too shiny and white; it smells like cat pee even though I can see my own reflection. It is too clean for me, so I feel dizzy and need to rest on a ride-on mower. A red-vested demon leans over me and makes noises in its words. I shake my head and say enough to make it move away from me. I can't understand its words because of the light and the buzzing and the smell being so strong. I sit on the seat of the mower; it is meant to be outside. But it has to wait until the snow melts and the grass wakes and grows and needs cutting. It has to wait until the thaw. I lay my head down on the cool metal greenness of the mower, and the store slows and then stops its spinning in my head. It must be time to go, so I walk on the clean floor beneath the blazing lights; I fight through the buzz like quicksand to leave the salt behind.

We are waiting at the cash register at Field-n-Farm. Uncle Peter hoists the sacks of birdseed onto the counter and the checkout girl looks at him. She has pink-stained lips and black spider eyelashes. He has a handsome face and a handsome crooked mouth. My mom looks at the checkout girl looking at Uncle Peter, then Mom concentrates on the seed. Uncle Peter stares at the seed.

Right now I can look and see: Uncle Peter took the photo in the basement. He was there when Daddy wasn't; he was there waiting when his brother finally came back. Candy bars are three for a dollar. Uncle Peter has the same mouth; he has no beard and no tobacco stains. The cloud had hidden him from my sight; it's like seeing love right before your eyes. Uncle Peter keeps his eyes low. When they rest on Mom's face, they really rest; his chest moves in and out slow, and it looks like he's remembering how to breathe — or how to see — again. Uncle Peter kept our garden the summer my daddy was away; Peter cared for Mom and taught her to walk again. Uncle Peter took the photo, and the harvest in the picture is his. Daddy ain't the only one with that mouth.

And it comes to me as if from the Lord: Peter could have been my father — or he could be still. But he couldn't and can't because my mom isn't that way, like the world is. It could have all gotten broken and ruined, but I'm sure Mom's heart was strong. Uncle Peter's got the same mouth as Daddy, the same mouth as me; Peter's mouth ain't straight. Somebody's mouth is lying.

I can see Daddy in me, even though he hides his crooked mouth. My heart is hurt the same way as his, so it hurts the same way for him. We are both soft. We are all too soft for this, too easy hurt. But when he looks at me, it ain't kindness. He looks at me with pity. And that's what he's got to carry. Jesus on the cross carried the same load; He had the same look and the same mouth.

But I can see Uncle Peter in me even stronger. We are eyes not needing lids and fingers without nails. We are trees without bark. He looks at me and knows I'm strong. He knows I'm his. Waiting for a daddy, for the boys, is like waiting on the Saviour. I don't know how long I will have to wait.

We all have something to be forgiven for. *All have sinned and fall short of the glory of God.* And *the wages of sin is death, but the gift of God is eternal life.* I am recalling all I can of verses of sin I know; I am remembering all I can of the sins of the world, my church, my family and my soul. I take them before Jesus and lay my sins down. I pile them up at the foot of the cross. It is cold, so I climb into the rusty truck and buckle my seatbelt. We drive home with my mom sitting in the middle of the seat. The clouds have covered the moon, and it is dark and the cold makes my hands tremble. Winter seems to last forever; the roads are slick with ice. But soon, in the spring, the deer will lick me until I am gone.

16

'SILENT NIGHT, HOLY NIGHT' IS PLAYING ON THE BROWN
Bakelite radio that rests on the corner of Grandma's kitchen
counter. All the local radio stations play carols during most of
December, but Grandma always chooses the Christian station
all the way from the Twin Cities as it plays hymns, choruses
and sermons to help us bake and cook. Even though the
reservation radio station is closer by, their music crackles as
it don't seem to travel good through the woods. I've played
with the dial without Grandma's knowing, and now she's busy
boiling krube on the stove and humming along to carols in
some Indian language. I guess Christmas is Christmas and we
all know the words, so it's alright just to hum along without
knowing.

We celebrate Christmas in the ways our people have always
celebrated Christmas: lefse, lutefisk, pickled pork, salted
herring, krumkake and krube. The lefse is a year-round treat,
thin crepes made of potato, served with butter sprinkled with
cinnamon and sugar. We even have a sugar shaker pre-mixed
with cinnamon just for the job. Lutefisk is slimy and shiny
both: dried cod soaked soft in lye, boiled in hot water, then
served with melted butter. All the smelly things — lutefisk,

pickled pork and salted herring — I leave to Daddy and Reuben. But I love krumkake: holiday sugar cookies crimped in a special-shaped metal pan. And krube is something different altogether; it is my favourite.

Krube takes the whole family. We peel potatoes, mounds of them, and then stuff them through a meat grinder. The grinder is hand-operated, not no fancy electric model, and it does take some pushing and pulling. Reuben and Samuel take turns winding the handle, trying to keep the metal pan set underneath in just the right spot to catch the dripping starchy water. The big bowl of worm-like potatoes then passes to us assemblers at the table. Naomi and I cover our hands with flour and grab mounds of the potatoes to mould them around a thumb-sized glob of suet or fat. Grandma says her people used to use bacon, but Grampa and her boys like suet. So we use suet. Grandma boils the flour-covered mounds until they float; they bob up to let us know they are ready. Later, we'll smother them in butter and eat them near whole or break them up and fry them again in milk with plenty of salt and pepper. Either way, krube sticks in the belly. I think it must be what manna from heaven was; there is no hunger after a few balls of krube.

That's how you tell what people are: their people do it a certain way and your people do it another. Grandma's momma was German, so she used bacon. My daddy's Norwegian so he uses suet. My daddy's people did not come to America; they came to Wisconsin. When they left the frozen fjords, the goal was to find the place farthest from home which was closest to home. From what they'd overheard in snatches of conversation on the long ocean crossing, Wisconsin was the place for a poor farmer to start again. When my great-grandpa finally came across the ice-crusted lakes, snow-sunken fields, and endless pine forests of the northwest Indian Head country, he knew that he was home again.

We are known by our food. Words, too, show a people. Daddy can remember his daddy speaking Norwegian around the holidays. *'Glade Jul! Hellige Jul!'* He wouldn't use it the rest of the year, though, as he didn't want the boys to pick it up. In the broken-down country schoolhouse that's slumping next to Mikkelsen's place, Grampa Ole got the strap from the schoolmarm when he used old-country language. Because of that, the boys didn't learn nothing but English at home. Only when their daddy would get real happy or sad did they hear the other. Sometimes he would sing to the cattle, just so he wouldn't forget the words. But we do try to keep some of the old ways: advent calendars to count down the season, gingerbread houses to decorate with frosting snow, prickly green pine trees with popcorn and cranberry strings, and red-and-white Christmas stockings hung by the fireplace.

After all the krube is moulded — all the balls stacked on the counter, waiting for their turn in the boiling salty water — Reuben, Samuel, Naomi and I start unpacking the nativity set. To prevent knocks and breaks, each piece is wrapped in paper towels from the kitchen and then wrapped again in last year's gift-wrap. Most every year, though, somebody comes out worse for wear. Unwrapped from his cinnamon-and-pine-smelling shroud, one of the wise men, the black-faced one with a purple and gold hat, is missing a part. He went in the box last year whole, but while he was buried, his hand must have offended him. I dig down deep in the box to find his missing part; in the far corner, mixed amongst a little pile of mouse droppings, his broken hand clutches his tiny, shiny gift. Reuben's got the crazy glue, so we start to mend him best we can.

Between gold, frankincense and myrrh, I know most about myrrh because of my library project at school. Last week before Christmas vacation, we all got to pick a topic to read about and then write a report. Since I like to sing 'We Three Kings', I picked myrrh, and I now decide that that's what this black-faced king's hand is holding. It's most like the syrup we get from boiling sugar maple sap; myrrh comes from the blood of trees. Sap flows from cracks in the bark, from the wounds of the tree. It is scent and it is holy; it is never just given away. Myrrh is more than perfume: it can heal cracks in the mouth and in the skin. I don't know why this king brought myrrh to a baby — I suppose Jesus' momma might have had need of it.

But the library book didn't stop there; it went back even beyond Bible times. There was a story of a sad girl, Myrrha, who ran away from her daddy. She didn't want to live and she didn't want to die. She turned into a tree. Nine months later, the girl-tree split open and a baby was inside; from the wound of the tree, the momma's myrrh tears dripped down and bathed her baby. It was a most confusing story, but I understood the end: like any wild creature — bird, wolf or other — the momma scented her baby so she could find him later. It seems that in all these old-time stories — Greek, Ojibway or whatever — something is always changing shape. I read other stories in the book: hands being chopped off because of apple trees; beautiful dresses made of the sun, moon and stars; young girls swallowed by the earth and being pulled by the hair. These things were a mystery and some were unspeakable: ice storms, bloody water and ashy smoke. These stories must be why Samuel and Naomi aren't allowed to read just any book at the school library. I read them, though, and at night I see them again in my dreams.

We have mended the king best we can and set him with the others around the nativity; you'd have to look mighty close to see he's been broken. Taking turns, one by one, we always put everything in the exact same place: Mary and Joseph, shepherds and sheep, cow and donkey, star and angel, and, finally, baby Jesus in the manger. We scatter hay and cottony snow over the scene. I can smell the roasted turkey and ham, and Grandma is calling from the kitchen; dinner is all perfect and set. The fireplace is roaring with heat, the gifts are under the tree, and the table is packed with food. We are together, all warm and safe. Now, we are ready to start.

Dinner is over and yellow ladybugs plop off the ceiling fan into the leftover mashed potatoes. The bugs are everywhere this winter, in the cupboards and beds and bathtub, and they stink when you squish them on the linoleum. Aunt Gloria says they have to watch the nursery babies close: when the little girls aren't eating the bugs, the little boys are pushing their spotted backs to try and make them spin or play music. Mom and Aunt Gloria are scraping and stacking dishes, finishing Christmas lunch, while the men and kids are relaxing with Grandma near the tree. Daddy brought in a beautiful pine for Grandma's tree: taller than I am with short, sharp, grey-green needles. It smells like a forest. Later, after we open a present each — mostly socks and sweaters — we'll head to church for carols and communion.

We hear it before we see it, Uncle Peter's fancy truck crunching slow down the driveway. As he parks outside the kitchen window, the overgrown branches of the evergreens planted near the turnaround stretch and catch the canopy of his pick-up. Green needles break onto the snow and ice crusted across the windshield; he's only cleared enough window to be able to drive over the hill. The passenger side is dark and bare. Grandma is sitting with Uncle Ingwald by the wood fire, watching the empty bird feeders out the window. She moves her chin down and then looks out through the glass again, pretending the truck in the drive didn't disturb the birds. The snowbirds flew up into the trees, but eventually they'll come back down again.

He's taking off his big boots in the mud room, Uncle Peter is. And now he pushes open the door and starts off smiling. I've never seen him cross that threshold.

'Merry Christmas.'

He already missed lunch. Acting like Peter being here is normal, everyone smiles and says hello — except Grandma just sits and looks out the window.

In a giant cardboard box, Uncle Peter's brought turkeys for everyone. The turkey workers always give bit parts to their neighbours at the holidays, but my uncle's got whole birds, processed and shrink-wrapped. They are huge turkeys; white plastic covers the featherless puckered skin. Unwrapped, they will be the colour of my flesh. With our family's turkey resting on my lap, I feel the cold from the pick-up seeping into my thighs.

'Merry Christmas, Momma.' Uncle Peter cradles Grandma's bird; he leans over her rocker to kiss her cheek.

'You stink of kerosene.' Grandma pulls her face away from her boy.

I notice the stumbling then. Uncle Peter is clumsy in his stocking feet but he's still grinning big. He's trying to catch their eyes, but nobody — not even my momma — will look at his face. I'm looking: his eyes are near to sleepy-shut, but his cheeks are up from the smiling and his head moves slow. His hand rests on the back of the rocking chair, fingers laced in the red crocheted blanket that usually supports Grandma's head. But she's up and moving now. Shaking her head and mumbling about the 'smell of death', Grandma brushes by Peter with her eyes set to cry.

'Ingwald, take the drunkard home.'

And then she's shut in her room. I hear the springs of her bed take her weight and a low sighing sound; except for the refrigerator noises from the kitchen, now the house is silent.

Uncle Ingwald don't move from his chair. He sits there staring and don't even look Peter in the face.

'I'll just leave the birds then.' Uncle Peter drops Grandma's and Ingwald's turkeys onto the seat of Grandma's rocker; it sways back and forth with the weight. His hip hits the arm of the chair as he turns around in a faltering circle and the blanket slips down the chair and shrouds the meat.

Mom jumps to her feet and reaches out to right the chair; she looks like she might cry.

Peter stares at my mom. The Christmas lights on the tree reflect in his eyes. 'Merry Christmas, Marie.' For the first time in my life, I see a grown man's tears.

Daddy jumps up and holds his brother by the elbow. 'Enough now.' And he takes the empty box from Peter's hands, and the man's shoulders slump. Head down but eyes up, Daddy says he's taking his brother home. He guides Peter through the living room into the kitchen.

We kids sit still, eyes down and trying to be small. Ingwald keeps his face toward the window, looking at the tiny triangle dents in the snow the birds make with their feet. Their tracks are stamped beneath the shadow of the feeder, mixed in with black sunflower seeds and cracked shells. He keeps his eyes on that snow.

Even when the Lord chooses to show Himself — causes His goodness to pass in front of our eyes and proclaims His name in our presence — we cannot see His face. No one may see Him and live. He has mercy on whom He chooses and compassion just the same. We do not know His ways and can only ponder. When the glory of the Lord passes by, He will hide us in a cleft in the rock and cover us with His hand. Look quick to see His back as He stirs and steps away; never try to look Him straight in the face.

17

I am scrunched up in the pick-up with Dad and Reuben driving around the neighbourhood. We are on our way into town to Ingwald's place for the church's regular New Year's celebration. Mom's already at the parsonage helping Aunt Gloria prepare, but Daddy always likes to drive past all the nearby homeplaces to get a look at what's changed in a year. A quick gander at new machinery or maybe a different barn colour gives him something to talk about with the old farmers during the party. We know the Svensen barn collapsed and burnt, and we sure don't need to drive past it. That change, from barn to ash, life to death, is too lasting to need to go and look at again. Every now and then, a tuft of ragged brown grass pokes up from the roadside, but the roads are slick with a layer of ice and then a light coating of snow. They aren't too bad for nearly January, but we are driving slowly anyway to get a better look at the neighbours' homesteads.

Daddy's always watching, learning our land. Before we were born, he was a sneak hunter, tracking deer by their marks in the dirt or snow. With seeing eyes, he can tell doe hooves versus wide buck track; he was a born sneak hunter with a natural gentle pace and the patience of a stone. He can rest standing while he listens to a doe drink from the river, and he can crouch quiet while a flitting bird lands near and a fat red squirrel gnaws acorns. When Daddy drives the deer toward us and we stand or walk slow, my brother leads me. Even though Reuben nods deep and taps his foot on branches that could trip me up, I tend to stumble through. I am not a born sneak hunter.

Driving the neighbourhood, we turn the corner where the Goodenoughs live. Their house is a green timber box wrapped in plastic up to the ground-floor windows. Sensing a bad winter is coming, they also got straw and hay bales stacked against the siding to insulate even more from the cold, blowing wind. Rusted tractors, camper trailers and half-built snowmobiles are scattered here and there across the yard. They must rob parts from the old machines to keep their new ones running. I've seen the old man hunkered on one of those sleds outside the grocery store; he waits on the snowmobile and smokes and coughs while the grey woman buys supplies. They don't go to any church that I know of, but I think their last name makes them Indians, part at least. Grandma said that maybe they are Catholics too. We don't see them much except buying provisions at the store during winter.

Across the road from the Goodenoughs is the former Nelson place, now the Bjorgen place. That Bjorgen is a good old farmer. He's from over by Mishtogie or somewheres, and so he ain't one of the original Failing families. He bought his farm fifty or so years ago, and he did marry a local widow so he wasn't a true stranger. Only one son is his; the rest came as a package deal with his pretty wife. He claims them all, I guess. That youngest boy with the red hair plays the fiddle real good; I've heard him at the nursing home when our church and theirs — the Methodists, I think — share nursing home service. Our school bus route is crooked, so he don't ride our bus. Because of that, I don't know that boy all that well. Their place is falling down a bit, but it always looks tidy.

Another mile or so, and next is the Turgeson place. It is calm and still with near a proud acre of yard between the house and the barn. That round white barn stands straight against the snow while the trees make shadowy dances against its side. It is already getting dark even though we've just finished supper. Grandma told me why Mrs Turgeson's mouth, her lips bitten and rough, is always tight even when singing hymns in church. I thought it was from holding her face straight when she helped the ladies of the church give birth, for she's a midwife. But it wasn't just that. Before I was born, Mrs Turgeson's daughter fell in love with the Goodenoughs' son. She even went and left high school and stayed with him — Evan, maybe — in one of the broken-down trailers that sit in the Goodenough part of the woods.

Just before hunting season and the first snows, she was home again already. She had bruised eyes and a big belly; her momma said rest but her daddy said she still had to pull her own weight. So she was mowing that big yard with the lawn tractor when Evan's truck came roaring into the driveway. She was running toward the house, screaming and holding her big belly, when Evan unloaded his shotgun into her back. Her daddy didn't come to see her buried amongst the weeds and fallen leaves in the country cemetery. When I watch him bow his grey head while serving communion, I see that fawn and that girl. My fawn taking a shortcut through the fence, and his girl taking a shortcut across the lawn; now the deer hangs as a cage of bones, and she is buried near a stone. When I watch

Mr Turgeson stand and pray, I see him holding her bleeding in the new-cut grass.

We set quiet in the truck as we go past that big yard; we just keep on driving. There's plenty of time to make it to Ingwald's house to help ring in the year. I'm very much looking forward to tonight, both for the fellowship and the rifle blasts from the roof of the parsonage. Although Ingwald ain't a veteran, many in the congregation are, and they always make their own fireworks. The singing of 'My Country, 'Tis of Thee' and other patriotic songs and eating goodies will take up the hours after supper until midnight. We will be in good company, and it is a good night.

But as we pass by, there is a Jersey cow — tan hide stretched tight across her giant bloated belly — sprawled out in Turgeson's yard. She's right in front of the big milking barn, only twenty yards from the gravel road that separates their land from a forty-acre piece my grandma's got. When we first drive near the farm, I think the cow is dead. But then I see her head lift and her lips shape a deep, hollow moan. We can't hear her with the pick-up windows rolled up tight against the snow, but we can all feel her. We drive on around the mile corner, but then it feels too hot and close in the truck.

Daddy, Reuben and I go back to the cow. Daddy turns the truck around and drives back to the Turgeson place. In front of the barn, he slams on the brakes and we slide to a halt. Reuben's opening the door before we are barely stopped. When he cracks open his door and lets one foot step outside, we sure hear her bellow real good then. Daddy jumps out but leans back into the cab of the pick-up to take down his rifle from its spot above the rear-view window.

'This ain't gonna be pretty, Ruth. Looks like a twisted stomach; could go either way.'

He is asking if I am sure I still want to come to the cow, and he is asking if I am prepared to help Mr Turgeson, prepared for what I might see. A twisted stomach can be ugly and there won't be much thanks coming from that stubborn old man leaning on the barn, his hands on his head and hatless in the wind. Even together in the yard, they are alone in this world, both the cow and that man. I nod my head, grab a few bullets from the glove compartment, and pull on my knitted stocking cap. It is part of being a neighbour. It might not be pretty, but it sure will be cold.

January

18

BECAUSE I MISSED THE NEW YEAR'S PARTY LAST NIGHT, I got to come and stay at Uncle Ingwald's place today. Well, I wasn't supposed to stay. First off, I was just coming to help Aunt Gloria and Naomi clean up from the party and maybe learn a little about the lace making they all do. Naomi did her 4-H demonstration on tatting, and Mom said 'oh, for cute'.

So, here I am vacuuming their good room and waiting to learn. Since it started blowing hard and the freezing rain came in good, Aunt Gloria called my mom and told her that they would just bring me to church in the morning. No need to make the trip — short though it may be — seeing I can just wear one of Naomi's old dresses to church tomorrow, and Mom and Daddy can take me home after the potluck. I don't know whether I'm happy about staying or not. At least Samuel has already left for hockey camp, so that don't prey on my mind.

Outside their kitchen window, I can only see blackness. I can hear the rain hitting the snow and trees and leaving a thick skin of ice dragging everything down. Tomorrow morning, there'll be broken trees and snapped electricity wires. The county will have to call out their men to do plenty of fixing.

That ice can do damage, alright, but the cold don't bother me much except for when I feel it freezing my bones. I guess it is the water. The water inside of us freezes up and makes a body hurt like it is too big for its own skin. Pulling a walleye out of a frozen lake must do the same thing. That fish — mouth, lips and pointy teeth all gasping for water — must feel the opposite of freezing. He thaws in the air, drowning being outside his cold, black water. His silvery scales break about in two, and he has to use every bit of his spirit to command his body to stay together tight. He has to be like Jesus, calling the storm to rest, rebuking the wind. He has to have faith strong enough to command the winds and the water.

Naomi is sorting her closet, piling up hand-me-downs on her pretty four-poster bed; after she is done with them, I inherit her dresses and sweaters. Fancy brands and fabrics, most of the clothes come from Aunt Gloria's fancy family out in California. The sweaters are always pink or purple, being colours Naomi, her momma and other swanky folk like. I like red, but I know ladies don't wear it. Naomi points out what sweaters can be thrown in the washing machine and what can't; it makes me think rich people must be dirty. She couldn't fit another sweater in that closet edgewise, crammed as it is with hooks and plastic hangers, but still, it is kindness that makes Naomi give me what she don't need — kindness and the thick-growing middle she thinks she's hiding.

Curled up on the bed like cats, we are warm and resting amongst the wool: Naomi leans against the foot and I stretch out along the head. Her room smells of lilacs and all other purple things, and there are even flowers in the curtain pattern.

I wonder aloud whether Samuel is having fun at hockey camp. When I ask, she moves her pink foot away from where it was resting by my thigh. She crosses her legs and starts unbraiding her hair. Tracing a rabbit of soft white fur sewn into my new sweater, I thank her again for the clothes.

'Do you think Samuel has any for Reuben?'

Naomi's loud breath out tells me no.

'Why do you always want to talk about boys? I think you have a crush on Samuel. Just shut up about him.'

That ain't fair and she knows it. I sit looking at my hands for a while. When I look up, she's got her hair all unbraided and it almost touches her waist.

'I wish I could sit on my hair,' she says. In front of the dressing mirror, Naomi shimmies her shoulders and hips. She's been watching television, pageants again, I can tell. She's peering at the mirror as she walks slow and ladylike, eyeing her reflection above the perfume bottles and hair ribbons lined along the shelf.

Staying quiet ain't getting me nowhere. 'I don't even like boys.' I got my sock off and I'm picking at my toenails. 'I sure wouldn't even want to be a boy.' My chest feels tight with me wearing this silly bra my mom brought home the other day. Mom said she could see me jiggle, and I was ashamed. I must be the only thirteen-year-old with saggy enough breasts to need to wear a bra. My nipples rub against the lace, and now I'm hunching my shoulders so that Naomi can't see. Everything needs to slow down, but it is getting all mixed up in my head.

'Do you remember when I fell through the ice, Naomi?'

Naomi's re-braiding her hair. With her hands tangled through and looping back and forth, she shakes her head no.

I ask her again if she remembers, and she looks up with mean eyes all squinting. She pouts, then nods a little as she finishes tying her hair with a shiny pink bow. Glancing in the mirror, she turns to the side and holds another rosy ribbon to one ear and then the other, pretending earrings.

'That was so long ago. I forget things all the time, Ruth.' She wraps the ribbon around her neck and makes a pretty sash. 'I'm forgetting this already.'

Naomi thinks she'll be Miss Failing when she is eighteen. The high school gym full of family and friends will witness her singing in the pageant, purple spotlight on her lacy dress and gospel song. Her hair will be piled up shiny and thick, and she'll smile in surprise and cry all pretty when they place that diamond crown on her head. She sees herself riding in the parade, waving from the royal seat carved in the back of a giant plastic bird. She'll reign atop Failing's Turkey Princess float, holding fake roses and catching the eye of a boy who ain't from around here.

But I know the turkey farmers pour that turkey crap in the river. I know it is drowning the fish and making folks ill. And I know — more than I know anything — no one's ever going to let Naomi forget who she is.

'Girls, come and see.'

Uncle Ingwald is calling up to Naomi's room from the breezeway that connects their kitchen to the plywood mud room. He's never home, always in church, visiting shut-ins, or working in the shed. Something must be bad.

'Now just you wait.' Uncle Ingwald's face is round and his cheeks are red; the scarred lines of his cheeks crinkle like frosting. His balding head is covered up with a winter-weight cowboy hat, and his eyes are shining.

It's done raining, but it sure is real cold. All of us, Aunt Gloria and prettified Naomi and plain old me, bundle up tight with jackets, scarves, hats and woollen gloves to head out to see just what has made this man come in the house. I'm worried, but seems like Ingwald aims to smile.

We follow him out to the shed, walking single file like hunters trying to limit their footprints on a path. The flashlight in his hand carves a road of light that we step into as we crunch and slip across the yard on the strange icy snow. Once we make it to the shed, Aunt Gloria reaches across the doorway to cut on the lights, but my uncle stays her hand.

'Wait, Glory. Now I'll show you.'

And then he does. Taking the big spotlight they use for shining deer, Uncle Ingwald lights up that yard like sun. He sweeps the bright light across the yard and shows us the twinkling ice that coats the world.

'Sugar snow.' He speaks real low.

Sugar snow it is with everything that is still standing frosted heavy with clumps of diamonds and crackled like icing. All we do is sigh and look at the beauty. When Naomi reaches over and puts her glove in my mitten, I catch her brown eyes and feel as if I might cry. And if I cried that would be all sweetness and beauty too.

'We used to blow bubbles, didn't we, Daddy? When I was little, we used to freeze bubbles in the sky on an icy night.' Naomi's eyes shine.

Her daddy nods and reaches across to her and pulls her

tight to him; since I am holding on to Naomi, I am pulled into his flannel jacket too. He smells like a man. Aunt Gloria puts her arms around us all, and we pause there together for a while.

As we turn to head in to start fixing supper, Uncle Ingwald's spotlight swings inside the shed and the light catches on ten or twenty eyes staring from the corners. In the cold air, my scared, quick breath in makes me cough. Uncle Ingwald's eyes are now wet from laughing at me and my fright.

'Daddy.' Naomi sounds like a little girl whining. 'Don't laugh at her when she's scared.'

And I am scared. Staring back at me from the shadowy eaves of that creaking shed are opossums clinging to branches and a fox with a pheasant dragging out of its mouth. There is a grimy muskrat and a mean-looking weasel stacked on a shelf and three old fish, maybe muskies, hanging on the wall. I got such a fright, I'm shivering in spite of myself.

Aunt Gloria tells Uncle Ingwald he better clean up his mess, and by mess she means me. I'm trying to laugh at being afraid of dusty animals covered in cobwebs. You got to expect taxidermy in a taxidermy shed, but those glass eyes just about shocked the life right out of me.

To make up for the fright, Uncle Ingwald is going to let Naomi and me help him with a pelt. Besides mounting most of the deer and other hunted animals around our neighbourhood, he also puts up fur from trapping. My daddy says that though Ingwald is home-taught and slow, he's about the best taxidermist and tanner he's ever seen. Working one or two jobs off the farm while trying to run a trap line — checking sets morning and night — a guy don't always have the time to flesh and skin out his own catch. So Uncle Ingwald takes care of it. He takes care of it right, as long as you don't mind waiting until after the Lord and the church, waiting until he gets around to it.

Lights on now, I can see animals in varying states of life all over the shed. Some new ones still got bodies, but most are pelts and parts. I know that my body is just a house for my soul, but seeing these inside-out animals with pink-grey skin stretched tight makes me wonder. Stroking my hand across a finished silky mink, I believe I'm knowing mink for the first time. Mink is soft almost to wetness, still and sleek; mink is not beady eyes and sharp teeth. There are other scalps — muskrat, weasel and skunk — stretched out on wood around the shed. Uncle Ingwald points out which animal is which as we can't always tell from the inside out. He explains while lifting up various just-come-in bodies or skins or pelts on boards.

'You got to case the fur, pull it inside out like a sweater over your head.' He says to take the skin, slit it from one hind foot to the other and peel it back up over the head. 'Now you got yourself a hose of skin, a cased fur. You don't case a coyote, fisher, grey or red fox, not a bobcat either. You leave them with the fur on the outside and prepare the pelt thataway.' Beavers are special too: skin them open by cutting down the underside, slit them from nose to tail.

Uncle Ingwald is happy out here in the tanning shed; he moves his arms — covered in wiry, red-blonde hair — like he does when he's really preaching. He points to chemicals in bottles on the tables, pats furry animals hanging from gambrels, and rubs a few slick skins pulled taut over fleshing beams. The fleshing beams are pointed boards that look like short skis, but skis with a strange glove of skin and fur. There is little blood, mostly skin, grey and pink skin and stripy fur.

Uncle Ingwald is pulling up a soaking raccoon, and he looks mighty excited. He is known for his brain tan and is rightly proud.

'Now what I'm rubbing into the coon, this is just a little brain tan.'

Naomi's momma don't like him cooking the cow brain in her kitchen, so he simmers it out here in a pot of water on the camp stove and then mashes it up good with an ice-fishing strainer. He likes the brain tan; it must remind him of his grandpa, Naomi's and my great-grandpa, putting up fur for neighbours.

'Not using chemicals for this one — just like the early folk around these woods and the Indians too — just using regular oil straight from the brain. Got to rub it into the skin of this coon, then I'll wait for her to dry and start scraping and working her. I'll work her until she's snow-white and soft as a girl's cheek. Take me a while, but she'll get there.'

Naomi can do it too. She can stretch and flesh an animal, scraping off every little bit of fat and muscle without even tearing the hide. She's nowhere as quick as Uncle Ingwald, but she is practising. I watch as her black-haired arms work a tube of skin and fur and her daddy leans over and guides her with his heavy hands. His pants press hard against her back while he talks low and slow of oil glands, stripping tails, rabies and such. I watch with my glassy eyes, sometimes pretending I'm Naomi; sometimes pretending I'm Uncle Ingwald. I stay still and catch dust on my hair.

'Don't work that section so much it gets weak.' Uncle Ingwald helps Naomi as she scrapes and cleans the skin toward the tail. 'One little bit of fat will spoil the whole pelt.'

You got to scrape out the insides to preserve the fur. That

animal is more than dead: it is empty, and this is the only way to pretend it is still alive. We all pretend together. Whether the skunk is stuffed and mounted with glass eyes and one foot raised up ready to step, or whether the pelt is soft and silky and ready to make a fur collar, we all pretend together that it is real. It will stay that way forever.

Naomi's arms are slowing; she is done for the night.

As we walk together toward the house, I worry about church in the morning. Just last Sunday, my uncle preached scary.

'There may be corpses amongst us this morning, corpses that haven't been buried yet.'

He told us to take out what is inside. He told us to reject the pretender who seeks to destroy.

'My eyes have seen Thy salvation. The Enemy seeks to eliminate and ignore. Woe to the scribes, Pharisees and hypocrites. Do not cleanse the outside of a bowl or cup and leave the insides full of rot. Pretending is hiding behind a mask. This is not a dead, empty pulpit!'

I ain't heard of nobody from the congregation dying, but I worry about bodies waiting to be raised from the dead. Week-long funerals with no burials have caused other Full Quarter churches to split; they splintered with cousins and brothers no longer speaking, let alone praying together on Sunday. We believe in Lazarus too; we believe, but I've never heard of us leaving a body in the sanctuary until it started to stink. Seems like flies are the end of our faith.

I wonder if our pulpit is dead and silent, and if our church smells of brain tan and blood. I wonder if I will feel black, furry raccoon arms holding and protecting me in my sleep.

Maybe their masked eyes will look at me brown and gentle, or blue and mean and they'll haunt me, hunting me through the night. Precious Jesus, please keep me warm and protect me from spoiling. Scrape me clean inside and make me holy. Wash me in Your blood, raise me from the dead and take me to live with You in heaven forever. Dear Jesus, all of these things are written on my heart, in Your Holy Name, amen.

19

His hand is behind his back. In almost all his navy slides, Uncle Peter's arm is crooked at a strange angle, tucked up and away and hidden from the camera. He's grinning wide and his buddies are laughing, slouching in their rumpled off-duty gear. And the ladies with them — long black hair looping across sundresses, bare shoulders and barely covered breasts — are sparkly-eyed with wet, pink mouths. I know without them saying: he's got a bottle of beer in that hidden hand.

Daddy and Peter and Reuben are smirking at the picture projected bright and big against the screen because they think I can't know. They think that I don't know about the liquor behind his back or what those wet mouths mean, but I do. They needn't hide it — well, maybe they should from Mom and Naomi — but they needn't hide it from me or for me. In the darkened living room, the slides of a teenaged Peter flash; the corners of the pictures glide off the screen and splash blue Pacific light across the curtains.

Plain winter light creeps in through the cracks between the curtains and the windows. It's unusual for the men to be inside during daylight, but this cold Saturday afternoon seemed a good day for Uncle Peter to remember the old times, his away times. Dad and Peter are on the couch together, and my brother sits before them on the floor. Naomi and I are sharing the recliner, legs up on the footrest to make enough room. After New Year's she came home with me. She was supposed to stay the night, but we're almost tired of each other already after just a morning of hairstyling and radio. So she called Uncle Ingwald to come and get her before supper. For now, I'm thankful for the slides and the break.

Mom is edging around the room, shelving blankets, folding clothes, and sending sideways looks to make me feel guilty. Cleaning is Saturday afternoon's chore, but my dust rag hangs clean and still between my knees. Naomi is supposed to be sorting odd socks — about the only job my mom trusts to the girl — but Reuben rests there without duty or blame.

Daddy lets Mom slip around the edges of the house, clanking pots and sighing, but he can't ignore the vacuum cleaner's roar.

'Marie. Marie, come set with us a bit.' And he grabs at her waist as she runs the vacuum near the couch.

Mom pushes his hands away but then smiles as he grabs her again and pulls her down, hard but catching her fall, onto his lap.

'Let's see all what Peter got up to, eh?' Daddy smooths her hair and wraps his arms around her elbows, pulling her close in a tight hug.

My mom can't help but smile, and she can't really get away anyway. She leans back against him and turns her face to the flickering screen. She's probably seen these slides before, all Peter's adventures while he was in the navy. But that doesn't mean she can't see them new all again: white sand and palm trees; fish with sharp faces and fanned fins; coconuts stacked like cordwood; and girls, girls, girls.

The colours flash as each slide jangles into the projector and I see the places so far away. He left Failing, my uncle, and saw people and things none of us has seen. He met folks who didn't know his name or where he was from, and no one knew he was one of us. No one even knew why he kept that hand hid behind his back. He left us, and could have gotten away, and still he returned. While the slides clink ahead, and Naomi braids and re-braids her hair, I imagine my way outside this place — outside this family and house. Me, lounging next to a boat with my shoulders bare and hair hanging loose; my mouth a wet, pink kiss. But there will be no slide of me hiking up my dress, the ocean up to my knees; there is no war for girls.

When the slides stop, Daddy slithers out from beneath Mom and opens the curtains. He heads into the kitchen. 'Coffee?'

And both Mom and Uncle Peter agree. Bored, Reuben pulls on his boots and goes out the door, but Naomi and me stay quiet on the recliner. If we are still enough, maybe Mom will forget the cleaning. Maybe we can waste all afternoon.

Uncle Peter and Mom rest side by side on the couch, talking about the oceans he's crossed.

'Sometimes I can't believe I've been there, Marie.'

And she nods and smiles and puts her hand on his elbow.

'Sometimes I can't believe I ever left.' My uncle looks down at his knees and back at my mother. 'It all changed while I was gone: you all changed.'

The sun trickles in through the window and shines on her braid, escaped wisps tangled and caught behind her ear. She is lovely and smiling, settled low in the sagging middle of the couch, chewing her lip. Mom closes her eyes and opens them like she's seeing old things new again. Sunlight streams through the glass and shows the dust in the air. The coffee percolator gurgles from the kitchen.

'Up, girls. Get to work.' And Mom springs forward off the couch, grabs my dust rag and play-swats me a little on the legs.

She's humming and straightening and moving about the room before I can even get on my feet. I'm not going to feel shame for watching the slides, for sitting and resting gentle for an afternoon. Once I've done my dusting, I've decided we'll be done. We are going to leave this house. Naomi and I will be outside in the cold and the light today. We are going to walk outside, even if it is just for a moment.

Naomi's wearing Christmas presents from her mother's people: snow gear, brand new every year. I've got on Reuben's old camouflage pants and Naomi's last year's jacket. The jacket is missing a snap. She is a frosted cupcake; I am a yard sale.

Carrying a cup of hot water from the house, Naomi wants to throw it in the air and watch it freeze before it hits the ground. She heard the television weatherman say it would work. I don't believe it. Not even cold this cold can halt and hold time.

'It ain't going to work.' I shake my head and walk toward Naomi. She's got her pink candy-striped gloves wrapped around the mug.

Her eyes darken. 'Yes, it will. The weatherman said.' She's even pouting. 'You don't know everything.'

She's always got to be right and, time to time, she gets mean about it.

'Do it then. I'm cold.' I stamp my boots.

'You ain't my boss, Ruth.'

'Somebody has to be.' What's gotten into her, I don't know.

'Well, nobody would ever pick you.' Naomi looks straight into my face with her black eyes. 'Nobody would ever pick you first.' And she pulls back her arm and throws the hot water across my chest.

The water is seeping into the jacket, but I can't feel it. I can't hear any noise or even smell the air. I can only see the frost forming across my chest, crisscrossing white and blotching the faded purple. I can only watch the freeze.

I can't smell anything with my runny nose, but I can see breath and steam leave my body and hear birds and small things cracking little twigs. I can see sticks and trees and pale blue sky, dead long grass stiff and glazed with frost like diamond dust. Dirt don't frost but leaves do. Some trees don't release their leaves; they just die on the stalk. My legs ache in the cold.

A horn honks and we both jump. Without either of us noticing, the church van has wound its way down our long driveway. Uncle Ingwald doesn't bother parking. Avoiding the slushy corners, he just turns around in the yard and then honks the horn again. She's got to go home now. As she moves toward her daddy, Naomi looks over her shoulder at me but she doesn't smile.

As I head for the house, I see Peter's truck is gone. He and Reuben have gone off together again. I hear raised voices inside. Pressing my frosted body against the siding, I try to listen to the goings-on inside the kitchen. My parents must've fought the whole while Naomi and I were in the snow.

'Shame you didn't choose the right one.' Daddy's slamming

pots and boxes around the kitchen, must be looking for his keys.

'That ain't fair.' Mom ain't even crying.

The keys jingle as he pushes the door with his hip. 'Money don't measure a man, Marie.'

She's holding firm. 'All I'm saying, all I've been saying, is that we need to fix the dryer.'

She's right: hanging clothes by the fire means we've stunk of wet wool all winter. Kids sometimes won't share a desk with me.

'Blood from a stone. I can't do any more than I can. I just can't make you happy.' And the door slams, and the warm air goes outside along with my daddy. He hardly ever says nothing, especially in a fight. His silence is worse than his words. He's headed for the truck and he didn't even grab his hat. He sure didn't notice me standing there.

Usually, we don't use words. We speak instead with eyes, head and hands: looking through, turning down, holding thighs. Folks move away to say what is necessary. My mother is soft and frightens easily. My father is not and does not. They stand and pray in our church pew. They walk up our dirt driveway, and the light between their bodies always shows like sun amongst the jack pines.

It is cold, inside and outside our house, and my mother is building up a fire. She banks the woodstove. The cast-iron stove throws and catches shadows, and I see more of that growing light of the in-between. Mom sits down on our soft sagging couch. Sometimes they rest there — my parents — near one another, not together but not alone.

I settle into a chair at the kitchen table to braid embroidery thread. Before we went outside, before the water, Naomi gave me some of her supplies and told me to make her a friendship bracelet. She was supposed to make me one too. Maybe she won't, but I still will: over, under, I weave the purple and pink strings. My wrist is smaller than hers.

When my mom is sad, she stays apart from us, restless and moving. She also sings. *All to Jesus I surrender; all to Him I freely give. I will ever love and trust Him, in His presence daily live.* She sits alone at the battered wooden upright piano, singing and playing old hymns and choruses, even some from her childhood days. *All to Jesus I surrender; humbly at His feet I bow. Worldly pleasures all forsaken, take me, Jesus; take me now.* Even when singing alone, Mom sings the second part, and that low alto makes the meaning soar. *All to Jesus I surrender; make me, Saviour, wholly Thine. Let me feel the Holy Spirit, truly know that Thou art mine.*

I've listened to her songs, the same songs, dozens of times; but sometimes I hear something new in the singing. I can hear it especially when her face is wet, like today. It is the sound below that helps me hear. *All to Jesus I surrender; Lord, I give myself to Thee. Fill me with Thy love and power; let Thy blessing fall on me. I surrender all, I surrender all. All to Thee, my blessed Saviour, I surrender all.*

When Mom finishes singing, I halt my braiding and remembering and cross to the piano. She's hurting. I lay my hands on her back and ask why she's crying. She won't answer.

'Do you still love Daddy?' I believe I need to know.

Her hands hit the piano, but soft like a sigh. 'How can you ask me that?' She cuts her eyes at me, and I'm ashamed

I spoke. Mom pulls the lid down on the piano keys, swings her legs over the bench and hurries away. She's in their bedroom now. I know she's standing just behind that door.

Every day we choose heaven or hell, and one day we will stand before the judgement seat of God. Life or death will be spoken from His mouth, and only then will we know for sure. All we know for certain is life on this earth. Until we see the Lord face to face in heaven, we haven't even felt real love. Mothers' love is the closest we'll get, though, and I can't imagine not having a momma.

My daddy told me that when he was in Alaska he saw a young moose trying to suck milk from its mother's gut pile. Nobody could drive it off for over a week, so the landowner had to come and shoot it before it starved.

We may not know true love yet, but I got to think that we're close.

20

UNCLE INGWALD IS DRIVING ALL OF US TO THE CABIN.
The old church van is a white Chevy with rust so deep that
I can feel the wind sneaking past the rags stuffed in the holes
in the walls. There ain't any carpet left on the floor, but we
got some of Grandma's braided rag rugs spread out. Red,
blue and green, they decorate the inside of the van and keep
the wind off our feet too. The van is packed, with Ingwald
and Daddy in the front seats, and Naomi and me in the back
with the supplies. Samuel is home from hockey camp; he and
Reuben sit in the middle. Even if we get skunked and don't
catch any fish, we got enough venison jerky, and cans of
cream corn and pork and beans to keep us fed a week.

I love going to Uncle Ingwald's cabin up at Cranberry Lake.
It's not really just their cabin, being that all the boys built it
with Grampa Ole back when they were just teenagers. No one
back home in Failing understood why someone would want
to leave their perfectly good house on the farm and drive three
hours every Saturday to slap together a shack on the edge of
a mosquito-bit lake, but Grampa sold one of the horses and
bought the land anyway. Now, most of the neighbours on
the lake are all lawyers, doctors and such from Minneapolis

or Chicago. Maybe because Grampa wasn't such a silly dirt farmer, there is a Rundhaug cabin stuck right in amongst them all.

Grampa's cabin is made of spare barn wood and some of the blood-stained floorboards from the butcher's shop in Failing. After the sheriff's wife got sick off of some venison sausages, the county health department came in to check on Seversen's shop. They made the butcher rip up the good oak floorboards just because there was some blood bringing out the grain. From what my daddy tells me, I don't know what else they were expecting to be on the floor except blood in a butcher's shop that's been there since the Indians, but we got a large part of our lake cabin courtesy of county health.

It takes less time to get to the cabin in winter. Summertime, we take the Rabbit Trail and wind through the old logging roads all around Cranberry Lake; wintertime, we go through. Not through, exactly, but on: on the lake. Once we get to the boat ramp, Uncle Ingwald steps out of the van and lifts up the rusty ice auger being used as a gate over the driveway. Then, we drive down onto the ice and cut straight across; County Road CL exists only in winter. Uncle Ingwald always drives in between the orange cones that the fish and game or highway department or some other such county boys put up as a guide. Not that they're guaranteeing your safety, the cones, but it helps to have a bit of a track to follow. When he's driving, my daddy goes wherever he pleases on the ice. He says he's got to listen to the ice and just hear where to go. He jokes with Ingwald that only the true believer will 'follow where the Spirit leads'. But whenever my daddy is driving on the ice, he still unbuckles his seatbelt and opens the windows; I believe his back-up plan is to follow the Spirit out the window.

Crunching across the snow, the going is slow. But when we make a turn, bending around a slushy spot in the ice, sometimes the tyres slip and provide a bit of excitement. Seems like Naomi's forgotten whatever made her hate me before. She's been all smiles today. With our legs in the air and our heads near the ground, Naomi and me hang upside down on the far back couch. Each time the van jostles, our heads almost touch the musty rugs, and we scream and laugh. I've got to sit up quick now or I'm going to throw up.

We are slowing down anyways. Daddy wants to get the fish-frying pan that's inside the rickety Cranberry ice shack. Close to the open water, the shack always sits where the fishing is the best. The van stops, and Daddy jumps out to trek quick across the frozen lake; he jumps out into the black.

I can't look over at Naomi; she's sitting up straight now. I can't look over at Reuben or Naomi's brother either. The boys are slumped against the van windows, and Samuel is melting ice on the glass with his breath. It's been about a month since I fell into Little Failing, so we can't look at each other — or worse, speak of it — and make what happened true. We all spent Christmas together, but then we weren't so alone and so close. I can hear him breathe.

It is quiet and darkest night.

'You guys still with me?' Uncle Ingwald turns around and checks on us. 'Your daddy will be back soon. It's just dark.'

My face must be pale and my eyes wide.

'He can see with the flashlight and the moon. It's a real bright night.'

I look down into my hands; in the moonlight I can see that

with my nails I've punched little half-moons of red into my palms. I unclench my fists and try to breathe. I just feel a little sick from the drive.

'I told you girls not to hang upside down like that. I've been saying it since Mishtogie.'

I start to gag and heave, so I scramble in between the seats, slide open the door of the van and puke. I've been eating squeaky cheese curds and saltine crackers and red licorice. I vomit all down the front of my shirt, and I tremble and gag. Naomi stays in the back.

It is my daddy who comes to rescue me. He steps out of the dark with the fry pan in one hand and the flashlight in the other. When he sees me hanging out the van door crying and carrying on, he tries to hustle on the ice and ends up falling flat on his behind. Because his hands are full, he can't break his fall and he groans a big '*Uff da!*' Uncle Ingwald smiles and Daddy thrashes in the snow like a trapped weasel, so we all see the funny in it too.

'I tried to get to you, Ruthie.' Daddy's eyes are wet and shiny from laughing. His hair is sticking up all over; that hat never can stay on his head. 'I did try.'

I'm too busy giggling now to be sick or scared or whatever I was anymore. It is good to make the most of things, to take the good with the bad, so that is what we do. That is what I do.

We'll have to make the best of it, all of us, together this week at the cabin. The outhouse is one thing and the weather is another. The damp and cold will creep into your bones during night or day, no matter which. 'Keep dry,' my daddy always says, and 'Stay warm.' So when we open the door to the cabin, the summer screen door catching wind and banging backwards against the outside wall, we get set to making our nest cosy.

While the boys start a wood fire smouldering in the potbelly stove, Naomi and I see to the blankets. Someone's beat us to it, though, making a nest. Sprawled across the old cast-iron bed, stuffing — from the quilts, pillows and mattress alike — has been picked out and scattered. Must be coon, skunk or just plain rats got in and made a whole mess of the bed. Every time I reach around a pillow, tangled feathers and fibres fall out in clumps. I can't begin to tell about the crap. We shake out the blankets and pillows as best we can; it won't be perfect, but it will be as close to warm as we can get.

Old as it is, the cabin struggles. My grampa built it good enough, but Wisconsin weather takes a toll on both the living and the dead. We've got baling plastic tacked over the windows inside and out, but still the wind sneaks in around the edges. To prime the pump, we've got to wrench on the handle over the sink a couple dozen times before the well will consider working. Daddy's got the water boiling on the woodstove: a pot holds our hot-dog supper, and the kettle will provide washing-up water both for the dishes and for ourselves.

Uncle Ingwald is moving a pile of old red-checked hunting clothes off of the green formica table. All around the edges of the table, there are chips gouged out: either from rambunctious eating or playing Zonk until bedtime, I don't know. Zonk is the dice game we play at the cabin; Grandma won't allow any semblance of gambling at the farm, but we play it loud and regular up here. Circling the table are many chairs: matching metal ones with green vinyl seats and some rusty blue ones from outside. I have the special wooden chair. It has my uncle's name carved in the arm, but he would swear

— if he swore — that he didn't do it. My daddy winks at me when I trace my finger over each of the letters. I'm sure I-N-G-W-A-L-D still remembers that undeserved whipping; I'm most sure the leather strap hanging amongst a mess of feed caps on that antler rack by the stove won't let him forget.

Daddy gives us each a hot dog in a bun, and we pile on raw onions, ketchup, mustard and pickled relish. There is a dish of Grandma's bread-and-butter pickles on the table and a jar of pork hocks too. Over the taste of my supper, I can smell damp mittens drying on the stove; their steam rises into the air and gives a wet-dog smell without us even having a dog. Next to the wood box just inside the front door, there are six pairs of boots drying upside down.

I gather up the fancy cut-glass tumblers and black-eyed-susan water pitcher filled with Kool-Aid. Grandma told me once that she saved coupons from the grocery for ever so long to earn up enough points to get this drink set. Daddy pours the hot water into the sink as the kettle is too hot and heavy for me to lift. I got to watch out that I don't accidentally bump the stovepipe in my clumsiness, or I'll have me both a scar and a memory from the cabin to match Reuben's from last year. Naomi and I wipe the dishes; my dishtowel looks made from a flour sack but Naomi's is a souvenir from a state fair.

After we wipe and stack, Naomi and I head up the creaky steps to play with Grandma's spoon collection. Through years of dedication to spoons — finding, buying and guarding — she's been able to gain a variety from across this land. She's got spoons from the Winter Carnival Ice Palace in Minnesota, the fantastic Corn Palace in South Dakota, and even one showing the carved heads at Mount Rushmore. On the stairway wall, in between an implement dealer's calendar from 1977 and a stretched beaver-pelt wheel from even before then, the spoons hang neatly in rows on an oak rack my daddy fashioned for Grandma one birthday. When we play spoons, Naomi and I do our best to push off the cobwebs from the rack and rub the tarnish from the metal. Each spoon is different: an enamel apple, gopher or owl squats at the top, or a bell or other such trinket dangles at the handle. We travel with Grandma to faraway places — Michigan, Illinois and even Georgia — just by holding and sorting her spoons.

From the sleeping loft, we can follow the light coming from the cracks in the floorboards and see the tops of our daddies' heads. Ingwald's near-bald one is hunched over the table; he is rolling dice with Samuel and Reuben. As usual, my daddy's straw hair is sticking up all over as he pokes around the back of the icebox, trying again to sort out why it growls and burps all night like a dying pig. The floor is covered in carpet patches nailed down with penny nails and linoleum leftovers from my Uncle Peter's renovations. Last year, Ingwald said that it was too bad that Peter had 'more money than sense or morals' but that it would do for wiping boots. Now I don't get near as many splinters in my feet from walking barefoot in the cabin kitchen, so I'm thankful nonetheless for the money, be it senseless or not. The morals are between Peter and his Maker, as far as I'm concerned.

We are settling into bed now. Downstairs, the boys are sleeping with their fathers: Reuben and Daddy on the pull-out couch, and Ingwald and Samuel on the bed. We girls are camping upstairs on our own. It is still except for the wind swaying the trees and the lake making ice. In the eaves above our heads, little mice or bats or some such rodents are scratching. But the sound is nothing like it is in summer when the cabin hums at night with pawing and scraping. As my body rests, my mind scrapes at me.

Tomorrow, after bacon and eggs for breakfast, Daddy will walk us through the woods along the same hunting trails he has always walked with his family. He will stop at each spot where he or his father or his brothers killed a deer. Again, he will tell us stories of Ingwald stripping off and swimming across the freezing river to retrieve a downed doe. Or of Grampa Ole driving deer through the woods, only to look down and discover he was straddling a black bear hibernating in a shallow cave made by the roots of a tree. Or of neighbours claiming the champion buck that Peter shot, because Peter was too lazy to track. And of all the boys living at the cabin for weeks on end — eating fresh fish and cans of pork and beans — being too little to help with harvesting chores and too big to stay out of the way. His stories are of fishing and shooting and trapping, stories of swearing and biting and fighting. Daddy's stories are stories of the good old days.

Sheltered by the wooden planks my grampa nailed and the patchwork blankets my grandma quilted, I lay here in the dark amongst the smells of the cabin. The air is both damp and dusty, but mostly full of the scent of men: socks, mud and blood.

It is most quiet, and whispery sounds of breathing creep up into the sleeping loft.

My mind is like the church van: my cabin memories squeeze out through the rust even though I have stuffed socks in the holes. Since I can remember, we've played games here: sleeping games; death games; even carcass games, where entrails are scooped out with hands and mouths. My mind won't let me sleep. What if what we think now is not what we will think in the future? Red hunting clothes used to keep you safe; now we wear orange. Can you change your mind just like that? We didn't use to have fishing seasons or bag limits or hunting licences. We do now. Can you fear heaven and hell at the same time? Can you love someone and hate him too? Can Jesus forgive you if you can't forgive others? Can you pray to Jesus without being forgiven? Can your soul have the stuffing scooped out of it?

I need to shake these questions off of me like leaves from a picnic blanket. I must shake myself as if shaking cobwebs from a quilt, spiders from the pillows. I will make the best of things. I will take the good with the bad. Even when red changes to orange, some things do remain. There is a place, deep in my heart, that remains unchanged. The hurt cannot seep all the way through; that is why I cry, so the water can't reach my heart, can't change my mind. I will not be made wet — damp and musty inside myself. My body will not betray me. But even my eyes won't let me rest either: I need it to be dark to sleep, but the light keeps leaking through the cracks in the floor.

When Samson went to Timhah with his mom and dad, he was attacked by a lion. *The Spirit of the Lord came upon him in power so that he tore the lion apart with his bare hands as he might have torn a young goat.* But he didn't tell them that. When he went back to the vineyard, back to where he was attacked, he found the carcass of the lion he had torn limb from limb. Inside the carcass, instead of mangled meat and maggots, were a swarm of bees and their honey. He held his hands like a cup and filled them with honeycomb; he ate it and his parents did too. But he never told them about the lion or where he got the honey. He just ate and gave the strange sweetness away.

The quilts are wrapped around my head, so I can barely breathe. I sit up and push Samuel away from me. I need to get air.

He touches my face gentle. I don't lay back down.

He pushes my shoulder, hard. 'If you don't let me, I'll go back to Naomi.'

Naomi? If Samuel could go *back* to Naomi, if he would go to his sister, that means that he has been to Naomi before. I know that what he does on me is not love or even making love, but I thought I was the only one. It hurts me to know that Naomi knows what he does on me. It hurts me most that I let him do it again, when I wasn't even protecting Naomi's perfect baby-girl life.

Even with the shame, I thought I at least was different now — maybe might smell different — but I'm not different; I am just the same as she is. Now, I am more like her than ever before; I am still just the same as them all.

I stare at Samuel. He is breathing heavy and sitting up on the bed. I tell him with my dark eyes to leave. And he does, creaking the stairs all the way down.

Naomi slept through it, or at least her shut eyes look like she did. But I've heard her sleeping enough to tell the difference. Her breathing tells me she's awake; she's just playing possum.

At my church dedication soon after I was born, Uncle Ingwald raised me up in the sanctuary and spoke a word of knowledge. He prophesied, 'This child will always follow the Spirit and reject hell.'

And I will. I will follow the Spirit out the window. I will reject hell. Hell is a place where you can't make the best of it. I reject hell, whether it is dry or wet, hot or cold. I reject hell now.

21

Tomorrow is Sunday, so today is our last day at the cabin. We will start driving home after lunch. Uncle Ingwald is at the table, working on his sermon. His black leather Bible is spread out in front of him, and he is writing notes while he prays and reads the scripture. He is reading of the widow in the second book of Samuel: her sons fought in a field and one struck the other down, struck him down to death. Her clan rose up to kill the remaining boy; they aimed to strike their names from the face of the earth. She called out to save her last *burning coal*.

Our Samuel and Reuben are outside cleaning fish, scraping scales and cutting, with Daddy. Naomi and I are settled on the bed, trying to decide what to do with a bird we found outside this morning.

Aunt Gloria has a bird feeder hanging in the maple tree, and one of the tiny winter birds must have misjudged his take-off or landing and hit the window by mistake. When we were washing the breakfast dishes, scraping off greasy bacon and eggs, I looked through the steamed-up window glass and couldn't see for a smear of feathers and blood and sweat. Naomi's got him wrapped up in a towel, and we are hoping that he didn't freeze to death laying there — assuming the impact didn't get him first. His soft sooty feathers were all splayed out on the snow and his orange beak was open just a touch.

Daddy said we shouldn't handle him, that we shouldn't get our scent on his feathers. Ingwald said that the Lord has His eye on the birds just as He has His eye on His precious children. Holding a hurt bird is a dangerous thing: he can scare himself to death. His little heart will beat right out of his chest. Praying for healing for this bird is like holding your breath, knowing you could just relax and breathe but being scared to quit hoping and let go.

Birds aren't safe; they can't even trust their own eyes. Loons will try and land on heat mirages rising up from blacktop roads; they'll mistake the mirrory haze for water and tumble wings and feet into the hard ground. And this little bird slapped straight up against sheer glass. Now his left wing hangs lower than his right; I wonder if he'll ever fly again. I wonder if he'll even breathe again through his hard beak. If God shows the same care for us as the birds, we are mighty deep in trouble.

I'm all upset, all up in arms. I can't think straight today; I'm having trouble settling on an idea or making up my mind. I can't separate the thoughts in my mind from the feelings in my heart. I can't choose between what is of the Lord and what is of the Enemy. We have to go home now. We must lay this soft-feathered bird down next to the outhouse and hope he ain't dead. I hope he's just playing possum. I pray that he will rise up and fly again. Maybe he already is in the arms of Jesus.

Every year, almost every bird goes home. Wherever they spent the winter — down south in the warm there or up north here hiding in the cold — when summer comes, it's back to the place where green is growing and violets and lilacs smell. No matter how far they've got to fly, they fly it right according to plan. She's got to flit with wings and beak and find another one just right for her heart, a bird that flies straight and strong with clean feathers and eyes. He's got to bring her twigs and such, branches that will bend to hold, and grass that will cushion the tiny eggs she's set on laying. Inside the nest, they'll have feathers — their own or otherwise, maybe one bright feather found on the ground, some lost blue spark to settle in with the plain padding — to soften the sharpness of the sticks. It is a long trip, this going home, but migrate means mate to most. And mate means eggs, and eggs make it worth the sore wings.

They rear the young, raising them on drowned worms and flying beetles. Every night the nest is more crowded with their growing, clawed feet and round heads bumping as they settle into comfort. Every morning just might be the morning that the breeze blows gentle and the rain don't come and the chicks finally try their stumpy wings. In the tree, the parent birds clutch the branch underneath their claws; they hold tight as they watch the babies slide away in the air. The babies squeak out their new voices and try to test their hearts with flapping. The old ones sit still, hearing their own hearts beat inside their feathers; the old ones rest and watch them fly. Then they're gone.

Near the end of summer, with blue draining from the sky and wood-smoke air changing all creatures' minds into fall, the birds come by new feathers. Soon, they are wrapped in plumage right for the flight. It is by kind, this gathering together, this making of the flock. They match beak and feather and foot: browns with white speckles stay with browns with white speckles; blues with blues; reds with reds. Together they feed to plump up and grow. They are ready to fly far to the warm or ready to crouch still in the cold. The flock lives and moves and feels together. They see themselves in each other's faces.

My hands are bunched up, crooked like the bird we laid down on the woodpile by the outhouse; even asleep, or maybe dead, he had his feet clawed up like he was remembering sitting on a branch. His eyes were open but not seeing and his neck was floppy. I didn't bury my face in his feathers. I didn't have to; I knew without even smelling that he smelled like a tree. Naomi and I laid that bird down outside, she with sniffing and crying and me with my lips pressed tight. She told her daddy she was so sad and now, even as the van jostles over the muddy ice ruts in the road, she slumps in her seat, deep asleep. She said she was so sad, but now she don't look it none. The van is warm and smells of firewood burning; our damp clothes are drying on our bodies as we ride. She was so sad, but now she sleeps. I am awake. I keep pressing my lips together and taste the syrup from the pancakes we ate for lunch. We are leaving the cabin and we are driving home.

The sun, stars and moon guide them as they go, but birds fly home with directions grown from their bones. They are born to it. That's how it goes with gifts. Hollow bones must be just like the anointing, something passed from mother to child. Grandma's bones are living now, but even after the

Lord takes her, they will live on in her people: Uncle Ingwald, Uncle Peter and my daddy. Her Holy Spirit power will got to go somewhere, though, and I know it won't go to me. Maybe Naomi will receive the fire.

They can see it, the elders, whether the anointing is upon you. When we pray for healing, the old men sway, groaning at the front of the church; with creaking knees they wander the pews, passing around the grape juice and cracker communion. Their wrinkled faces look with their eyes into my bones. I can see into them too: secret sins — beer, beatings and such; and smushed plans — taking over the farm, marrying the girl, leaving the other behind. But it comes down the bloodline either way, the curse or the blessing just the same. We don't always get to pick. As he raises his hands in prayer, Uncle Ingwald's eyes shine just like Grandma's. And Grandma says her boy Peter and Reuben look just alike. But she's wrong: it's me that has the man's mouth. Samuel ain't the shepherd of his people; even I can see that. He won't lead no flock. He won't lead no sheep anywhere but astray.

I listen from the van window, but all I hear is the crunching of the tyres. January is near enough to silent: most of the birds are away. But I'm waiting. I'm anxious for their return. For I've got plenty questions. If all the birds of a kind are the same, how can they tell who's flying at the front of the flock? How do they decide who leads the flight? And if a bird is left behind, either up north or down south, what is he to do? He can't just join another cluster. People see it on you, what is your kind. The same ones leave together, whether leaving home or coming back. They all fly the same. It is easy to see, even from a distance, who belongs.

I wake because of the cold breezing in behind Reuben's back; he's climbing out the sliding door. We've stopped moving and the van doors slam quick. It's almost dusk, that still purple time of long shadows and no sound, and the doors scraping shut echoed like gunfire. Reuben's joined Samuel and our daddies at the edge of the road, standing near the banked-up snow in the ditch to get a look at the problem. With the back of my hand, I wipe away our breath that's fogged the window. My daddy's on his hands and knees by the back wheel. Uncle Ingwald and the boys are crouching behind him, looking at what he's looking at, and shaking their heads. I can't hear them, but I don't need to. We've got a flat.

It isn't until the back doors of the van are pried open and let in the wind that Naomi stirs, looks around a bit, and then snuggles down again under a blanket on the back seat. Samuel is taking down the spare, and Reuben is moving our suitcases so they can get at the tools and change the tyre. My brother has already shed his jacket: he gets so heated up, even outside. When he throws it up over the back seat, the coat flops down on Naomi's head and she finally wakes up all the way.

Reuben tries to sound annoyed, but his cheeks are red and his eyes are excited. 'I ain't jacking up this van with you girls in it.' He don't mind changing a tyre, even in the snow. Pushing and pulling in this world is something he knows and likes. He's ready to sweat.

Naomi, still sleepy, is struggling into her jacket; she's got a sleeve inside out. I slip into the back seat to help her, manoeuvring the armhole of the slippery pink plastic. Her head leans onto my chest, and I smell her hair, dirty but sweet like a barn kitten.

'Let's move, girl.' I talk soft.

She doesn't want to go into the cold, but we have to lighten the van.

'We'll find tracks.' And I know it is almost dark and that we won't be following deer or rabbits nowhere, but sometimes a lie can't hurt. We creak open the door and turn our faces into the wind.

Snow is falling light but steady on our shoulders. Reuben's hands are callused and gloveless in the cold; he waits, holding the jack, while Samuel struggles to loosen the lug nuts. Our fathers watch and stamp their feet. I can hear Samuel's breath, pushing in and out, as he strains against the metal. His arms pull at the wrench, but he can't force the lug nuts free. It is snowing harder and the light is failing. Samuel is stepping on the wrench, jumping against the metal with his foot, and still they won't budge. His breath surges, great gasps sucked in and then cast out. Even in the dim light and snow, I can see his breath. Finally, Samuel throws down the wrench.

'God almighty!' He swears loud enough for us all to hear and hits the side of the van with his fist. 'Christ!' He walks off along the road.

Naomi and I gawk, trying to make our bodies small. Daddy stares at the snow caked behind the front wheel; he moves up and starts kicking at the dark and gritty ice. The snow is still falling and we're still stopped, so Uncle Ingwald pushes his lips together, shakes his head and starts toward the back tyre. But Reuben has already taken the wrench and is grappling with the lug nuts; he twists and pulls, twists and pulls, and he breaks them free. While Naomi and I huddle together trying to stay warm, Reuben positions the jack and lifts the van. He removes the lug nuts and tyre, fits the smaller spare, replaces the nuts and lowers the van. Watching him is like watching a good dog. My brother is still tightening the nuts, crossways and back, when Samuel returns.

'Sorry, I couldn't.' He speaks to no one in particular. Samuel hauls the old tyre over with him, handling the rubber with his gloves.

Ingwald walks over and roughly pulls the tyre away from Samuel. My uncle's face is partially covered by his wool hat, but I can see his eyes and mouth. I have seen this anger before. He spins the wheel around and wipes away the snow; there is a bulge in the rubber, a large pucker that gave way beneath the weight of the vehicle.

'Worn through.' He speaks like from the pulpit, his voice holding the words slow and heavy.

Ingwald is almost always disappointed, seeing more than we can see and knowing more than we can know. He picks at the small stones embedded in the tread like they were rubies, carefully slipping a few into his pocket. The snow has stopped falling, but the wind is whipping up the flakes that fell earlier. They are not yet packed hard into the ground. Swirling in the air, the snowflakes sting my face. Ingwald loads the tyre into the back of the van and closes the door with a dull thud.

22

WE HAVE BEEN HOME FROM THE CABIN TWO DAYS. I DON'T know what to think or what to do, but I will not curse the work of the Lord. There is danger here like we've never known, and I must not remain silent. Following the old fence line along Grandma's river, Naomi and I trudge through the snow. It is that dying part of day when the snow glows blue, and the trees wait skinny and black against the sky.

The wire is supposed to show you where not to step. Grandma says that as soon as the boys were old enough to toddle, Grampa traced all the quicksand on the homefarm with barbed wire. Tangled with dry weeds and rotten posts, the fencing is still there; circled sinkholes lie behind the old tobacco shed, between rusting cars inside the junkyard and amongst the deer stands deep in the woods.

Dwindling light seems to bring my eyes into focus; if need be, I supply my own contrast by narrowing my eyes. Last year, when Reuben and Samuel built a darkhouse for spearfishing through the ice, it took me no time to see clear through the water into the muddy weeds. Darkhouse shacks are special-made to shut out light; the walls are thick and sometimes even chinked. Only in complete shadow can you peer into the man-sized hole and watch the fish swim by. Most locals hang a carved wooden decoy high in the clear water to make the pike come up close. Throwing the tiny metal spear into a passing fish takes some practice, and it's not unheard of for folks to drop white fencepost caps into the hole to provide focus points for eyes numbed by dark water. Of course, it ain't legal to sink extra help — neither is spearing walleye if you ain't Indian — but that don't mean it don't happen.

Blue snow and black trees; black water and green fish; contrast helps us see what is changing before our eyes. And so, narrowing my eyes, I've been meaning to walk with Naomi for weeks now. Walking together side by side, not looking face to face, loosens our tongues. My boots feel heavy with the mud and snow, and my arms are cold and numb.

My heart is heavy too. 'You are round.'

'I am.'

'How can you be? You've never bled.' She must know that much.

'Maybe I don't need to bleed.' Naomi winds her way amongst the evergreen trees.

'What can we do?'

'I don't know. Maybe pray.'

Clinging to the edges of the river, sharp, thin ice is trying to span the distance between the mud and the thicker ice. Deer have stepped cautiously across the broken edges to get to the thawed patch in the middle; the current keeps the middle open and the deer pause there to drink. Bare branches scrape my face, so I hold them back and let Naomi pass under my arm. Walking through the woods, you can either make someone's way easy or let the trees slap them hard in the face. She holds her face straight and she speaks soft.

'Always, his breath smells like hot dogs. His hands bruise my wrists.'

I keep my eyes turned to the ground, watching my way across the snow.

'Most times like a hound, from behind. Sweat drips off his forehead and trickles down my back. Sometimes he can't keep it strong enough, and sometimes he can't finish. When he's done, he shivers like a man possessed.'

My boots slip on the ice. As I lose my balance, Naomi's arm steadies me. I need to know where.

'In the woods, in Babylon. In the ice shack, in the darkhouse, in the hunting stand. Up at the cabin, up in the haymow. Under the dock, beneath the pews.'

Nowhere is safe, but she ain't no baby. Why didn't she stop it?

'I never thought to fight.' She lets go my arm and looks me square in the eyes.

I know before she opens her mouth, but she's got to tell me, tell me what she never could say before, never could say aloud. Either way, it's too much, but my heart can only bear one answer.

'Samuel.'

Now I need to know when.

'Since I can remember.'

And I know I wasn't even first choice.

Naomi bends from her middle and vomits on the ground; the brown splash melts a path, sinking through the snow. Surprised, I breathe in deep, but catch only the scent of pine needles. My mouth is dry and tastes sour; there is nothing left to ask or answer. So we pray. I take Naomi's mittens in mine. God can make a miracle: the baby can leave. We pray for the way, and we pray for the end.

With the same measure I judge Naomi, I'll be measured myself. There is no need to judge. My eyes don't see right that way anyhow. Something evil in me wanted the fault to be on my brother, to know that I was something to somebody. But the bigger part of me knew — even hoped — it was Samuel. Reuben did not touch this girl. When Samuel said he'd go to Naomi, I hoped he was lying just to make me jealous. But what I did to save her didn't save her at all; Samuel and me are just plain damned to hell.

I hold this in my heart: we must wait for the Lord Himself to weigh and measure. And it might not be us that will bear the load; I can see some of what is truth. *Do not give dogs what is sacred; do not throw your pearls to pigs. If you do, they may trample them under their feet, and then turn and tear you to pieces.*

It is cold and we are still walking but now not talking. The snow is starting to drift, banking up alongside the trees and blowing right across the road. Crossing the field nearest to Grandma's barn, I almost lost my boot. I stepped down deep, deeper than I thought it should be, and brought up a sock instead of a moon boot. My pants were still tucked around my leg, tight around my ankle, but a stocking foot can't compete with this weather. Right away I stepped down hard into where my boot was when I lost it, and I got lucky. I'm still walking with two boots, even though one set of toes is frozen. My mittens are tucked into my jacket sleeves, but wind keeps slipping up my wrists. We were going to lay ourselves down on the ground and make snow angels, sliding wide wings and kicking slippery robes with our arms and legs. But it is too cold, even for joy; my eyelashes and nose hairs are sharp.

After our woods walk and talk, Naomi and I want to go in and have Grandma give us something warm to drink. We stomp up the creaky steps to the boarded-up porch, screens covered with plywood to stop the winter winds. Hockey gear — a duffel bag spilling pads, a taped-up stick and unsheathed skates — is slumped by the doorway. Samuel is here. We scrape open the kitchen door and smell both baking and boy. Grandma's round back is to us as she pulls bread out of the oven, and Samuel is at the table, socks hanging off the back of his chair and bare feet on the braided rug. Grandma believes in dry feet, and Samuel loves fresh bread. Their deal is clear.

Samuel is tilting his head strange to slither in bread, yellow butter catching in the corner of his mouth. Bustling about, Grandma slides two more pieces onto plates. When I sit at the table to start buttering my own bread, I can see what is twisting the boy's eating. His front tooth, on the left side, is broken clean in half. It ain't ragged, like a rotten tooth that has crumbled; instead, it is sharp-sliced and square.

'Hockey practice. Took one in the face.' Samuel is mouthful and proud about the puck; it means he had some time as goalie, his great plan to become popular at school.

It won't work. He's too bad for the Mennonites and too good for the normals. And the Fundamentalist and Baptist kids know him too well already; his spark is wearing out. Samuel is wedged halfway between heaven and hell: he is stuck in high school.

I am eating my warm bread, and Grandma is spreading honey on the piece cut for Naomi. The girl won't eat crusts, so they have been trimmed and piled on the wooden breadboard. Samuel's half-tooth reminds me of a girl from Iowa who visited our Sunday school last summer. Someone's cousin, she had a black smear in the blue of her eye. I kept risking glances at her, trying to figure what was strange, what was broken. And she saw me. She fixed me with a stare straight from both eyes, smeared and plain: *I can see you looking.* But she didn't take it hard or none. She told me about being little and the cat claw and the prayers of the righteous. She lived it all as testimony, and that's how I took it. Samuel's tooth is just the same. I sneak looks at Samuel, trying to look deep enough to see the brokenness in him. Trying to tell if he is too far gone to ever come right again.

Naomi has finished her bread and has plopped down next to Grandma. Side by side on the living-room couch, they are reading an old seed magazine and making grand plans for the garden. Grandma is anxious to get to the dirt this spring; she rubs her hands together, crepey skin smoothing like mud wet from early rains. Naomi's honeyed hands stick to each page as they pick tomato and radish and squash. I pile the plates in the hot soapy water in the sink. Samuel strokes his tooth lightly with his thumb. Grandma sees rows of geraniums and pansies. Naomi don't want to go home.

What I don't understand is how you can grow mushrooms and raspberries out of the same dirt, water and air. No one planted them there, but they still spring up alongside the old horse path. Even with seeds: who tells the seed what to become? Take a handful of pumpkin seeds and a handful of cucumber seeds and plant them in the garden. It takes faith. A body must have faith in the seed and faith in the rain and faith in the sun. Once the spindly sprouts shoot through the soil, it is hard at first to tell what you sowed. The green vines are hairy and curly both; it ain't until the flowers lose their bloom and the fruit begins to form that I can tell what's what. A more experienced gardener must know right away, but I haven't seen too many seasons of planting or harvest. I guess I'll learn more along the way.

Wrapped in a pink crocheted blanket, Naomi and Grandma are purring together like cats. I watch them from the kitchen, the way they hold their heads near and smile, always sharing some secret. I wipe my hands on a dishtowel and lean in the doorway.

Naomi is blooming like there is no stopping her. Honestly, she has been sick to her stomach and pretty tired, but the Lord has granted her an easy way. Other than peeing all the time and being a bit teary and crabby, she is still my Naomi. Her face is pink and shiny; Grandma just said that Naomi 'glows with the love of the Lord'. I felt like growling and saying that her breasts must be full of the love of the Lord too, because they sure are getting swelled up fast. Naomi lifted her shirt and showed me before, so I know. For all her spiritual gifts, Grandma sure is missing something right now. Can't she tell that there are two souls dwelling in the little brown girl settled on her lap? Can't she see the work of the Lord? It is right before her eyes, but she has not eyes to see.

Jesus taught this about the kingdom of God: all man can do is scatter seeds on the ground; the work is done — seeds sprouting and growing — while he sleeps or toils, just the same. Alone, the soil generates the grain; we don't know how, how it grows from seed to stalk to head then kernel. When the grain ripens, he reaps it with the sickle. Man doesn't grow the grain, but he cuts it when the harvest has come.

23

MY EYES SEEM LIKE THEY'VE LOST THEIR COLOUR. IT'S NOT like the blue has drained from them, but that I now live in a black-and-white world. We got about six inches of snow last night, and she's still blowing out there this morning. The dark pines are weighed down with thick, heavy snow, and I think that some of the boughs might even break. Naomi and I are looking out Grandma's front window watching the white come down; although Samuel went home when Gloria came by in the van, we stayed the night. The fire was too warm to leave. Winter is already too long, and we've all got months to go yet.

With my missing colour, I also miss birds: feathers swooping, beaks chittering, tiny feet hopping about. It's not like they've all gone south. The downy and red-bellied woodpeckers are still hammering the trees, and there are quite a few black-capped chickadees scratching at the sunflower seeds on the ground underneath Grandma's feeders. But we haven't seen a mourning dove nor heard their low *coo coo* since their hunting season in September. Reuben and Samuel took a few beside the barn, but when they brought them in to Grandma, she wouldn't help the boys cook them up. It was sad to see their floppy necks hanging down the side of their fluffy, smoky feathers; limp and dead, they looked so small and not even worth eating.

Not all the winter birds are shades of grey and black. Last year, Grandma's tree was blessed with a pair of cardinals; the lady was a brownish-red smudge, but the male could take your breath. He was a beauty against the snow with his deep-red chest puffed against the cold. He would lift his pointed cap high as his black-lined eyes held a steady gaze. They haven't come back this year, though, and the feeders are too close to the house to pull in the pheasants, so this winter we're stuck with only blue and black on white on snow: blue jay.

We come by our love of birds honestly; Grandma gave it to us in her blood. Sitting on hardback chairs, side by side, Naomi and me keep watching those birds pecking at the snow. They make tiny tracks with their cold feet.

I wouldn't shoot one, but I sure wouldn't feed one neither. I just can't bring myself to like blue jays. With their bright blue feathers lined with black and white, any beauty they bring to winter is rubbed out by my memories of the pain they bring to spring. I've seen one steal a mourning dove's nest, peck out the eggs, and then lay her own eggs in the spaces left by the dead. Blue jay mommas will munch on newly hatched robins; blue jay daddies will rip up mice and frogs to take back to his naked, blind babies. He is a thief, and he is a liar: his voice can pretend to be a hawk or a killdeer. Around the blue jay, you can't trust even your own ears.

There must be a special kind of cruelness that pushes a body to kill a baby; to crush a helpless egg is beneath even an animal. What kind of mother can crunch through a damp, downy chick and then fly back to her brood?

'What kind of mother will I be?' Naomi is smearing the window with her hand, trying to clear the fog.

I place my hand on her swollen belly, hidden below her thick sweater. Her stomach is stretched tight, bloated like a new bruise forming underneath the skin. My finger traces the shadowy line falling from her belly button into her skirt. I've got to convince her.

'Don't worry, girl; you will not be a mother. I believe God's Word, Naomi, and God's Word says that He loves us. What kind of Father would He be, if you were made to become a mother?'

I don't tell her that I wonder too: what kind of mother can she be?

When I am a mother, I will be a killdeer. My nest will be a slight dip in the gravel; my mottled eggs will be still and silent as stones. My babies will be born on their feet, eyes wide open, prepared to fight. My chicks will hatch covered with black-and-white feathers; our wings are ready to fly. No soul can come near my nest. I will scream my name and lure danger away, dragging a wounded wing: *kildeeah, kildeeah!* Maybe I don't so much miss colour in winter; maybe I miss sound.

It would be better to drown like a worm in a mud puddle than to put a child to sinning. I'd rather have stumps instead of hands or feet than burn forever in hell. Blindness to the streets of gold in heaven would be better than seeing the lake of fire. Worms will live forever in hell; they won't fear drowning there. We all — the saved and unsaved alike — will be salted with fire. Once we lose our saltiness, can we be made salty again? We must stay salty but remain at peace.

Naomi is crying again. She never used to cry. She has chewed her nails down to ragged nubs; she has scratched at her face, scraping down any bump, pimple or otherwise, flat as a scab. She needs me so. Gently, I wrap my arms around my girl and hold her close. I have to be so careful with Naomi. She is like a robin's egg I found on the ground last spring: pale, fragile and broken.

24

January, even at the wailing month's end, ain't even close to spring. In Wisconsin, the winter has scarcely taken hold. Sometimes, especially in the dark low times of the night, I warm myself by thinking on things of spring. Tonight I lay in my bed, nothing but dark through the window, while the wind moves and moans outside.

Last year during calving, I helped with a cow. Straining with pain, on her knees, the black-coal-spotted Holstein was all torn up. She just couldn't hold. Daddy was helping Turgeson with the stuck calf. The chains rattled. I held the spotlight from the corner of their old barn and listened.

'Least it's out.'

And it was: fresh, filthy with blood. I couldn't hear if there were breaths beyond the men. Maybe it lived; maybe it died. The calf lay silent when we left the barn.

Springtime makes nothing willing to wait. Before it's hardly warm enough, yellow-stain dandelion heads push through mud to struggle for sun. The petals scrape new through the dampness. Dandelions are just a weed, but they get anxious too. Like fresh-born garter snakes, green-striped and only just strong enough to move, the fierce babies break out of their mothers. She has carried them all winter, deep inside and near her pumping heart, to keep them warm and safe in their eggs. They break their shells inside her and wriggle away. She is left with the abandoned ragged membranes. When I put my heart inside her emptiness, I know she don't regret carrying them — the extra struggle for warmth and food and safety even in the season of least — but she fears for them on their own. Always, there are hawks and owls and ravens.

I put my heart inside the animals and even inside the ground. When the world presses too hard, I don't press back; I fly apart. By the Holy Spirit, I move beneath their outsides and push within them.

In earliest thaw, the river can't decide if it is winter or spring. Some days, the white-cloudy river ice'll be only just thick enough to hold a skinny deer drinking, away from the shoreline; other days the ice will be thawing, cracking up, slow floating toward the edges. But then the same rains that melt the ice will refreeze it thicker. It is a confusion that I cannot sort even from within the current. The water has outgrown its home; it is fighting the ice. The changing seasons will bring blessed release. But the river will not wait; it always pushes, especially in spring.

These are secret things, and they are sacred. We are to *go into all the world and preach the good news to all creation. Whoever believes and is baptised will be saved, but whoever does not believe will be condemned.* In the name of Jesus, signs and wonders will accompany us: we will drive out demons, speak in new tongues, take up venomous snakes and swallow poison. Our fingers will not be blackened by the fangs, nor our tongues by the deadly drink. Instead, we will lay hands on the sick and they will be healed; we will call out praise to the Saviour with our mouths.

My people don't know about my travelling, my minutes and hours inside the dirt and clouds. It is my sign and wonder alone. Even Grandma and Mom and Naomi don't know. If they knew, it may not be called holy. But it might.

Come May, when spring finally arrives in the northwoods, I will be waiting.

After the thaw, the spring flows will fill the streams and rivers and lakes until the lost water is brought home. The water will be cold, clear and icy. In the lakes, the walleye will swim shallow in the weeds and the peepers will be peeping in the mud. Swimming the shallows to spawn, the crappie can be found in the weedy bays and in the bulrushes. Deeper water hides the largemouth and smallmouth bass. Muskie, too, will be spawning in the deep lakes, the clear lakes full of cold water. But the panfish will swim in the warmer water and the bluegill will be nesting. Trout will be swimming the rivers, gorging themselves on the hatching insects. Some larvae survive only seconds.

When the spring is late in coming, when it is cold even into the last days of May, the birds and the flowers and the trees are late as well. The songbirds and warblers do not fly north soon enough, and we wait up here while they wait down south in the warmer trees. The birds linger for the better winds. The late spring slows the blooming of the flowers but it also slows their death. The flowers and trees delay for rain and sun; they hold tight their buds. But once it happens — the rain and heat and wind combining to crack open all those waiting — the music that happens is spring. Mosquitoes buzz, frogs chorus, and toads trill their happiness. Spring peepers peep.

More than the trout and walleye and more than the crappie and bluegill swim in our waters. The thaw ain't just the shiny fish, gleaming bronze or brass or silver in the sun. The thaw ain't just the muskellunge and sauger, all sharp fins and teeth. In these waters are creatures that can't be believed until they're seen. Although I've moved my heart inside many of the fish — seeing the larvae hatch in the moaning weeds and hearing the flies' buzzy dance on the filmy water — I now choose different where I can.

Today I can, because I feel her down deep in the mud beneath the water, underneath the January ice. The lamprey is moving softly, just rocking with the slow currents that tunnel in the muck. She is eel-like in her jawless body and gliding movement, but someway remains a fish with only dorsal fins slid low along her back. And she too is dreaming of spring.

Once we attach, all our anxious thoughts peel off like scales. Until this host is empty, we — the lamprey and I — have all we want. Complete, without need of smell or sight or sound, we are whole. Touch and taste brought us to this host: a plump, mature walleye, she must be near two foot long. With our bony tongue, we rasp a hole into the side of the host; she feels it, we can't pretend she don't. Then our teeth bore into and past the scales and sharply sink into her flesh. We — the lamprey and what is me but is not Ruth — are a funnel of sucking and biting teeth. Our teeth circle without end.

But it is not only need that brings the lamprey to the walleye, and it is not only greed that shifts life from one to the other; it is more like admiration or even love. And it is more than a little jealousy. It ain't her pointed teeth, funny cones protruding from a gaping, low-slung jaw. It ain't her splotchy olive-yellow top, blotched with black, or her white belly. Not even her rough scales with biting ridges or the cutting bones that guard her gills are what the lamprey envies. We envy the eyes of the walleye.

Rolling in the sockets, the eyes can only just be held. The marbles flash silver, guiding the walleye to the dim and deep water during the bright day and to the shallow shoals and weedy bays during the night. Given muddy water or cloudy skies, the fish will risk the light, but glare usually keeps her deep in the dark water. And in spring, when the flowages break up the ice, the walleye bite will last as long as the cool weather does, as long as summer is willing to wait. The walleye feeds and thrashes and feeds again. She prepares for the spawn.

And the lamprey and I are with her, the walleye, as she swims where she needs to go. We trail alongside her like a streaming coil, but straight in our body. We drain her. She swims to a sloping gravel bottom along the river's rocky shoreline. There they wait for her: fish with dorsal fins glinting metal in the sun. She blinks; the shine, at first, hurts her eyes. She is weary, already, with her burden: us and the eggs. The males approach, pushing us backwards by her nose. There are many of them, seven, and the male walleyes rush around her and tangle themselves with us; we struggle to hold our place. The water is a snarl of fish and fin and lamprey. Pushed and prodded on all sides, the female walleye is finally satisfied with the labour and turns on her side. She lays her eggs and the males discharge their milt; it is over and we all, God-like, swim away. It is days until the female dies and the lamprey and I release. It is weeks until the eggs hatch; it is a cold spring. I come back to winter where the lamprey lies in mud.

Knowing what I know now — since the lamprey and our spring dreaming — I will not swim inside walleye. I can, if I want to, but I don't and I won't. Sometimes, even I know when to leave well enough alone.

25

Rolling over, my sleeve catches against the frost on the window aside my bunk bed, but the glass glows silver. The frost glazes the panes both inside and out, and the snowflake pattern is now traced in sharp gold. It must still be darkest night, but I feel someone call my name. If we are deep in night, why is the icy window turning gold?

'Ruth. Ruth?'

I hear the call again but am more awake now. I reckon I'm not being chosen, so I don't answer with *here I am; you called me* nor *speak, Lord, for your servant is listening*, but I answer just the same. 'Yes, Mom?'

'Ruth, get out of bed and come downstairs. Turgeson's barn is burning.'

I struggle out of bed and try to wake up, but I can't seem to put my clothes on right. I can hear Mom rushing through the house, pulling on her jacket and boots. The door between the kitchen and the garage opens and shuts: she's starting the truck. The woman won't wait forever.

When I open the door and climb inside the vehicle, Mom is wiping the fog from the inside of the windshield.

'Where's Daddy?' I don't barely feel awake.

'Peter came to take him to the fire.'

'Where's Reuben?' He must've gone with the men.

'That's a good question.' Mom clicks her seatbelt into place and starts backing out of the garage. 'I don't know where that boy is.'

I know only enough to keep my mouth shut. I pull the seatbelt across my body and stay quiet.

Up over the hill at the Turgeson place, I can barely make out the stars as the sky is so bright. The faded-red barn lights up the sky and snow, and smoke streams out the haymow. The freezing air is cloudy with smoke and ash and whispers. Ladies from neighbouring farms, coats wrapped over their nightgowns, huddle murmuring next to their pick-ups parked alongside Turgeson's long driveway. Each time they speak, I can see the breath leave their mouths. The men are in the yard trying to salvage what they can of the machinery near the barn. I see my daddy run toward the tractor. I don't see my brother anywhere.

She's starting to come down now: the barn timbers are breaking away and burning in spiralling heaps toward the ground. I can hear the rafters creaking, men yelling, and animals bellowing too. A wave of heat rushes past my face, and a smell of fiery grease, manure, burnt hair and rot runs up my nose. The cattle are burning.

Mr Turgeson, stomping past bare-chested with only slippers on his feet, tries to run back into the barn. The men catch him on his way, and I can hear him sob. He is a proud man, but most he is a farmer, and he knows each cow by name. He swears not to go back in so the men release his arms, but he takes off for the barn again. Finally, they tie him to the clothesline post with baling twine. He slumps against the pole, his hands pressed to his ears, but I know we can all hear the stock screaming.

With its foundation of hand-laid river rock and fieldstone, this barn stood when Mr Turgeson's daddy was a boy. The same post he's bound to now used to mark a halfway point from the house to the barn; his folks would wrap a rope from house to post to barn to make sure they'd make it out to milk in winter. Even when a blizzard blew white beyond what he could see, no man could bear to hear the Holsteins moaning from the barn due to lack of milking. Following the rope through the hip-deep snow, they held on tight to make sure they'd make it out there and to make doubly sure they'd make it back home. The post let them know, both ways, that they were halfway there.

The night slowly turns to day as sunlight comes up over the pines. The barn is now just a pile of black wood as steam and smoke rise off it to mix with the falling morning snow. My eyelashes catch snowflakes and my teeth chatter. The birds have started to make their morning sounds; they call to each other. *Look at the birds of the air; they do not sow or reap or store away in barns, and yet your heavenly Father feeds them. Are you not much more valuable than they?* There is something here about being chosen: Job to suffer, Samuel for service. Eventually, we will all hear our names called.

There is a yearling calf, furry black on white, bleating and scrambling in circles near the muck yard; she must be all that's left. I know the best I can do is pray, so I do.

The Lord is my Shepherd, I shall not be in want. He makes me lie down in green pastures; He leads me beside quiet waters; He restores my soul. He guides me in the paths of righteousness for His name's sake. Even though I walk through the valley of the shadow of death, I will fear no evil, for You are with me; Your rod and Your staff, they comfort me. You prepare a table before me in the presence of my enemies. You anoint my head with oil; my cup overflows. Surely goodness and love will follow me all the days of my life, and I will dwell in the house of the Lord forever.

Late morning, and the Turgeson house remains. At least the fire didn't get her too. That big yard must've spared that hard silent woman being turned out in the snow, turned out to stand alone next to her man staring up at the cloudless cold sky.

Mom and I have gone home and come back. We brought sandwiches — venison sausage and cheddar — up from our house to help feed the men. The Turgeson woman takes the plate with a soundless grimace. In the dusty four-season porch, apples and kindling stacked here and there, she has made a table of an old door laid across two sawhorses; with her bony hand, she slides our sandwiches onto the peeling-paint door next to the Rice Krispie bars and two-gallon jugs of milk brought by earlier women.

She hands back the empty plate with a mumbled, 'So's you won't have to come back up the hill,' and then rushes us outdoors. When the ash settles, she is going to feed all the volunteer firefighters and helping neighbours this one time, it seems, but she ain't going to like it more than needs be.

As the screen door slaps shut, we stand in the yard's grimy

snow, smelling smoke and gasoline. I can see the woman staring out from the shadows, porch protecting her from the wet and cold; her tight lips press together and her eyes sit blank: loving-kindness is absent from her way.

Looking at me, Mom rebukes my thoughts. 'Ruth, we can't weigh what others carry, but her load seems heavy enough.'

And I think about the many women Mrs Turgeson has pulled panting through labour, and the many boys and even girls she's pulled out screaming, and my heart is heavy. I lower my head as we walk toward the truck, weaving our path amongst piles of scrap board, metal cogs and the like. The drag in Mom's leg leaves a strange pattern in the snow, separate from the trails of the other visitors to the house. I could follow her way without watching her walk; I could cipher it just by knowing her old wounds.

It is after sunrise but before noon, in the middling part of the morning where the sky is a fogless clear blue and the sun streams bright enough to blind. I rub the back of my sleeve across the inside of the truck's windshield to wipe away the condensation settled on the glass. While we wait for the truck to warm, we watch the work spread out across the farm. Men are raking piles of smouldering remains, tamping out any glowing embers. My daddy drives the tractor, lifting wet and freezing hay bales from the wrecked barn toward a pile near the road. Uncle Peter is there too, herding horses away from the burnt rubble to a makeshift corral fenced with what looks to be white tape. Steam loops up from the trotting horseflesh, and the same vapour marks each guiding shout that leaves the men's mouths. Over all the waste — cinders and debris and carcass — there rise whorls of smoke and mist. The farm is a hazy battlefield.

Mom and I both jump when Uncle Peter opens the passenger-side door.

'Hate to disturb your sleep, ladies.' In he climbs, sweating in his shirtsleeves and sooty, but smiling just the same. He pushes his hair from his face and leaves a black swipe across his forehead and nose. 'Run me down to the homefarm, would ya, Marie?'

And so Mom clunks the truck in gear and we back out onto the road. Caked ice in his steel-toed boots melts next to my feet as we drive down to Grandma's. Peter's on a mission for a battery.

'Those horses of Turgeson's will stay behind the tape thinking that it's wired, but only for a time. Be better if it was more than memory keeping them within bounds.' He reckons a spare battery in our barn might give the right current until the electricity returns.

Mom hums a little and clicks her nails on the steering wheel. 'Electrical fault then, was it?'

Failing loses a heavy share of barns and outbuildings. Bad wiring work or hay put up too early or critters eating through the wires usually split the blame.

'Shame to see so many head go with the barn,' Mom adds.

Turgeson's luck was doubly bad that the fire took when all the cows were under cover. Out in the yard, at least more would have survived. In stanchions inside the burning barn, the heat and fear must've been awful. Kicking hooves and rolling eyes, it would've been a gruesome confusion beyond my mind. To just see a calm hundred-head herd of Holsteins confounds the eye: black and white, black and white, black and white. How they know one from another, I don't know. But to each, its friends and relations must be as dear as ours are to us. And the spots on a Holstein are the same as fingerprints, the same as snowflakes; no two cows are exactly alike. All beasts know our own.

'Could've been electrical, maybe not.' Peter don't know what caused the fire. He turns his head from staring out the side window, watching the road whip snow and gravel beneath our tyres, and looks aside at Mom. 'He'll get back up again. Turgeson's not one to stay down.'

They share a smile as we pull into Grandma's farmyard. Chimney smoke spirals up and away from the roof, and I can almost smell the loaves in the oven.

Uncle Peter slides out of the cab; he'll rummage in the barn while Mom and me visit with Grandma. 'No need to track muck through her kitchen. Give me a quarter hour and I'll be set.' Peter ambles toward the barn and so we gather up jackets to make the short walk to the house.

Grandma's in a flour-covered apron and waiting at the kitchen window. She waves to us as we crunch across the yard. Her head turns as her eyes follow Peter's path to the barn. If she were a shepherd of a hundred sheep, she'd leave the ninety-nine on the hills to try and find the one that wandered. If her boy ever returns to the Lord, she'll be happier about his salvation than about the rest of us never going astray. But, in truth, she isn't willing to lose any of us to the Devil.

Men's voices raised in anger travel swiftly over the snow. Mom and I turn to see Uncle Peter pushing Samuel against the side of the barn and Reuben trying to get between. As they scuffle, a huge icicle falls from the eaves. What the boys are doing out here, I'd hate to guess. I think back to the early time when Peter prayed aside a weak fire with two puny babies; he sat there and called out, feeble and fearful, to an unknown God. Whether watching or hiding, those boys were behind the barn then and now.

Peter is waving his arms as Reuben stands between him and Samuel. The boys jump on the snowmobile and roar away, spitting dirt and slush beneath the sled's skis. Too far away to hear, I don't know what Peter said to the boys, what his accusation was. I only know I saw anger and fear; I saw it just as plain as I know men sweat and heat rises.

February

26

SHE WAS STILL IN HER ROBE WHEN HE FOUND HER. THREE days ago, Uncle Ingwald went to pick up Grandma Esther for Sunday morning service, and she was lying dead in her bed with rollers in her hair. She's sinned; I'm real sure of that. When she was a young girl, just about my age, her mean daddy told her to take a sack of kittens and throw it in the river. She couldn't do it, just heartless drown the mewing grey fluff-balls, so she let those kittens out before throwing the empty sack in the river.

When her daddy asked if she had obeyed, she answered true. 'Yes, Daddy, I threw that sack in the river.'

And it wasn't until the kittens came home that she got a whipping. Then he made her drown the kitties in the family's cast-iron bathing tub. Grandma said that she held those babies down in the water and wept. So she has sinned in her life, but she's been saved too. I know that to be true just the same.

I come to the garden alone, while the dew is still on the roses. And the voice I hear falling on my ear, the Son of God discloses.

She is in a box now. At the front of the sanctuary, she is in a box with so much make-up on her face it would drive her to anger and to sin anew. When my mom passed by the casket to get to the organ, she was horrified to see the colour caked on Grandma's cheeks and settled in her wrinkles. Mom took the handkerchief straight out of Daddy's pants pocket, spit on it and wiped most of the make-up away. Mom also put Grandma's glasses on her face.

When I said that it just didn't look like Grandma in that box, Mom got real stern.

'That's because it isn't. That there is just a painted-up shell. Don't let me hear you talk like one that ain't got no hope, Ruth.'

So it ain't Grandma up there in that box. But it is important that she don't have too much make-up on nonetheless. It's why I make my mom swerve around cardboard boxes in the road: I'm afraid there might be a litter of kittens in the box. So she swerves for me; she swerves for empty boxes.

He speaks, and the sound of His voice is so sweet the birds hush their singing. And the melody that He gave to me within my heart is ringing.

Uncle Ingwald leads the service with prayers, psalms and hymns. He hasn't broke down once, even when his brothers did. My daddy has been red-eyed and quiet-crying since Grandma died. Uncle Peter don't even try to muffle his cries; as he pays his respects in his worn blue suit, he leans and practically throws himself on the casket. Whatever woman's with him now has to hold him by the elbow and steer him to his pew. We grandkids are in the second-to-front pew behind the grown-ups. Reuben, Naomi, Samuel and I are squished up toward the middle aisle, and our current cousins of many colours sit dazed and staring along the rest of the row.

Against Ingwald's strong advice and wishes, Uncle Peter dries his eyes and pulls himself together enough to speak. Steadying himself, tall and straight, he grips the edges of the wooden podium and closes the Bible resting atop it. He speaks of the totems of the Ojibway: crane, catfish, bear, marten, wolf and loon. Just sniffing slightly, he explains reindeer, rattlesnake, black duck, goose, white fish, pike, lynx, eagle, moose, sucker, sturgeon and beaver. He tells us that the rivers underground are the veins of our mother; water is her blood. She is life and fertility. She is Mother Earth, and we who are here — especially we who are native — are home. Just like Grandma Esther prophesied, Peter has come home. He has just gone further and deeper than she ever could have believed.

I'd stay in the garden with Him, though the night around me be falling. But He bids me go; through the voice of woe, His voice to me is calling.

Now it's Uncle Ingwald's turn to look dazed. He is trembling with anger; the little vein in his temple bulges and his nostrils flare like a heavy-breathing horse after a gallop. He steels his eyes against the room and leads us all in the Lord's Prayer. Grandma walks in the garden now with her Lord. Her gentleness is matched by the Saviour's touch, and she will know no pain forevermore. As for me, I think I would just run the bathtub warm. I don't need no bag or box. Stroking them nice and holding them down, the little kitties would just drift on off to a breathless sleep, a gentle deep sleep in the warm water.

And He walks with me, and He talks with me, and He tells me I am His own. And the joy we share as we tarry there, none other has ever known.

We sit at Grandma's house, the entire family, eating the buttered flour-dusted rolls filled with ham and turkey that the faithful brought by the dozens. Daddy's hand rests on Reuben's shoulder; they slouch together, almost snoozing, in the living room on the lumpy couch. My brother has pained eyes but has not cried. Mom and Aunt Gloria are busying themselves in the kitchen. From the clinks and scraping of glass, I'd hazard that they're cleaning out the refrigerator. Ingwald and Naomi are flipping through the pages of Grandma's calendar, reading her daily notations. There are records of the progress of her annual read through the Bible; interesting variations in the temperature and precipitation; daily sightings of bird species including number; and records of phone calls especially highlighting prayer requests and answers. Samuel sits with me near the bird window. We stay a ways apart, both from them and from each other. We watch the dirty grey snowbirds scratch beneath the feeders.

Of course Uncle Peter didn't come in the house. He drove his woman home, along with what appears to be her children. Where he finds these creatures, no one knows. And what we do know is limited to inheritance: the woman is white and the children ain't, so that makes none of them his, by nature anyway. Peter don't pay no nevermind to inheritance one way or the other; those about him, he'll care for, regardless of blood or skin. Except, it seems, his own; he's off with them now when he should be sitting here with us. She was his momma, whether he likes it or not. His blood and skin are a match to hers and he should be here looking after his, and his inheritance, instead of looking after those that got no claim.

'There's enough put by here to last us all five years.' Mom is calling from the pantry off the kitchen.

Aunt Gloria is bent deep in the chest freezer, restacking, as I slide by to help take inventory. Mom is right: the pantry shelves are laden with sliced and dried apples sealed in plastic quart bags; glass jars of peaches, tomatoes and sauerkraut; and row after row of homemade pickles — some cucumber, some pepper, some beans. Paper labels tell content and date, with a couple jars collecting dust since I was born. The handwriting gets scratchier each year and the canning done from this fall is only identifiable because the names can barely be read. Grandma's hand shook so, but she still laid by for our provision.

'With the meat, we'll all just take what's ours.' Gloria's got the cold job: separating into plastic bags whose is whose. Store-bought from them, venison from us, and the rest — pounds and pounds of beef, practically a side of pork, and that giant shrink-wrapped turkey — from Peter. 'You know he won't take his. He won't take it back. But I'll leave it just the same.'

Grandma's last year's Christmas coat hangs empty on a hook near the door. My aunt is wearing the matching blue gloves she stole from the pockets. She sorts and piles carefully, making sure each bag is full of wrapped meat before reaching for an empty sack.

Naomi wanders in the kitchen, bringing Grandma's wall calendar with her. 'Who's gonna feed the birds?' Not looking up from the page, she asks of no one in particular.

Grandma sliced oranges for the orioles and smeared grape jelly on plates for the hummingbirds. She hauled seed for the little hopping birds, and shot at coon — and once, even a skinny black bear — when they tried to raid her feeders. She kept up the seed all winter; she kept an eye on it like she watched the river ice and the deer and the muskrat and the weather. She watched the beavers build, and the ice tear away. She watched that river close. Naomi don't ask for certain from anybody; she asks this of us all.

Shoving aside a plate of powdery sandwiches and peanut-butter bars, Naomi plops herself and the calendar at the kitchen table.

'No more desserts.' Aunt Gloria looks up from the chest freezer and glares at Naomi. At least she's finally noticed the girl's getting a bit thick in the middle.

Why the churchwomen keep bringing food, I don't know. It must just be trying to be help to somebody. Bringing food to the dead or keeping birds alive in winter, either way it only matters to the hands that are feeding. The dead don't care, and the birds die just the same; they die just the same, only later.

'These jars need emptying, Ruth.' My mom hands me a dusty few from far back on the shelf. The tin tops have puffed up, so it means it's bad. The insides have gone rancid. As I scrape out the pickled beets, a syrupy smell — like kerosene, but sweeter — rushes out the jar and fills the kitchen. They've gone bad; they've been gone awhile.

'Your grandma, girls, lived a long time. She honoured her parents, respected and honoured them, so she was given a long life.' Uncle Ingwald is leaning over Naomi's shoulder. He has wrapped her braid around his hand, and they are reading Grandma's calendar entry for the first day of the year.

There, in and around the square marked for the date, she has written all our names. Near these names are brief prayer requests for the family, the country and the world. 'Peace, joy and hope.' Grandma called out these things to the Lord. She called them out, knowing she'd be heard.

'She was a woman of prayer, my mother.' Ingwald keeps reading them out. 'Faith, long-suffering, gentleness.'

And she was, Grandma Esther; she was a mighty woman of prayer. Earlier, when it was just my mom and me at the house, Mom picked up Grandma's prayer notebook and set it aside. In it — in the same scrawl that obscures the dates of peaches — are recorded prayer requests and answers for the current year. But that private notebook holds a different list from the open calendar on the wall.

Grandma's hand had written *Naomi, vanity (Gloria)*; *Samuel, pride (Ingwald)*; *Ruth, anger (Eric)*; *Reuben, envy (Marie)*; *All, fear (Unknown)*. She knew her grandchildren — and our line — and so she prayed. And she knew that bad blood can skip; sometimes the bad travels by the heart alone. But she didn't know what I believe: my anger has a different source and my anger is also my strength.

Mom put it away with the older notebooks in the cedar hope chest in the bedroom. Not quite hidden but still stored away, in amongst the crocheted doilies and embroidered handkerchiefs, there is a deep stack of spiral-bound paper written in an ever more shaky hand.

'Your grandma rarely forgot others' trials, but she often forgot their victories,' Mom said. Then she asked me to keep this pile between us, to keep it not from the others but for another day.

And that's fine with me. I've finished scraping the beets and washing the jars. They are stacked and drying on the counter where Grandma won't be making bread. They don't need me in the kitchen any longer, so I return to the window to watch the birds. Samuel sits there still, picking his teeth and keeping watch. He is watching the winter birds swoop from the bare-armed trees; he is watching the little ones scratch for seed. I look out at the black bark and then down to the scraping of the nails on the icy snow. If birds are as close as we know to angels, I think it would be something every heart must dread. For angels carry more than feathered wings: they are tipped with beak and claw. And that sharpness is something we all should fear.

27

PEOPLE ON THE LAND LIVE CLOSE TO THE BEGINNINGS AND ends of life. Death ain't a scary something that creeps in now and again in the night, slipping away with a surprised somebody and leaving shocked folks behind in the light of the morning. We are people that raise, hunt and butcher; meat don't come wrapped up nice. Well, it does, but you got to peel off the feathers or fur and fat to get down to the bone. Meat is wrapped just like my soul: sometimes there's got to be a bit of blood shed before you get down to it.

Not that I wasn't all torn up by Grandma's homegoing; I was. I am still. But Failing's no place to be if you can't handle the comings and goings of this life. The Lord giveth and taketh away, and folks help each other along the best we know how. Being friends and all, Daddy shot Turgeson's dog late last summer. Why they didn't have a gun in the house, I didn't understand, until Grandma told me the deal about their daughter getting shot up. So when their dog started running deer, Mr Turgeson asked my daddy to take it behind the barn. So he did. It shouldn't be that way: their dog was a malamute and near to half wolf, but it was raised by regular farm dogs that don't chase or herd deer. I don't know how he learnt it;

maybe it was just in his nature. But that's the kind of friend my daddy is: when your neighbour asks you to shoot his dog, you do. Someday, you might hope he'll repay the favour. There is a reason for it all.

Flesh just got to make room. Look at the Indians. They moved over for us, and I suppose someday we'll have to move over for someone else. I wonder if we'll move to the reservation, and if we do, where will all the Indians go then? I hear folks talking about the goings-on out there in the woods. I hear talk about the drink and even drugs and how that casino out there is taking farmers' money and ruining lives. I guess them Indians fight; I heard somebody even set their boy on fire and burnt his whole face off. But I don't have no cause against them, and I sure don't know where the blame lies. I like to hear their drums and singing on that radio station and see them now and again. I hope they keep dancing — dancing in their spinning, whirling way — even if they are just dancing to make sure there is still room for themselves here on earth.

Leaving earth and going to heaven is a walk we all got to take. Sooner or later, we're going. It's just a matter of how and when. I'd like to be dead and buried now. I'm not afraid to die, to move over and on and make room for the new. But I am afraid of not dying and living past the rapture. My family will be taken up to heaven, and I might remain behind. What if I am left? What if I wake up in the middle of the night and my mom's nightgown lies crumpled and empty on the bed, and what will I drink if the faucets run with blood instead of water? Maybe I deserve to be left: I sin.

Sometimes I read books that speak of tens of thousands of years upon the earth, and sediments and fossils, and even amoebas turning into frogs and them changing into monkeys and then monkeys eventually becoming us. I know I shouldn't read the Enemy's lies, but the book was in my science class. I guess that's why our church hopes to grow a Christian school ministry. Then, we kids wouldn't have to learn that kind of science. We wouldn't have our faith challenged none. But I like to read, even those kinds of books. Sometimes, deep inside my mind where I think no one else will ever know, I think about the earth millions of years ago. I know the Lord can read my thoughts, and for that I am ashamed. No one else knows that I think on these things, so I do from time to time. With one hand on the earth and one hand reaching toward heaven, I tear between the two, suspended between death and life.

When bad things happen — death or blindness or some other such pain — the sin can't always hang on a boy or his parents. Sometimes it happens so that God can make a miracle. *As long as it is day, we must do the work of Him who sent Me. Night is coming, when no one can work. While I am in the world, I am the light of the world.* And after the rapture, the saved will be together in heaven. They will have eternal bodies of perfection in paradise, and sinners will have eternal torment in hell. We will be right back where we started, back in the perfect image of God. We are doomed now without Jesus. We are damned to hell, all because Eve ate the apple and tricked Adam into eating it too. All because of sin, there is pain and hate in the world. But God has compassion on us; he forgives us if we are covered in the Lamb's blood, the blood of Christ.

When I worry at night that I will be left behind or that I will go to hell, I pray and think about heaven. *He will wipe every tear from their eyes. There will be no more death or mourning or crying or pain, for the old order of things has passed away.* But when I awake from a dream that has me screaming, I don't know if I seen things to come or things already passed. Just to make sure, I sometimes ask Jesus into my heart over and over. Mostly, I want to hold Grandma's soft hand and smell her warm breath again, and folks can never be too safe.

Why it was Daddy — not my mom — who came to help me wake, I don't know. Maybe because she was feeling poorly or he was up anyway, but right when I woke, he was standing next to my bunk. His head is still taller than where I lay, all scrunched up and sweaty under the quilts. He peers into my bed and touches my shoulder.

'I'm alright.' I try to sound calm and still. 'Just a nightmare; it's gone now.' I didn't know it was a dream until I woke up cold. I woke up scared and shook and slick with my own sweat.

And I think he will go straight out of my room, my dark room with only me and the wool blankets and the frost freezing on the window. I know he will walk out, just shake his head and turn and leave; I will be alone with the night wind outside shrieking enough to rattle the panes of glass. But he stays.

'You were screaming, Ruthie.' He pulls back his hand and he switches on the lamp fastened to the wooden side of my bed.

When I first got the bunk beds, I couldn't reach the bedside lamp from my top bunk; Daddy rigged up a clamp so that I could keep reading at night. The bulb is yellow and sends a circle of light onto my face. He can see me now: eyes red and scratchy and lip chewed down to bleeding. He ain't happy with what he sees, me screaming at night with proof of tears.

'What's troubling you?'

From his crooked mouth and his fingers twisting at his beard, I know he's hurting for me. But where would I start, if I told him what's wrong. And where would I ever end? He won't move, my father, unless I give him something to take.

'Just Grandma.' I speak soft, telling the truth even if the missed-out bits make it part a lie. 'I'm worrying on heaven and sin.' I speak the truth and even as I speak, my eyes tear with thinking about what can't come out. I think about Grandma and her praying, twisted belly cows, and the girls who bleed in the yard. There's folks that get the chance to come back to the Lord and there's those that don't ever. There are stains that won't be washed away with the blood of Jesus.

His eyes are wet now, so he wipes at them with the back of his hand. Daddy's momma has gone to Jesus and he can't think about it anymore or any other way. 'Peter should have kept his mouth shut.' He's angry but still crying. 'My mother was a woman of faith.' He pats my arm again and reaches for the light. 'She wasn't ashamed — the Indian thing — but it wasn't something anyone needs to worry about.'

He shuts off the light, still talking as he walks toward the door. 'Grandma's in heaven with Jesus.'

And then he is gone.

The wind is howling and my room is dark. There is still my father's smell at my bed: soap and sweat. While I lay waiting for sleep to come, I remember last spring when that big black-and-white malamute would rush across the fields. Turgeson's dog would run with his tail stretched flat, legs scrambling in the muddy furrows made by the plough. He'd chase the new fawns as fast as he could until he tired. After, he'd come down to our house so I could pat him or feed him a bite of venison sausage. To help him shed for summer, I'd brush his long tangled fur with a rusty sheep's comb. I've kept that hidden too. Out there in the garage, I've got an old pillowcase full of his fur. Mixed together, it isn't black and white. Once fur is scraped away, it makes something more like grey.

28

WE ARE IN THE COLD KITCHEN BECAUSE NO ONE LIT
Grandma's stove. The family is gathered together again,
remembering Grandma and her ways. 'Gentle and good',
'loving and strong'; no one says 'stubborn' but we all share
sly smiles knowing we're thinking it just the same.

And the talk turns. My daddy and my uncles are worried
about the land and the barn: leases and fallow years, dividing
and selling. The men are speaking — even Peter's in the
house and is having his say — and Mom and Aunt Gloria are
listening and nodding. Reuben and Samuel are set at the table,
and Naomi and me are standing behind our mommas' chairs.
There is an empty seat at the head of the table; it is where
Grandma sits. All the women are quiet, but we are there
nonetheless.

Uncle Peter leans back in his chair. 'Just so everyone knows:
there'll be no hunting or trapping either way.'

'You can't be serious.' Daddy puts down his coffee cup.
'That ain't fair and you know it.'

'That's the way it'll be.' Uncle Peter sounds certain.

Reuben shakes his head and looks as if he might yell or cry
or both. Samuel's face is hard to read; he might just be pleased.

Daddy can't believe it. 'Peter, Momma's law got buried with her. You can't keep me and Reuben from these woods.' His voice is angry.

'Let's see if I can't.' Peter's voice is calm. 'And this ain't about the boy.'

Ingwald looks up from his Bible for a moment. He scrapes his chair back. 'As the eldest, perhaps I should have a say here? Peter, you might farm the land, but Eric has a right to the woods and his machinery in the barn.'

Both younger brothers turn their heads to watch Ingwald's mouth form the words.

'Maybe buying me out is the best way for you boys to keep me out of your affairs.' Ingwald lowers his eyes back to his Bible.

The other men exchange looks across the table. The women sit in silence.

I am not ignorant about those who fall asleep; I do not grieve like the rest of men, who have no hope. Jesus died and was buried and rose again; just like Christ, those who have fallen asleep in God will be raised up by Him. And those of us who remain awake — we who linger at the coming of the Lord — will not go before the sleepers. *For the Lord Himself will come down from heaven, with a loud command, with the voice of the archangel and with the trumpet call of God, and the dead in Christ will rise first.* After they rise up — the dead shedding dirt from their skin and breaking the vines that hold their arms — after that, the saved will rise up into the clouds and touch our Jesus riding high in the sky. *And so we will be with the Lord forever.*

'Mind your own way.' Uncle Peter is more than angry; his voice is hard and we can hear him. He is in the doorway separating

Grandma's kitchen from the porch, moving his hands high. Peter points his finger sharp at his brother; Ingwald is drinking coffee and resting calm with legs crossed at the table. 'Ingwald. You, mind your own way.'

Whatever brought on Peter's anger, we missed when all the cousins went outside to get snow. We were going to make snow ice cream; Mom and Gloria already mixed the eggs, sugar and vanilla. As we stamp our boots on the porch and pull off our snow clothes, Peter surges through, angry as a wet cat.

He grabs Reuben's arm. 'Keep your gear on. Let's go.'

My brother replaces his cap and follows orders.

Peter's truck tyres scratch and spin black muck up onto the clean white of this afternoon's snowfall.

Gloria is refilling Uncle Ingwald's coffee cup as Samuel, Naomi and I file into the kitchen. Steam rises off our clothes while we huddle near the stove. Finally, someone saw sense and made a fire; the coals are just starting to glow and heat is pushing the crispness out of the air. Mom is leaning against the counter, still holding the blue bowl ready for the snow, and Daddy is resting his elbows on the table. His coffee cup is empty too, so I reach for it, but he stills my hand.

'Did that need to happen today?' Daddy is looking straight across the table at Ingwald.

This table in this kitchen held almost all their boyhood meals: breakfast oats, ham sandwiches and chicken dinner. It was here, a thousand times over that they read their daily bread — cardboard scriptures from the little plastic loaf that rests in the centre of the embroidered tablecloth. I keep my eyes on those faded, knotted birds picked out in blue and green thread.

'There was a better time for that.' And Daddy stops speaking.

Mom places the bowl on the counter. 'Nothing was said that can't be taken back.' She almost whispers. 'Peter didn't mean —'

'He didn't mean?' Ingwald interrupts her. 'With his pagan poison and discontent?' My uncle is almost spitting. 'Peter dishonours our mother.'

Ingwald is crying now, great sobs pulling his arms down onto the table, his head slumped over his hands. Beneath his weeping I can hear the whirring and tick of the cuckoo clock; it chirps the hour as the bird slides in and out of its wooden nest.

'And the unfounded accusations? Against my family?' His voice is pitched high but soft, like a whimper. Ingwald picks his head up and looks straight at Samuel. The boy is standing in wet socks and a red long-underwear shirt, his jeans dripping a puddle on the floor. Samuel's face changes from pale to whitest white as his father pushes himself up from the table.

Ingwald rounds the table and stands directly in front of Samuel. The boy must look up, as his father is still several heads above him.

I'm frozen at the stove with Naomi; we are like night animals caught in light, stunned into stillness. I'm using only the corners of my eyes; no motion can be seen. My mother and father do not move and neither does my aunt. But this stillness is not calm. It is not the eye of the storm; instead, it is the space before the great reckoning: the clouds hurling thunder and fire, the mighty cleaving of the earth, and the boiling of the churning sea.

'Samuel.' My uncle speaks with a tongue of fire burning atop his head and in his mouth. 'Are you setting fires? Did you burn Turgeson's barn?'

Samuel's eyes shine black, and he does not flinch; he keeps

his eyes hard on his father's face. 'No.' The boy leans wet and steaming by the stove. 'No to all your questions.' Ringlets of blonde hair are puffing up as they dry, and we can all smell the wool. Samuel breathes normal without any sign of fear, without any pause or searching; he is well and warming at the fire.

'And that's the end of it.' Ingwald puts his hand on Samuel's puny shoulder, capping the bone with flesh. The man holds on tight for a moment and then releases his grip. Ingwald glares around the room and his face flushes red again. 'Peter's waited a long time, but he won't sow division amongst us.'

And my uncle walks back to the table and drinks his lukewarm coffee. Aunt Gloria and Mom start folding the snow into the vanilla mixture, clinking their spoons in the bowls, and Naomi and Samuel sit down at the table. My daddy gets up, but keeps his head pointed at the ground; he walks quiet through the kitchen into the pantry and brings back some of this fall's maple syrup. The pails of snow have been melting; the ice cream will be soupy and strange. But we'll all pretend it's alright. No one dares speak. I stay warm at the fire.

Last spring a starving black bear was roaming our land. Grandma had seen it across the river weaving amongst the white pine planted by Grampa's people. The bear was tall and long, would have been six foot if he stood. Winter fur was coming off in mangy clumps where the bristly new was poking through, and he walked a bit unsteady. Could have been he was just dazed like they are when they first awake, but then Grandma got out her binoculars. Instead of pointing them at the bird feeder, she aimed them at the bear and saw that he was hurting. She got a good look.

He was caught. He was plain stuck and he was dying. Must've been some syrup dripped down inside a plastic jug or somebody pure mean put some meat in there. Otherwise there was no reason for his head to be wedged like that. The bear's whole head, triangle face and ears and eyes, were trapped inside a plastic jug. The opening must have been just big enough for him to force his way in, but too small to pull out. The ears would've been the sticking point and his sharp teeth couldn't help him much, not in that position, pushed close to the plastic base. So for however long was as long as he lasted, he had wandered the woods without sight, sound or smell. And without eating — and barely breathing — he was ready to drop. But before he lay down and died, he was giving it another shot; rubbing his head against the pines, he was straining to pull his way free.

Grandma called the DNR boys, but it didn't seem they were interested in this particular natural resource. They said they'd come and shoot him if she'd like. Grandma said she'd shoot her own bear, thank you, and called my daddy. He came down the hill and made her a deal: they'd try for a while, but then time would be up. He had better things to do than rescue bears. It took a while; sometimes they were too close to danger or too far away to help. And close enough to touch was a hard balance. But eventually it worked: Daddy lassoed and held him just long enough for Grandma to get ahold of the jug. When she pulled, it came off with such force that she landed on her bottom as the bear shook himself, blinked his eyes and — as Daddy released the noose — walked slowly away. Grandma held the jug and Daddy the slack rope as they watched the bear's backside slip into the woods. Nothing held his neck anymore.

29

Amazing grace! How sweet the sound, that saved a wretch like me! I once was lost, but now am found; was blind, but now I see. 'Twas grace that taught my heart to fear, and grace my fears relieved. How precious did that grace appear, the hour I first believed. Through many dangers, toils and snares, I have already come. 'Tis grace hath brought me safe thus far, and grace will lead me home.

I DON'T KNOW IF THE LORD IS SAYING YES OR NO, BUT I KNOW He needs to start speaking louder now. She must have started bleeding heavy on the bus ride home from school, because when we got up to get off at the homefarm, Naomi left a dark, red stain on the vinyl seat. In between the pain, she keeps saying that God heard us and He is answering our prayers. I know that He hears, and I believe that He answers; I just think I'm having a hard time hearing His voice over the sound of Naomi.

Straight off the bus, I hustle Naomi up through the yard into the screened-in porch; Grandma's house is lonely now, but at least we'll be out of the weather. As I try to push the front door into the kitchen, the door handle don't turn. After the funeral and the family meeting, someone must have locked the house; I didn't even know that door had a lock. Through the window, I expect to see Grandma peeling potatoes at the sink: scraps floating in a basin of murky water, peels piled on a newspaper spread out on the counter. Instead, I see casket flowers sitting on the table. With the florist-wired roses and irises smashed together, dying without water to drink, the kitchen must smell sickly sweet. It makes me glad we can't get inside: I want to keep the kitchen in my memory with the smell of spring lilacs and baking apples.

Even a garter snake knows you can't have a new thing lying around outside in the cold. She'll carry her eggs inside her, come hunger or fear, and won't give them up until the babies are ready to wriggle free. I've got to find us a nest; there's got to be room for us somewhere. In the corner of the porch, three brown-paper grocery bags sit on the flaky-blue bench. Mom and Gloria must have made a start on sorting out Grandma's clothes for charity. Looking farther and further away, Naomi's brown eyes are coal-black. It don't feel like she's even standing here with me anymore; all that's left is a girl-body, empty and trembling. So I grab the first bag without even looking in, take her by the elbow, and decide to head toward the barn.

Parked smack in the middle of the entry, the dusty tractor is taking up too much space. We can barely squeeze between it and the wooden workbenches piled with oily chainsaw and snowmobile parts. My hand brushes the pitted concrete wall; it is damp with cold. There's no room here for us. Naomi ain't going to like it, but we'll have to go up. I tell her, but she don't say no. She don't say anything at all until she is pulling herself up the ladder into the haymow. She is scared, and she is hurting.

She is crying. 'Oh God. Oh my God.' And she sure ain't cursing; she is praying and praying hard. Her grip on the metal rung seems a bit shaky, so I start to help from behind. As I hold Naomi's bottom, a trickle of warm water seeps into the sleeve of my jacket.

She's really panting now and keeping up a stream of prayer. 'Oh God, oh Lord, oh Lord.'

The boys' fort is the closest, so we struggle toward the stacked bales. As soon as I settle Naomi down on the hay, I shake out Grandma's give-away bag. There's a half-finished quilt and scraps from her patchwork basket, a couple flower-patterned baking aprons, and — wrapped in the blue wool coat her boys gave her for Christmas — Grandma's worn leather Bible. The hay is warm but scratchy, so I spread out Grandma's blue coat and help Naomi slide over onto it. The slippery lining is cool to the touch, and Naomi's forehead is next to boiling, so I think it may give her some comfort. Grandma's Bible props up Naomi's head. I wrap the pieced quilt around her body and hope that it will calm down her shivering.

She is hot and cold at the same time. 'I'm so thirsty, Ruth. I'm so cold. I'm so cold and thirsty. Oh Lord.'

Oh Lord, I don't know what to do.

Even though I don't want to leave her, I feel like I can't just stand and watch her suffer so. I climb down through the opening in the haymow floor and look around the barn for anything that might help us through. I don't know if what I bring is better than what I leave behind; I can't even see clearly for the tears in my eyes. My arms are shaking as I climb back up the ladder, but I've got some help tucked in my pockets: a rusty skinning knife, some baling twine, and an icicle I broke off the side of the barn. Maybe she can suck on the ice.

As my head rises through into the haymow, I struggle to catch my breath: there is much more than hay here now. Blood is weeping from Naomi; she is still, so still, laying on her back with her legs surrendered and spread wide.

At first I fear she is dead, but then the baby takes hold again. Naomi's body tenses with the next swell of pain, and I hear her praying again.

'Help, Lord. Give me help.'

I guess that I'm the closest thing to an answer to prayer that she's going to get, so help I do. Daddy will only reach in and pull when a lambing ewe starts to roll her eyes into the back of her skull, but Naomi's way past that now. There is a head: black hair slick with blood. We try to rest, but the rhythm is too powerful; it is a heart beating, in calm, steady control, all from the inside of Naomi.

And then, it is all over all at once. With a great rush of blood and water, into my hands slides a tiny baby: eyes, nose, arms, fingers, legs, knees, feet, toes. She don't scream; not the momma nor the baby. Naomi lays panting, spread out like a field-dressed kill. She is so little, the baby: her elbows work, and she has long, dark eyelashes. She is a tiny kitten, curled up in my hands, tender and mild in this quiet night. The barn swallows have stopped their swooping and no scurrying mice can be heard. The only sound is the barn creaking in the wind. We are three little girls alone: just me and Naomi and this still, silent child. I use the twine and the knife. I offer the baby to Naomi, but Naomi won't touch her. Naomi won't hold her.

She can't even look at her. 'I won't name her. I don't want to have to forget her name.'

Still, I can't just lay this nameless baby down. Someone has to tell God and Grandma who she is so that they can recognise her face. The light is fading, so I raise her up high to get a better look at her. I still can't get a good enough hold on her features, so I walk toward the hay chute and struggle to slide open the heavy door.

It is windy and cold; snowflakes swirl around me as I stand high above the farmyard looking out into the dark, deep night. I talk to this girl.

I hold her out toward the woods. 'These are our trees.'

I hold her out toward the farmstead. 'This is our home.'

I hold her out toward the river. 'This is our water.'

Finally, I hold her out toward the heavens and tell Grandma and God. 'This is our baby; hold her now.'

And then I let go.

30

WRAPPED IN A FILTHY QUILT, I GUARD FROM HIGH ABOVE THE farmyard. I watch now, as God does: too far away to hear, too nearby not to see. From the north, two angels are flying through the snow. Their strong wings are tucked beneath plaid barn coats, their golden halos darkened by orange hunting caps, their holy feet shrouded in boots. Snow flies before them as they roar across the cornfield, circling broken stalks with shouts of joy. Their snow machine screams over the icy gravel road and slides to a halt in the middle of the farmyard. They have found her; they are here to take the sacrifice.

They stand. The quiet angel bends to retrieve the body; the fierce angel knocks the body out of the arms of the quiet angel. Words are spoken, loud words, but I still cannot hear. Their words are spoken with puffs of smoke; their breath is hot to the cold night air. I think they voice a blessing that must be spoken by the two over the one. Pain comes with this sacrifice: the quiet angel is now on his knees, weeping over the body of the one. The fierce angel's hands knot into fists. His eyes sweep the farmyard; his eyes see all. They burn through the snow and melt the ice. They burn straight through my body. His eyes see all that has gone before and all that is yet to be.

The fierce angel snatches the sacrifice and pushes away the quiet angel. They wrestle for the body; the quiet angel will not let go. He must be fighting for a blessing too. He pleads with the fierce angel for mercy; he begs as if he is asking for his own life.

We are shrivelled leaves clinging to the trees until the wind and our sins sweep us off the branches. Our righteousness is like a leper's rags, filthy and unclean. No one knows our names or hopes to hold us; we call no name and never reach out our hands. For the Lord has hidden His face and allowed our wasting; we are dry and dying because of our sins.

We must come before God the Father stained with the blood of the Child. Fierce Angel roars away through the snow, the sacrifice balanced on his lap. Quiet Angel kneels in prayer next to a red stain in the snow, but as he raises his eyes to heaven, he sees only me.

To put back together again something broken is harder than it was first to make it new. I wasn't there when Naomi was conceived, somewhere in the dark jack pine forest, the tall trees swaying with jagged broken tops and long brittle needles. That final push and groan was not in me, but at the moment she was made she was whole. Now she is shattered and unwound and wrecked. What it will take to bring her back — unbreak her — is beyond what my mind can imagine. And all I have are my small hands.

The wood framing the hay chute is solid, so I push my fingers into its hardness. It brings me back to this world.

Turning away from the gaze of the angel — Reuben — still kneeling on the snow, I look for Naomi and I see her. She has wrapped herself in Grandma's coat, and the wool sticks to her where it is wet with blood. She does not whimper. The hay beneath where she rests is red. I do not know the way, but if there is one, I will find it. I've walked pathless before.

'We got to get you help. I'm going to get help.' And I rush over to her and hold her head to my knees. She is not weeping but she is not here. Eyes open, she pushes her head into my legs, like a baby calf nudging for more milk.

Her blank eyes and her low breathing are all that I have to know that she is not dead. But when I turn to leave, she grabs my knees and pulls me down on the hay; her clinging is so tight. Her nails push into my arms. There is no pride in Naomi now; she is silent and broken before the Lord. The gifts of the Spirit are not present and neither is her soul. She cannot bear even my eyes upon her, and hides her face in my chest; my eyes burn holes into her heart, so I look away, up into the beams of the barn. High above in the eaves are the mud nests of sparrows, abandoned for the winter. The birds have spackled them together with mud and spit and hay; here they will lay their eggs and raise their young. Their homes are safe spaces, refuges in which to rest, but they are just earth and water. They would crumble easy enough.

All I can do is hold this girl, keep her safe and tight. I rock her body and brush away her tears, warming her and humming and praying in tongues. I am in my right mind, even though the Spirit is pushing hard to take hold. Naomi thought she was chosen, but I know now for certain: I am the one to bear the load.

I am not afraid of blood. I have seen enough blood in my life, so I'm not afraid of the blood. It smells of life and it smells of death; it spreads and spreads and spreads. Her soundless, almost breathless crying is more than enough: it is repentance and she will be justified before God. His tears drip down his face and roll off his nose. There is no weeping in heaven; the angels must come down to earth to cry. Quiet and peace, peace, peace descends on our souls. There is sin and there is blame, but they are not here in this lofty place. We have been given a way. Even in the midst of my confusion, I remembered. I opened the mouth and looked before she flew. I opened the mouth to check for fangs.

Obey the Word of the Lord, or you will be killed. That is my sentence; I have pronounced it myself. Thus the Lord speaks and thus speaks the prophets, they who speak the Word of the Lord. *Therefore it is your life for his life, your people for his people.*

And we three sit together in the hay: my brother, me and what is left of Naomi.

Reuben pulls away from our crying tangle of arms and legs and crouches nearby. Stuttering, he holds his hands across his face. 'Why didn't you tell me?' He sways on his haunches, wiping his eyes. 'I knew — I guess I knew some — but I didn't know about her.'

'What do you mean?' My head pounds, and I taste salt.

'We could have fixed this.' Steam rises off Reuben's jacket. 'He said you weren't being hurt, and that he'd never touch Naomi. And Samuel said he'd tell the truth — about the fires

— he'd tell that most of them was just me.'

I can't quite keep my mind still enough, but my brother's words try to slip into gaps in my memory: times the boys weren't where they claimed, gasoline smells on their clothes. The barns left by our grandparents were hand-hewn and hard-won: trees taken with axe and crosscut saw, logs skidded on ice with horses, fieldstone basements made of field rock. The boys burnt them, and then Reuben traded me to Samuel. He traded me to save his own skin. He traded me to keep Naomi safe.

I cannot look at him. He is not my brother.

Reuben clambers up and starts screaming, roaring with no words, directing his sound at the barn roof. He hits his head with his hands over and over; his grief is breaking him into noise. He screams until he stops.

When he is finished, and the sound again is only the hay-chute door rattling against its iron clasps and the wind outside and the creak of the barn timbers, I release my hold on my tender Naomi and turn my face to Reuben.

'There was nothing to be done.' I am certain of this, and hold my eyes hard on him. 'Nothing happened here. Nothing that was your fault.'

It is made so as I speak it. I stare at his eyes and keep him still. And the wind stops moving outside and the eaves still their groaning and the chute door stands silent.

I begin to remake Naomi, to push everything back into place. But Reuben breaks again, with his knocking at his head and his screaming. He did not move before, so why must he shake so now?

Reuben screams at God and swears against His name. Then he screams against the Enemy while rejecting God's way. And he screams until he falls down on the hay, slumping with his face buried between his knees. After he has sat there awhile, next to the gently rocking Naomi, he lays down in the hay. He is curled up like a baby, with his hands cupping his groin. He is finished. And now I know what I had hoped against: he is all he is, and he is not enough.

I cannot clean Naomi with my brother stretched out beside her. I will preserve her dignity. So I wait. There is no hurry here.

As we rest in the silence, I mumble prayers unto heaven; the Spirit indwells my soul. I can see my hands moving, fluttering in front of my face, but I am not making them move.

There is no sound except the language of angels.

31

AND MY EYES REMAIN GIFTED FOR THE SEEING. THE SPIRIT shows me the fierce angel. He has four faces: the rage of a man, the power of a bull, the lust of a hound, and the cruelty of a bird. I see him, screeching and flying like a bird across the silent fields. His wings swoop over the cornstalks that lie flat and shake with fear before him. He is the avenger: he brings pain disguised as love; he changes his squawking call to that of the hawk. He is blue on black on white on snow: he is Samuel.

And now he moults his feathers. He flies high above the frozen world, twisting in the wind and the snow. Sharp feathers from the jay fall like blue fire from heaven as he stretches his wings wider and wider until he bursts through the overstretched skin. He is born again: his new, broad wings scrape the sky with black, glossy feathers, and his sharpened talons leave scars. Upon his head are no feathers — he is red-naked above the neck. He is black on red on red on snow: he is vulture.

And he flies past the dark, standing pines. They drape their branches across the river; they shadow the ice with their arms. He does not bring it, but he delights in death. The stench of his food will call enemies to the nest; he must be careful to hide it well. His favourite is the eye; it is the choicest morsel. He is helped by decay; he patiently waits until his beak can break a softened hide. He vomits the carrion. Here the body will be well hid; her odour will call no one. Here he will keep his silence; his hunger is satisfied, for now.

And he leaves no totem, not on rock nor tree. He leaves no marker to guide those who would chase or mourn.

It is almost finished and then we will not speak of it again. Reuben hauls over the last red-brown scraps: he's bundled and stacked the dirty hay like cordwood. Deep in the corners of the haymow, the straw will dry brittle; mixed with rat crap and dust, it will soon crush into dirt. Nothing will remain behind. My brother's face is scratched and smeared with blood and dust; he looks like he wrestled a bobcat. That will wipe away. He has not spoken since I told him his job; he has just scraped the floorboards clean and hidden the soiled things away. He is able, thick back bending and strong arms scooping. His sweat began at the beginning.

Naomi is still shivering, lips murmuring nonsense as her teeth chatter. At least she is making sounds, even though this is from the cold now, as the shock is done. The snow was all I had so I used it, rubbing handfuls of white across her legs and the rest. It was blown-in snow from the triangle piles that grow at the widest cracks in the wooden walls. Snow that has fallen from heaven and has been taken by the wind is clean. It is clean and cannot be made dirty, and it helped her pain. We are going to leave this place, so she must be decent. I hold up Naomi's jeans, but they are beyond saving. Turning my back to her — even though she isn't looking, isn't even really here — I take off my hand-me-downs and replace them with her ruined pair. Already stiff, the hardness makes me struggle; I'll throw them into the burn barrels when I get home. I help Naomi into my too-small jeans; they'll do until she gets home and maybe no one will notice the change. She is shaking, but clean and warm. We will be alright soon. I tell her 'breathe in' and she does, and the zip goes up only partway and she groans. The button won't hold and hurts her so; partway is close enough.

We will leave this barn even if Reuben and I have to carry Naomi down the ladder. We will end this and be free forevermore. My brother walks toward me, crying again, the tears making white tracks down his grimy face.

'What about these?' With his boot, Reuben nudges a small pile at my feet: Grandma's coat, Bible and quilt are all that remain.

I can't just leave these things — no wolves or coyotes will scavenge them away — I have to take care of it. There is blood on my hands. But my mind aches with thinking of a sanctuary for the hurt and the wounded, and Grandma's own pile: heads and hooves, ribs with meat still sticking, all spilling out of torn plastic bags. A head with a horn still attached and the other side ripped straight off. Some of them does and fawns, mostly bucks missing horns: bloody holes burrowed in the meat and soft fur between their eyes and ears. Curled-up hooves spilt out on the riverbank, picked-over bones lying right where Grandma was fixing to rest and remember and look at the water.

I hear her voice: *I made up my mind — swaying there amongst the blood and the fur and the dirt — I made up my mind.* The sins are on both sides.

'Leave them.' I will not lose Grandma's way. 'Just leave them alone.'

And we do: the coat and book and quilt will remain. Naomi can walk, but she still can't talk. She can ease herself rung by rung down the ladder. We weave through the milking parlour of the barn where the concrete floor is cracked and patchy and the manure gutter is full of leaves and dirt. I guide Naomi around Grampa's broken tractor; it is filthy with dust and old grease. Past the stacked buckets, Reuben is leaning near the window; he listens and looks and no one is there. We will walk through the door. We will walk through the snow and be saved.

The world drowns in the tears of the broken; everywhere that shadow and light remain, there is no comforter; the tormenters own power. Without fear, I speak it aloud: *The dead, who had already died, are happier than the living, who are still alive. But better than both is he who has not yet been, who has not seen the evil that is done under the sun.*

32

TODAY IS SUNDAY, AND I HAVE FASTED SINCE FRIDAY. SINCE the haymow and the angels, no food has passed my lips. Last night while I sat quiet and still at table, Daddy looked at me strange, but Mom admires my commitment. She doesn't know what's on my heart, but she always believes in prayer and fasting. She believes I'm preparing my heart, getting clean. She's closer than she can know.

But we can never be forgiven, never get clean again. There would always be talk. Even if some man would take her — for her family, her smile, or whatever reason — she would always be beholden to him. For men, a struggle is something that can be overcome, and by overcoming be made stronger. To confess and conquer is of the Lord, as long as his damage can be undone. A man can say he's sorry and mean it; even more, a man can be believed. But for us, it would never be forgotten, never forgiven. She would always be stained.

Today is Sunday, and it is like every Sunday before: braided blonde hair like rows of field corn; callused hands held up to Jesus; babies crying in their mothers' arms. Like always, the church smells of cow, sweat and soap. But this Sunday is Baptism Sunday. At the front of the sanctuary, my Uncle

Ingwald smiles at a shaky grey-haired man in a too-big suit. The man is new to our congregation, and today he's being baptised. He's giving away the whisky, trading sorrow for joy. The pulpit has been moved so we can all see the baptismal tank sunk deep into the stage's floor. Uncle Ingwald leads the man into the water and asks him to examine his soul. The man's face looks frightened: he didn't see this coming.

I have examined my heart every night since I can remember; even as a little girl, I would recount my day and seek out my sin. And it is often a self soul-searching. At church, I coloured in my own judgement with paper ladders of smiles and apples, ranking my obedience and kindness. At home, I admitted not just fighting but pride. At kindergarten — droop-shouldered with shame — I handed back crayons I accidentally took home, and I was alone there. Not that they ever leave you alone, even beyond church or home, but that they don't need to accuse you of nothing much once you can walk. They know they can't be there all the time, so they trick your mind into being them.

But the man just stands there with the water lapping at his waist. My uncle stares at him with burning eyes and waits. The water drips, and we wait. And we wait until the man speaks and tells of his pain and sin and sorrow, and eventually it is enough. Uncle Ingwald wraps his arms around him and takes him down deep below the water.

I'm having a hard time knowing what is real: birds with floppy necks, dog fur in a pillowcase, a grave surrounded by leaves, and a mouth without teeth. When I close my eyes, I see coyote fangs and starving ticks. When I open my eyes, I see the same.

All that I know is this: they believe that this water will bring us to God. I don't know if it is real, but I believe it is needed. I believe we need to wash this all away. I have decided: now is the time. I take Naomi's hand and take us up out of our pew. Now is the time for us to be baptised. After we emerge from the water, we will again be clean.

Naomi and I stand together before the church.

Uncle Ingwald holds up his hand. 'Girls?'

'We came to get clean.' I match his eyes. Naomi waits silent.

And my momma is crying at the organ, her arms shaking. The music stops.

'With your permission?' Uncle Ingwald asks across the church. Daddy looks at Mom and then he nods his head yes.

Aunt Glory in the front row says, 'Thank you, Jesus. Thank you, Lord.' Tongues fly up from her as she gets up and wraps her arms around Naomi.

The voices of the congregation echo the sound. Like the waiting time before a storm, the air presses on my skin. Naomi's fingernails dig into my palm.

And Uncle Ingwald commands us as he commanded before: examine your soul.

And we do. We testify of our salvation and desire to walk with the Lord; we answer yes to any questions asked. I want to be clean; I truly do. But there is a dark pain inside me, a place where the water can't go. The old will fall away and all will be made new, but I carry this stain and cannot and will not wash it away or forget it. I just wish I'd kept proof of something, something to know what happened and what didn't. Maybe hair or I don't know.

Water streams down her black braids and seeps onto her already soaked back; Naomi climbs up the stairs out of the baptismal tank at the front of the sanctuary. Behind her, she leaves a trail of damp footprints. Draped in a soggy towel, she stands with Gloria's arms wrapped around her. Gloria don't seem to notice that Naomi is wet; she must be numb as well as blind and dumb. Gloria don't seem to notice anything.

Before the entire congregation, Uncle Ingwald has just finished baptising 'the child of our hearts'.

My turn is next to go under the water, *in the name of the Father, and of the Son, and of the Holy Spirit.*

As Ingwald grabs my shoulders, I know that I should close my eyes — now is a time of the spirit, not the body — but I can't squeeze them shut. I want to see for myself what is beneath the surface.

Water covers my body just like the snow blankets the ground, like the clouds hide the sun. My old spirit dies under the water, and I am waiting to be reborn as I take my first breath after breaking the surface. But before I come up, I see whatever is hidden. I see all that is buried under the water, under the snow, under the mud, and under the ice. Water flows and fish swim beneath the river's ice, and they are not alone. Communion is blood and body, and baptism is water and body.

But this Sunday, Naomi's blood is in the water.

My head comes up from the water. As she stands before farmers tired from morning milking and devout farm wives, the mothers of many children, Naomi's chest streams with holy water and breastmilk. It takes blood in the tank, water changed into wine, for Gloria and Ingwald to open their eyes and see what's underneath.

It is so hard to hold a secret tight. Like water carried in the palm of your hand, it will always leak out. But this dripping water cleanses us; we are clean and baptised now. Naomi and

I have proof of our salvation. God knew before, anyway; God has always known. But now, we are comforted by the Third of the Trinity: the Holy Spirit will guide us and always be with us, and we will never again be alone. We weren't alone, anyway, though. Wherever we went and wherever we will go, we are always three: Naomi, me, and what was our silent secret.

We are in the wings, behind the altar's baptismal tank; there is space here only for extra chairs and hymnals and maybe a waiting angel in a Christmas play. But the women swarm with lowered eyes and arms crossed, their dresses clinging to their legs and ankles. I am still dripping, wet in my dress and barefoot. The carpet on the altar don't reach into these small rooms, and my feet scratch along the uncovered chipboard. There are nails holding it down.

And Naomi and I have promised each other; we promised with our eyes. The women swarm us, smelling like violets and vinegar; they ask, and they decide without knowing. Aunt Gloria is holding Naomi tight and Mom is trying to peel them apart.

'Hush now, hush now, girl,' Gloria murmurs over and again while she rocks and squeezes hard.

Naomi sits with eyes closed and a blanket wrapped around her skin; the wet is soaking through the cloth. And my mother is gently pulling at my aunt's hands, sliding her own hands beneath the bony fingers and between their pressed bodies. Naomi's hair is dripping; water drops slowly hit wet on the floor. As they splash, I can see them true: they break as wasted eggs, laced with black blood. It seems no one else sees the dark. The women see only the water.

'Let's get a look at her, Glory. Let's see what can be done.' Mom has separated the two, and with a push sends Naomi to me to mind. 'Settle now, Glory. Sit in the chair and pray.'

And we leave my aunt there, attended by the ladies of the church.

My mother takes Naomi and me by the shoulders and herds us behind a curtain. Mom is crying as she walks away. We alone must face the woman who knows what is unclean.

Mrs Turgeson is there. Her dry lips are in their straight line, and her eyes stay flat. She pulls me and Naomi toward her. Behind the curtain shrouding the stacked chairs, there is a gap only big enough for us three. Wordless, the weary midwife pulls back Naomi's blankets and towel and then reaches beneath the wet dress, pushing deep between the trembling cold legs. Her hand comes back bloody, and she wipes it on my towel. She is calm and unhurried in her manner; she is used to both women and the problems of our sex. She alters her gaze. Again her hand drives out from her body, but now it aims on me: beneath my wet dress and into my legs, her rough hand scrapes inside my panties. Her fingers come back wet, but they come back clean. It is baptismal water that leaks from me.

She wraps up Naomi and looks at our eyes. 'Tell me who.'

Naomi crumples down into a chair with her hands over her eyes, tears squeezing through her fingers.

I shake my head at the Turgeson woman, and she shakes hers back at me. I close my eyes and ask for words to speak.

There is simple peace in my mind; even with all the singing and prayer in the room and Gloria moaning beneath it all, there is a peace within my heart. I rock on my feet. I wait. And after a moment, I think Jesus gives me words. Two are better than one; we help each other stand. When we fall, we pull each other up. Together we lay down and keep warm. It is cold sleeping alone. We together can defend ourselves. A cord of three strands, braided together, is not quickly broken.

But then, as I open my mouth, nothing; there is nothing but a gentle hush in my head. As I listen to the wind blowing inside, Naomi begins to murmur.

'*Hebesheba nonna. Hebesheba nonna. Op it littlemoftastompka, hebesheba nonna. Keptilitforngorna keshnor link gup nonna fortuntintin. Jujkilop my organa rotyu. Jujkilop gorthu jus. Horphush young, most upostable ruk danke!*'

There is silence now in the room. Over the tops of the chairs, the women are listening. There is silence in the room, but not in my mind. I swirl in pieces, seeing swallows waiting near the river amid clear air and blowing wind. The birds swoop down to the water, slicing nearby in loops. One flies into the water and one crouches high up in the branches of the low-hanging tree. The water swallow does not drown, and the sitting swallow laughs; she takes joy in the slaughter.

I open my eyes and smile. Looking from wet Naomi and then straight to the harsh woman, I open my mouth to speak these words as the Lord has given them to me to speak.

But before I can bring the word, Mrs Turgeson cuts her eyes cruel at me. It ain't enough for the woman, and she takes my shoulder and shakes me. It ain't enough that the Lord has spoken, that Naomi is broken. It can't be done for her.

'That won't work. That won't work with me.' Mrs Turgeson pushes those lips together and tries again. 'I'll know. If you lie, I'll know.'

There is no moving her. Sunlight in the room shifts, and I look at my feet. They are still cold and dripping on the wood. The water beads for a moment and then soaks down, disappearing into the floor. The water would taste sweet.

From her chair, Naomi reaches over to take my hand. We both shake our heads. It is freezing.

And the woman shakes her head too. 'If you are going to hold this, girls, get set to hold it tight. Don't ever say it, not even to each other, not even in prayer. You're through the worst. You're through the worst, and going back would be harder. Swallow down hard now, and don't make a sound. Swallow it down.'

She pats at her dress, smoothing the patches of damp, rubbing at a small smudge of brown-red at the edge of her sleeve. She folds the white towel with the finger smears, careful that the wiped colour stays on the inside. She breathes deep in and out, sets her face, then Mrs Turgeson leaves us with the chairs.

After pausing with the Turgeson woman and whispering awhile, my mom scuttles behind the stacked chairs with dry clothes. We strip off the wet and hold our matching Christmas angel robes in our arms. I don't think there'll be a potluck today.

'Her monthly, that's all,' Mom whispers to me while unbraiding my hair and rubbing a towel through the length. 'That's all it was, all this fuss for nothing.'

Smiling and re-braiding my hair, my momma hums and sways and play-acts for me: that she always dresses me, as I stand trembling and dumb; that she always soothes Naomi with clucks and song so that the girl can still her fingers enough to button. I don't know whether to be relieved or more worried; our secret can't sleep forever.

But we are pretending that all is well. Forgetting about mother's milk, we are pretending it was just blood.

We are pretending so it can be.

33

At the altar, Samuel is recommitting his life to Jesus and praying for the indwelling of the Lord.

When Naomi and I finally emerged from the wings at the front of the church, dressed again and dry, most of the congregation had already left. A few men, holding their feed caps and looking at their boots, lingered at the back of the sanctuary waiting for their women. A scattering of boys and girls ran laughing and bellowing in the fellowship hall, but most everybody was gone.

After our baptism, while the ladies rushed the stage, Uncle Ingwald had begun to pray. And then the ancient organist had begun to play, so the people had begun to sing. Once Samuel started moving, folks set to making their way out, grabbing Bibles and jackets as quiet as they could. Some elders stayed, but the rest left. Samuel had responded to his daddy's call for sinners and walked the aisle all the way from the back of the church. The boy didn't give a reason for coming forward, but he didn't have to. He's forgiven: his sins are as far from him as the east is from the west.

Just as I am, without one plea, but that Thy blood was shed for me. And that Thou bidst me come to Thee. O Lamb of God, I come!

I come! Just as I am, and waiting not, to rid my soul of one dark blot. To Thee, whose blood can cleanse each spot. O Lamb of God, I come! I come!

And now Samuel's breaking down, trying for baptism in the Holy Spirit. He wants a flame atop his head and he needs a prayer language; he needs the power. With his arms outstretched and a pinched look on his face, he waits at the front of the sanctuary with the elders of the church around him. They have laid their hands upon him and are praying in the Spirit as Samuel pleads with God. Uncle Ingwald stands behind him, eyes raised in prayer and voice lifted to heaven. He is ready to catch his son should the boy be slain in the Spirit and be overcome, just fall out. But Samuel merely sways with the men in time to their gibberish. Some of them spit as they speak. I believe I can see spittle on the tops of Samuel's shoulders and some seeping into his clean white shirt.

Relieving the old lady, Mom is now playing the church organ. Her head is down, but she is singing 'Just as I Am' like we always sing. Daddy is in the wooden pew with Reuben and me. I am crumpling the bulletin, creasing it back and forth over the requests for prayers and notices of thanksgiving.

Aunt Gloria puts her arm stiff around Naomi in their pew, second from front. Naomi hasn't had barely a minute alone since she coloured the baptism water. Her momma must be afraid that she will leak again if she isn't there to hold her together. Outside of the midwife, no one has said much to me. I don't think they want me to find out where babies come from yet. Truth be told, I don't think they want to know either.

We've waited long enough: Samuel shakes and tears start flowing from his eyes to his cheeks. He's got a ghost in him, alright. He is moving his lips in a mumble, and I can almost hear his new words under the church's celebration.

'Praise the Lord!'

'Hallelujah, Father!'

'Thank you, Jesus!'

It don't matter who says what anymore. It is always the same voices saying the same words.

It is always the same: he has them in the palm of his hand.

My hair is still damp even though Naomi and I came out soaked and dripping probably four hours ago. No one will leave this place.

Our parents are swaying, arms raised in prayer, at the back of the church. Except my daddy keeps his arms low, like a fighter, hiding his head. Facing forward and only stealing glances, we can't see clear as Reuben and me are in the second pew, and Samuel and Naomi sit in the front.

We can't hear much either from this distance, only bits of 'and sin could not wrestle control of our ...' and 'return them to wholeness for Your ...' and the like. When Ingwald is most fervent in prayer, he forgets the ends. He don't finish his sentences, but the Lord must know nonetheless.

Hunkered deep in the pew, Reuben is cutting his nails, paring them down like an apple, with his pocketknife. He's already shaved bits of callus off his palm with the same blade and pulled out slivers with the tweezers. He's sat still for about as long as he is able. Naomi sits motionless and forlorn; her braid trails a dark damp patch down the back of her robe.

At the front of the church, Samuel looks straight ahead, trying not to crack his knuckles.

And I listen and I watch. And I know.

Our parents are praying — I can hear them — but I know without hearing.

The sins of the world are many. There is sin in our church. My family is stained by sin. With the travelling of my soul — into the fish and birds and trees — I blaspheme the Holy Spirit: this is the unforgivable sin. *I am the way and the truth and the life. No one comes to the Father except through Me.* I don't believe. I hate. These are the sins of my soul.

Samuel stands and stretches. At the sound of his father's voice, he starts to walk to the back of the church and reaches out those arms for Naomi. The boy smells of sweat and piss.

'Let's get.' He grabs her elbow rough and pulls. There is no change; he still wants to go home.

I don't need him to say nothing to us, and I'm ready to hit him. But others are more ready.

Reuben beats me to it, holding Samuel down. Snarling and spitting, my brother halts his hard fist an inch from that squeezed face and halo hair. 'Never again, you hear me? Leave her alone!'

Reuben is going to do it, hit Samuel and break him. Cowering, Samuel can't push him off; his arms aren't even pinned down, but he can't break the hold. He can feel scared now, his breath struggling out and the weight on his chest. He can't stop what he's got coming. No one can. Samuel barely fights back, but he doesn't have to.

He speaks soft, just loud enough for Reuben, Naomi and

me to hear. 'You ain't so innocent.'

And it is enough. Reuben can't hit Samuel: my brother's afraid that the boy might split and the truth with spill out. He needs to keep those fires quiet; he traded me for Samuel's silence. Reuben didn't love me at all. Nobody did; nobody does.

Reuben's fist is still frozen in the air. But the men are there before I let my breath out; my daddy tries to pull Reuben away. There is a rush of men and dragging apart and a noise like a tornado in my head. When I open my eyes, my brother's shoulders shake as he is held by our father.

Samuel scrambles upright. There aren't even marks on the floor.

Our family is going home; Daddy has both Reuben and me by the elbow. He steers us down the sanctuary aisle toward Mom, standing wide-eyed and crying at the door.

What Ingwald says don't matter now. Calling to our backs — 'broken vessels of clay' — he can go hoarse all he likes. He can't make us believe that Samuel is part of God's plan, can't make us forgive the boy and forget what happened. Ingwald's 'thirst no more and pouring out Christ's side' can't follow us home. There's enough blood — by family and the Lord — to cover the sin, but there ain't enough to make us thankful for it.

Whatever it is, it is done. The blood and water flowed and the sin was forgiven. It is done — again — and we will speak of it no more.

March

34

SUNDAY LASTED FOREVER, WITH THE BAPTISM AND ALL THAT came after. We hardly got to sleep last night. And it is dark through the window, but it's morning nonetheless. It is Monday, so it is school and all is well. Mom made us porridge, and we read scripture; she squeezed my hand extra hard at 'amen', sighed heavy, and passed me my scarf. Reuben and I went out the door and down the driveway. When I turned around, Mom wasn't waving at the window.

Because we are the first ones on the school bus, Reuben and me always get our pick of the seats. Used to be, depending on my morning mood, I either sat at the front to watch the kindergarteners play or sat toward the back to listen to the bad boys curse. This cold morning, I no longer have that choice; there is only one seat for me.

Walking down our long driveway, with Reuben hanging behind cracking frozen mud puddles, I know that he wonders — about Naomi, about me, maybe about her — and that his gentle way won't allow him to ask. There is nothing left to say, anyhow; not much is left in my mind or memory to speak. We must come together now to hold this secret, and keep it forever down deep in our hearts. If we are obliged to no longer sing, or laugh, or pray, we must stop our singing, laughing and praying. If I am obliged to sit on the stain for the rest of my life, I will sit on the stain; that is the least that I owe.

Snow has fallen overnight: white covers up the dirt and broken crops. As we drive by in the bus, the fields are still; sometimes the long, slipping tracks of a rabbit whisper across the flat snow. Snow piles in the corners of the roofs of the turkey barns. The metal looks frosted: cold, dull rectangles packed with murmuring birds; steam pours out the air holes punched high up on each side.

They aren't beauties, the crop turkeys smushed together in the stinking sheds, with their white-yellow feathers dragging in the dust and crap. Nasty, beady eyes, thousands of them, peer out if you get close to their air holes. Their gobbles sound like they're drowning as they stare up at their dim day lights and false moon nights, barely blinking. Workers on the farms must cut back their beaks, so the birds don't pluck themselves to death or start on eating each other. I've heard tell that they'll die from water down their throats if they are allowed outside in the rain; the clouds will catch their attention, and they won't be able to drag away their eyes.

These are things I hear, though not things I've seen, and I'm beginning to appreciate the difference. I'm starting to wonder about some of the things I hear and have heard, and I might not believe anything anymore unless I've held it in my own hands. Even then, I might decide not to believe that it is true.

At the parsonage stop, Naomi and Samuel climb on the bus. She is pale and shivering, but she slides in next to me, by the window, like always. I meet her smile with a smile, just like always; she is a true friend to me.

Samuel slinks all slow into a seat across the way. His curls are squashed under a camouflage hunting cap. He is sucking on an orange, hurrying its thaw after it froze during the wait for the bus.

We drive on and pick up more regular kids at all the regular stops. Under a highway bridge, I feel the temperature drop in the shadow. No sun can sneak through and warm what is beneath a bridge; under a bridge, a river might never melt. A cold shudder snakes through my body, and I watch as Naomi melts the window frost with the side of her hand. She melts bear paws, dog tracks and baby feet.

Deep in the woods, in the bramble near the rivers without bridges, the beautiful wild turkeys are strutting and gobbling. Come spring, the hunters will be out, camouflaged head to toe, settled dead still in their blinds waiting. They lure the brown-black jakes and toms, clucking and purring, trying to call them in close enough to fire. Only their eyes show, the men lingering in the branches. They cover their clammy, white faces so the wild turkeys won't spook; they cover their frozen, red hands so the wild turkey hunters won't shoot. Turkeys can see colour, and folks fire quick at blue, red or white. More than one empty-handed hunter has come home, or didn't ever come home, because of a shotgun blast straight into his face or chest.

We are what we are, and always will be. *No good tree bears bad fruit, nor does a bad tree bear good fruit.* Look and see and know: figs don't come from thornbushes and grapes don't come from briars. *The good man brings good things out of the good stored up in his heart, and the evil man brings evil things out of the evil stored up in his heart. For out of the overflow of his heart his mouth speaks.* Good or evil, it is there in the tree; good or evil, it pushes out the same.

I want to be like the happy girls — the Indian girls with long black braids and the normal girls with stubby ponytails — holding hands and skipping toward the school. I want to sing, laugh and sometimes pray. Naomi, Reuben, Samuel and I could look the same as everyone else on the bus. We walk, talk and sleep like everyone else.

My boot catches on the edge of the bus's stairs, and I fall onto the concrete and bite my lip. I am okay, but my lip is cracked. 'Shit! Shit!' I say as I spit blood into the snow.

Naomi looks at me with wild eyes, afraid of my cursing. Hear me now: I am just like everyone else. Samuel grins at me, and then walks away onto the playground with one of the little kids off the bus; he is always hunting.

We are always hunting when spring comes to Failing: we shoot songbirds, chukar partridge, Canada geese, wild turkey and whatever else is within reach of our shotguns. I hope we all go pheasant hunting this year and turkey hunting too. I pray we see one of the strange, white turkeys that are rumoured to be hiding in the wild. Folks say that they are escapees from the sheds, albinos or half-breed wild turkeys. But I know that the ghost turkeys are spirit birds with beady pink eyes and sharp claws who hunt the hunters. The pure-white wild turkeys wait for a boy with blood-red hands to stalk them through their woods. Then, the spirits will tell the other hunters to fire. We should be out in the woods; we need to be out amongst the good trees. Our hands might redden with cold, but we will be safe; we will be safe under the shadow of the Lord's outstretched wings.

At recess, Naomi walks slow to our spot. Away from the regular kids, we hide near the elementary school playground. We've sat on these swings a thousand times, pushing back and forth, pumping our legs toward the sky. We've swung and sat and sung, day after day, racing our hymns into the sky. But today, she is dragging her boots along the ground, leaving a long trail behind her that looks like a limp. It is one of those bright sunshine days that make a body think it's spring. The ice is shining and sparkling but dripping, trying to reflect light while it still can, while it can still keep itself together. But there is a darkness on her. Naomi finally makes it, slumps down on the leather seat farthest from me and holds tight to the chains. She keeps her feet on the mud and doesn't swing.

When she waits like this, it makes me mad. She wants me to ask, but I won't. Naomi can pink-lip pout and shoulder huff all she wants, but if she needs something she'll have to say. I start swinging, moving my legs hard and making the chains clank. She is chewing her nails, down to the nub again; as the swing set sways, she gnaws the corner of her thumb.

'Ruth.'

I slow my swinging but say nothing.

'Ruth.'

That thumb of hers — all her nails, in fact — won't look good in her Miss Failing princess wave.

'Do you think I have a call?' She moves her legs a little now, swaying in the muck.

I slow my pumping legs and just ride the swing natural, until it stops gentle on its own accord. I put my feet on icy snow. 'It ain't Grandma's.' And I look over at her to know that she gets my meaning.

If she's got a calling from the Lord, it's her own because she didn't inherit it from Grandma. It isn't lack of bloodline or the anointing: Naomi's our blood because we chose her and the Holy Ghost power can fall on whomever He chooses. But Grandma's mantle — what Ingwald calls down and claims for Samuel — her gifting is mine and mine alone.

This is what I used to pray against, ask the Lord to take from me. But now I know that I am an instrument in His plan, a tool for His way. I have tasted of the tree of good and evil, and still I remain. I will walk the path, but my way may not be their way. The scales have fallen from my eyes.

But she isn't claiming through Grandma.

'I've healed myself.' She looks over at me and nods toward her skirt. 'It's done.'

And I nod back. If she was closer, I'd take her hands in mine.

Across the swing set we stare in a hard look and agree together in prayer. The ice atop the swings is dripping water down the chains and onto my hands. It is new water, unfrozen just at this moment. It is ice that is moving for the first time. My hands are wet and shake with the cold.

Recess is over, so we head back inside.

Unless you are most near, any shadow brings cold. No comfort comes unless you push in close enough to touch. And the turkeys in the sheds can't. In the sheds it is all unblinking eyes, low murmur of cackle, feed scramble, peck peck. There is always the gouge and the peck. With the wing dragging and the torn claw — injuries that never heal — the night-day-night is endless. The trucks move in the dark, when the turkeys are alone with their blue-bulb moon.

The birds will be herded toward the truck, and onto it, and we will move forward. All of this will happen without ever being touched. Endless until the end.

35

AFTER A WEEK OF COLD DURING A WEEK OF SCHOOL, LAST night the moon shone white and blue on the icy snow. But today like yesterday, the yellow sun is shining hot like spring; snow is melting into mud, ice is breaking up and the rivers have started to run. Even with the snow, March began like a lamb and is staying gentle. The sleeping animals have started their waking.

We who remain are still sitting around Grandma's table like old times past: Ingwald and Gloria, Naomi and Samuel, Dad and Mom and me. But we aren't playing cribbage or telling tales. We wait in silence. And Uncle Peter stands solid in the room.

Honeycomb ice, like that straddling the current, is not good ice. Neither is black ice: when the colour turns, that's the sign to go. Ice is as living as I am. And it speaks. The ice moves on the river and lakes, making sound as it breaks up and floats away. Taste of snowmelt in the water is a sure signal of spring. But at this moment, right at this moment, spring could stop. As small as she is, just starting, this melting season could end. Winter still touches the trees and the shadowed river with cold hands. Beneath the bridges is the last place to thaw, or it should be.

But we are a people who are ever hearing but never understanding, ever seeing but never perceiving. Our hearts are callused and hard; our eyes and ears are closed. Otherwise — if our hearts were soft — we might open our eyes and ears. Otherwise, we might see and hear and understand with our hearts, and Jesus would heal us. But the ice is unmoved: it will stay or thaw according to the season. The ice will hold or shift according to time. Weather does not care to know our hearts.

This is what Reuben was looking for at daybreak in the mud along the river: stone arrowheads, bone fishhooks, lost tackle, early wildflowers. This is what he found snagged on a tree root: an impossibly tiny baby girl, wet and bloated, but held in near-perfection by weeks in the frozen, icy river.

Reuben didn't bring it in the house. She needed to stay in the barn. And she is wrapped in my brother's hunting coat: he came back freezing with the wind screaming through his bones and the snow slicking his skin. He found her and brought her home, and then he got someone to help.

Uncle Peter called us all to Grandma's house, just told the grown-ups that it was 'life or death'. Once we came, he took the adults one by one into the barn and showed them what the children didn't need to see, what we already knew: black hair and lashes, tiny pink hands. Peter didn't take Naomi or me, just stared at us with those hangdog eyes and then looked away. The women came back crying, and the men came back grim.

Peter hauled Samuel out there last, and they were out there a long time. When they came back, the boy's lip was bleeding.

Peter put us in the kitchen and stood beside the door, halfway between the inside of the house and the porch. He didn't take off his boots, but stood there with his big arms crossed and still wearing his cap. There is a tiny smear of blood on his forehead; he must have wiped his hand. All I was thinking was that the small things of this world are smaller — and mean more — than I would have ever thought possible.

Hummingbird eggs are like peas, and when the chicks hatch they buzz about like bumblebees. But their momma isn't much bigger: she weighs only a penny, and her wings are black and shine metal green. She sucks her nectar and sap through her straight pointy bill and she'll gobble bugs whether they're flying through the air or climbing on leaves. We sit at the table waiting for God to tell us what to do. That momma will even grab insects from a spiderweb, and then go and steal the web itself to stick together her nest. Her eggs rest in a cup made from lichen, feather and dandelion thistle. She takes fur from dogs and hair from horses; she patches it together with spiderweb.

'Ruth!' Uncle Peter yells my name and stamps his hand against the doorframe.

And I look up from the table and see his eyes angry at me. 'Tell them.'

And what would I tell? Who she is? They know she don't belong to my skinny arms. Do they want to know how she flew away?

'Ruth, you can't just sit there forever.'

But there is nothing for me to say.

I think about the hummingbird and spiderweb glue

holding moss and fur together. She sleeps deep and barely alive, almost frozen in the night. When she wakes, she bathes in leaves, fluttering her wings against whatever is wet and glossy and green. And she'll die fighting — struggling against a frog or a giant spider — not sliding gentle along their killing throats. There is no proof of anything but spring, and that is beyond what I could say or understand.

Gloria's hands are folded and resting on the table, and her eyes are shut. Ingwald stares at the door. Samuel is blank and still; his lip bleeds. Naomi's head rests on the table; her braids lie limp atop the tablecloth.

My parents sit squashed together; Daddy's arm wraps around Mom's shoulders.

I look Peter straight in the face and do not speak a word.

Peter shakes his head at me and at all of them, and he turns his back on us. 'This is what you want?'

We remain silent.

Peter will not stop. 'You know, I saw it on that boy — a darkness — the day I met him.'

Uncle Ingwald looks up. 'Which boy are you talking about?'

'Your boy.' Peter turns to face his brother. 'There ain't nothing wrong with Reuben.'

'You sure about that?' Ingwald's voice is proud and mean.

Peter's hands are fists, and his eyes are on fire. 'Don't speak against him again. You know what I meant.'

Ingwald pushes his chair back. 'Last I remember, there were two baby boys you set naked in the snow.'

Aunt Gloria starts to speak. Out of the corner of my narrowed eye, I see Ingwald rising up. I think he might slap his wife — or maybe Naomi or maybe me — but my daddy stills his arm. All I hear is weeping: Gloria, Mom and Naomi.

All I see is Samuel: mouth shut tight, icy-blue eyes staring straight ahead.

Ingwald shakes off my daddy's hold. 'You sure you didn't see something in the other boy beside that fire?' He points at Peter. 'If a curse is being carried, it's Reuben carrying your blood.'

There will be blood spilt, of this I am sure. But Peter says nothing. He tucks his fists under his arms and looks at the floor. He does not deny anything.

'Reuben is my son.' Daddy's voice is hoarse, almost crying. He looks across the table at Ingwald. 'And I'll kill you if you ever say different again.' And I believe him.

The wind outside the window screams against the glass. Stubborn snow clings to the cornfields, white holding fast tight to stubble and stalk. Golden sticks hang with broken elbows, waving in the wind, shaking in the cold; they linger in the field, stripped.

Ingwald sits back down. All the women wait in silence. My mother looks at her lap; Gloria touches her arm.

Peter isn't angry, more sad, and he stays — almost waiting — at the doorway. I see my mother look long at my uncle's back, and next at her hands clutching the tablecloth. Then Peter is on the porch and the kitchen door slams shut behind him, and there is no way ahead or back or any which way anymore.

But my brother's big knees bump under the table, and his chair scratches back. Reuben gets up and follows Peter out the door. He's done his time sitting and he's finished with unspoken requests. As he leaves, I know he has made a choice forever. He'll be freezing out there in the cold.

My daddy and Ingwald sit down again, flanking Samuel;

Samuel stares at a water stain on the wall. There are men here who can only wait. But when God did not move, Reuben did. There is a frozen baby in our barn, and they don't know how she got there. But my brother knows and he will wait no longer. I believe he'll never call upon His name again.

And then they start asking.

They are asking and asking — and now demanding — but we aren't telling. They believe I can't hear them calling my name or asking me questions.

Naomi weeps and cannot speak. They know.

I fly out the window with my eyes. Mixed in the crystal powder and the left straw, blood smears into meandering crimson trails, tracing the path through the white of a tiny Trinity. It is a yearling deer with three whole legs, spindly brown, and one torn off at the knee. Sharp ice didn't cut it off, as flesh wouldn't have broke that clean. He must have caught a wayward bullet before winter set in. Here he is: a genuine miracle hopping through the field, right before our eyes. We only have to look to see. On he hops, picking through and nosing for missed cobs. He's nowhere near the edge of the field, yet he's nowhere near done.

36

LONG DAY SINCE MORNING, SINCE REUBEN FOUND HER AND brought her home. We sat hours at that table; the stove went out and no one relit it. Shadows darkened Grandma's kitchen, but no one switched on a light.

'Burn it.' That's all Samuel said when his daddy asked him what we should do with the baby. 'Burn it in the barrels behind the barn. Grandma's barn will burn easy as the others. Ask Reuben.'

Ingwald grabbed Samuel by the front of his shirt and pulled him to his feet. We all sat and watched them struggle. Ingwald slapped Samuel's face over and over, and the boy didn't cry out or raise a hand to his father. The only sound was the slaps — over and over and again — until Gloria stood up straight and the weight of her coat sank her chair down onto the linoleum.

'Enough.' She barely raised her voice. 'That's enough.' She bent over and pulled on her coat, buttoned Naomi into her own jacket, and left the kitchen.

Daddy stood and reached for my mother's hand. She nodded at me and we wrapped up and left too. As I walked through the door onto the porch, I looked back into the kitchen. Ingwald still held Samuel by the shirtfront, and Samuel still looked straight ahead. The room was cold and quiet. It was mostly empty.

Outside, without a word, Gloria has gone to the barn and brought back Reuben's coat and what it holds. She puts Naomi in the passenger seat and then, cradling the orange bundle, my aunt climbs into the backseat. Mom speaks to Daddy and he gets a shovel. Mom and I sit in the middle of the van. Daddy breaks off the top of a crabapple sapling out of the yard. After piling the tree and shovel in the farthest back of the vehicle, Daddy starts up the van and honks the horn. Ingwald walks from Grandma's house with Samuel following, and they get into Daddy's truck.

We drive in silence in the van; the wipers swipe snow from the windshield. Once past the driveway as we speed toward town, Gloria's voice sings soft from the back of the van. *When peace, like a river, attendeth my way; when sorrows like sea billows roll. Whatever my lot, Thou has taught me to say: it is well, it is well, with my soul.* Instead of a funeral organ, she is accompanied by the clicking of the wipers and the shovel knocking against the rear window. We all join her — even Naomi — in the final refrain. *It is well, with my soul. It is well, with my soul. It is well, it is well, with my soul.*

Making like we're at the church to plant a tree in Grandma's memory, our family gathers under the pines of Babylon. Planting a tree in March is like spitting into the wind, but here we are, scraping snow away from beneath a long-needled pine. Like an unspoken prayer request, we all knew without saying what had to happen next.

Ingwald has said the words and made the ground sacred. Gloria's tears are watering it and making it holy. Naomi is nothing; she is not here except in body. She is the same as it. My daddy is holding on to my mom's arm; she is white and shivering and her shoulders heave with sobbing. I am still and holding the sapling; I can feel its pulse in my hands. Face blank but eyes sour, Samuel has the shovel; his daddy makes him dig.

When the Lord shall come again, His second coming will be a time of great rejoicing for all those who remain. Enduring suffering beyond imagination — beasts with raping stingers, blood flowing like water, death the only release from tribulation's torture — the faithful, both living and dead, will be caught up in the air with Jesus. For the graves will break forth, and we shall be redeemed.

The ground is frozen solid. This will take some time.

'I didn't do nothing,' Samuel is whispering.

When a guy plants a tree, he wants to be careful. Reuben and I found it last year before I shot my deer: an oak, pin oak maybe, with a tie stretched taut around its centre. The looped label wouldn't stretch, not anymore, so the orange plastic dug into the bark. That scar was worn deep. Reuben cut the bind off the tree. Seemed we both heard it breathe relief.

They finally get it under, beneath the snow, barely into the ground. The men lay the shovel atop the small dirt heap, beside the leaning sapling, and go into the church. The men enter the sanctuary.

Mom pulls us inside the church doors and into the fellowship hall. I wish I was hiding in the coats, but she settles me on a folding chair. She sits between us. She puts Naomi and Gloria side by side on folding chairs and touches the girl's cheek for a moment.

She asks me. Mom asks me if she was mine. She knows better. She wants to ask more but she can't. When I say no, she nods. Mom leaves me be. Then Gloria asks Naomi. When Naomi says no, she is looking at me with wavering eyes; her hands twist their purple mittens.

The hair tells, though. That wispy black hair matches, and it don't match me. The women don't leave Naomi. Mom sweeps her skirt underneath her legs, kneels down before Gloria and Naomi and takes their hands in hers. They are in a whispering circle.

We should always wear orange, then and now. For Daddy and Reuben, hunting gear is all the warm clothes they got, but my brother ain't here and he don't have a coat no more. The deer see the shapes moving through the pines, but their eyes can't see orange. The danger is the other hunters. And wearing the colour, letting the others know you're there, is the only way to stay safe in the woods.

They break the circle and I see the women's eyes and I know Naomi told them, just like I saw that Reuben told Peter. Each eye holds a new darkness, a deep hole in colour that is wide and empty and more lonely than before. Naomi gave it away to them — Gloria and my momma know — and for that I will never forgive her. It is her hurt to share; I suppose I know that much. She can tell them about her brother and her belly and all about the blood. But the tiny elbows and ankles, that part is mine; that moment of no weight that I gave to that child — no matter what Naomi said — is mine forever.

Mom opens her mouth to speak, but Gloria is quivering and mumbling loud. 'No one can know,' she says.

And my mom says, 'Of course no one can, no one will.'

'About the baby.' Gloria's hands are holding tight to the folding chair.

'About the baby.' Mom is an echo. And then her face changes; this isn't about the baby in the blanket. 'About Samuel?'

Yes, about Samuel. Gloria only nods. No one knew what Samuel was doing, but no one knew what he was, what he was made of. My mother's eyes move from Gloria to me and I can see her mind travelling too. Back to California, when there was a miracle born.

Gloria speaks. 'Samuel wasn't early.' I hear the words, but then there is silence and there is a bright spot inside my mind, like a star exploding. 'We sinned, Ingwald and me. We weren't married yet. We fell, and Samuel is our shame. What you must think of me.'

'I think I knew that anyway.' Mom gently sweeps the tears from my aunt's cheeks. 'And it doesn't matter. You are still my Glory, and we can still pray.'

But they cannot pray because Gloria does not stop.

'My false miracle is Naomi's curse.'

'Glory, the Lord gave Samuel to you.' Mom is almost holding her breath.

My aunt is a ghost, so pale she looks like she is going to vomit.

'And the Lord used him to stop the bleeding,' Mom adds.

'And did the Lord use him again?' There is sweat across Gloria's forehead and she holds her stomach in pain. She is groaning and squirming on the metal seat. Her dress is soaked through.

My mother cannot answer. She gets up. 'Alright, Glory. Let's get you to the bathroom.'

My aunt stands and my mom holds her; they move slowly to the ladies. Naomi waits alone on the chair. Swinging her legs, she sits next to the metal chair stained with her mother's blood.

There is an end to miracles. Naomi sees me, and it is like she has just realised I am here and her eyes are the same as they always were. They never were like mine. She sees me and she calls me nearer, pleading, but I don't come to her. The space between us is an undying shadow.

She is still mine — always will be — but I will never trust her or Reuben again. For all that Samuel is, at least he never told — not about nothing. And for all that I am, I never will either.

37

INSIDE THE SANCTUARY, HIS SHOULDERS STILL DAMP FROM snow, Samuel is kneeling at the front of the church. Ingwald is weeping. He and Daddy wait together in the last wooden pew. Both sit straight and tall like schoolboys, and my uncle's hands grip his knees. After she helped Gloria in the bathroom, Mom settled her in the nursery. Then Mom told Daddy about Naomi, and Daddy told his brother. Ingwald hasn't spoken since; he cries without sound, tears sliding along the scars on his face. All of them could see me if they were looking; I'm standing right before them.

Ingwald rubs the back of his hand across his eyes. 'I need your help, Eric.'

Daddy looks straight ahead.

Ingwald pushes up from the pew, bracing his body on his brother's shoulder. 'First, I need your forgiveness. Your son is yours. Sometimes, we choose our burdens.'

And my daddy moves his mouth to speak but says nothing. He swallows it down.

After nothing changes and no one moves, Ingwald says, 'Call them.'

Because he does as he is told, my daddy calls together the

elders of the church. Ingwald is seeking direction and comfort. He is seeking healing for Samuel. We must examine ourselves as to whether we are in the faith. We must test ourselves; this is just a test. *Come now, let us settle the matter ... Though your sins are like scarlet, they shall be as white as snow; though they are red as crimson, they shall be like wool.* The request don't go out on the prayer chain; this is a private matter before the Lord.

While we wait for the elders to arrive — old men leaving their suppers cooling on kitchen tables, young men rushing through the evening milking — I walk like a ghost through the church. Gloria grieves in the nursery. She can't send out the call for help; she can't even stand, let alone speak. Mom rocks my aunt like she is a newborn lamb. I put my hands to my ears and peek out the nursery door. In the church kitchen, my daddy leans by the phone. He stood and made the calls for help, but even he looks small and lost.

They gather now in the rusty pick-up trucks and the old cars we drive in winter. We tend to drive beaters in the snow because of the good chance of hitting deer or sliding off the road. And the road salt eats out the paint anyway. The prophet Elisha healed the water of the land with salt: he put it in a new bowl and then threw the salt in the spring. The Lord healed the water; nevermore would it kill or make barren. *And the water has remained wholesome to this day.* The church parking lot fills with the tarnished vehicles of the saints. They have come to lay hands upon the sick and to anoint him with oil. Jesus used spit and mud to heal the blind; He used blood to heal us all.

Farmers keep their chore jackets separate at home — hanging in mud rooms or piled on porches — to try and keep the cow smell out of their town clothes. I don't think that they know it ain't working: even with hair wet from the shower and clothes that have never seen the inside of a barn, the smell of feed and manure clings to each farmer like fur on a cat. I'm not bothered; it just smells warm to me.

The elders have gathered and are making coffee. Murmuring to each other bits of what and where, each man passes along what he knows. When late men push through the double doors, stamping boots and breathing out cold air, their high greetings are met with downcast eyes and hush. They know pretty quick that trouble is here. Coffee drunk and cups stacked in the sink, the men sigh with their shoulders and head into the sanctuary. Ingwald and Samuel await them there.

From my peeking, I'm set to slink behind, hoping to hear the goings-on without getting caught. I am with the women in the nursery; near the cribs, Mom and Aunt Gloria are slumped in rocking chairs, and Naomi has curled up in one of the toddler beds. My leaving won't bother them none; they are weary and need to rest.

As I'm sliding one leg out — stocking foot only, my snowy boots dripping on the mat — I again hear the creak of the double doors, the push of wind, and the voices of men. Daddy stayed behind in the kitchen, quiet for some time, but now two other low talking voices have joined him there. I feel the cold enter the church. In my daddy's asking for help, Uncle Peter was the last call he made. And Peter brought Reuben with him.

These men have forever stood, brothers, shoulder-to-shoulder. My daddy has always had a way with wood, so he helped how he could. As a boy, he built a pulpit — hammered together two-by-fours, crooked but strong — for Uncle Ingwald to preach to birds, deep in the pines behind the barn. As a man, he's worked construction — barns and bridges, a dock for Uncle Peter, and some cabins — throughout the northwoods. He's had sore muscles and sore hands, slivers stuck deep in his palms. And when I had a sliver in my finger, he'd help me pull it out. But Daddy would usually wait with his own sliver, worrying against the moment that it might break halfway through the pulling. He'd rather let it grow out, allowing the skin to harden. The skin will push it out.

As the men talk, I feel the seeds beneath my skin: the tiny spots of sand or grit that wait for me to pick. I rub the seeds and feel my nails start to scrape.

And Peter tells my brother to speak.

Reuben does: falling from the sky, riding quick across the snow. He is weeping, but he needs to have nothing to fear. 'I set the fires, not alone — Samuel was with me sometimes — but it was me.'

My daddy puts his head in his hands; he does not speak.

'Our neighbours?' Uncle Peter's voice is fierce. 'All Turgeson's stock?'

Reuben's voice is shaky. 'I started just with the wrecks — whatever fell I burnt. And Turgeson's pump house was all we were trying to light. It all just lit up.'

I see cows straining in agony in the heat and smoke. Pulling on their chains, rolling and trying to kick through the concrete and stone walls.

'Why didn't you let on?' Daddy's hurt.

'I tried. I tried to tell you in prayer — my unspoken request. I just couldn't say it. I never hurt those animals on purpose.'

His voice is failing but still he talks; my brother breaks again. He's wide open. 'And Samuel didn't hurt just Naomi.' Then he tells them my name.

The older men get low and slow; I hear both my uncle and my daddy.

Daddy's crying. 'It ain't your fault, Reuben. And I don't give a damn about the barns. That boy hiding in the sanctuary — Samuel — he's the one, always been.'

'Shouldn't have to come to it, but it has.' Uncle Peter's voice is certain. 'We need to fix it for good.'

'How?' Daddy looks at his hands.

If a guy falls from a stand — out poaching deer or some such — he might land on a twig, be impaled and be finished. Or his gun might go off in the tumble or finally when he hits the ground. Hunting accidents happen: maybe attacks by bear or coyote, or trips and necks breaking it could be. Or shooting a rock and having the bullet ricochet.

Daddy built hunting stands for himself and his older brothers all through our woods. There's hanging boards tangled in weeds or clinging to the high crooks of trees.

We need to check the shotguns for turkey hunting — that'd be believed. Uncle Peter remembers. 'It's certainly time, overdue even.' It's patterning instead of sighting-in: check the spread or adjust the choke.

But I'm busy with my nails in my hair; the dandruff looks like the tiny parts of flowers, stamen and petal. Maybe pine pitch stuck my hair together; the clumps are hard to break.

And the twenty-gauge shell is smaller but the plastic lip is wider than the twelve; the lip could be shaved down just enough to fit.

'Stuff the shell down the break,' my daddy is thinking

out loud. 'Maybe with a rifle cleaner; most men don't even check their barrels, a boy won't.'

The twenty would stop the following shell from travelling down; she'd bubble up then probably banana-peel. Standing to the sides would be the most dangerous; he'll have to watch out. Peter knows to be careful.

Make sure the sides are clear, so that the shot goes where it's meant and get her done. The barrel will blow, just explode. Samuel needs to shoot the gun.

I'm hoping on leaving now, just walking out of this place, slipping over to where the boots are stacked. Some men don't take them off, but most fear tracking mud or manure through the sanctuary. Icy bits melt down the treads, the murky water sticking at stones and grit. Farmers' boots are different than factory workers' or the slick bottoms of a stray accountant. The soles show their owners. Samuel carries a twelve gauge for sure.

When Uncle Peter sees me, I stay silent. What I saw and what I know — then and now — it is inside me. The men can see me and they can ask; I can't help that. My family can stop me from leaving — pulling my arms from my shoulders — but what I did is mine alone.

They stop pulling when they sit me down firm, but they don't need to worry about me none. I have kept my mouth shut and I always will.

Reuben is bawling and saying he is sorry.

'We'll protect you forever.' My daddy is stroking my hair, trying to comfort me. 'No one's ever going to know what happened, not to you or her, not even to him.'

Peter looks at me, and his eyes have changed. He don't see me clean anymore.

What they want from me, I will not give them. I'll nod about Naomi and I'll nod about Samuel, but about me they won't get a word. They can just keep on asking; I'll sit here as silent as a stone. Their flannel and wool steam in the heat.

All Reuben's eyes do is cry. Thick shoulders quivering, he weeps.

Daddy holds Reuben's hands. 'All we have left is Jesus.' He doesn't sound certain.

Peter shakes his head. 'Nothing makes sense in this place.' He looks around the church, at our felt banners and cracked oil paintings. 'Give up this crazy chase.'

Daddy waits. Reuben weeps.

Their voices blend together and pull apart, and I leave them as they argue amongst themselves on the metal chairs. Inside my head, tangling ropes swim, twisting and pulling tight against me. I pull away and start floating around the ceiling, sticking close to the tops of the walls. I'm flying, but I'm afraid that I'll come crashing down hard to the floor. So I open my eyes and go into the nursery. I go to find Naomi.

38

MOM AND GLORIA BOTH SLEEP IN THE NURSERY ROCKING chairs; their heads hang down, chins touching their chests. It is night and this horrible day will not end. Folded and bent like a fawn in a field, Naomi still dozes in the toddler bed. She needs to wake now.

'Girl.' She hears me but does not move. I touch her knee. 'Naomi.'

She opens her eyes. There is a hollow in her, like I can see into her mouth and all the way down. 'I'm hungry.' She moves her knee away from my hand and curls her body tighter.

'There's nothing to eat.' I touch her knee again. 'The elders are in the sanctuary. They're in there deciding what to do.'

And I do not expect it, but she awakens and uncoils. Naomi gets up and walks out of the nursery.

We hide in the back of the sanctuary. Naomi and me are laying on our bellies, low and flat like coyotes on the pews. Our faces are opposite, almost touching; I can hear her breathe. I sometimes sneak a look over the top of the seats. We will remain quiet. We will be witnesses to the healing power of the Lord.

They are still praying. I'm keeping my mind on anything else, taking myself out of this church, out of this family, out of this Failing. But they remain here; they stay. At the front of the sanctuary, the elders hold their hands down on Samuel hard. Ingwald's words are mixed: forgiveness and healing and the unforgivable sin. He speaks in the language of sinners and in the language of angels. They are praying for the healing power of Christ to come down and heal him, to heal Samuel.

'Hear us, Lord; hear our prayer.'

Samuel won't weep or thrash or nothing — he is just waiting for it to be finished. He stands underneath the weight of their hands; he is unswayed.

They finish praying. Nothing's left.

Straining from the back pew where we hide, I can hear them murmur amongst themselves. Broken-down farmers, tired loggers and bored factory workers, the elders reckon that they know the Bible and Jesus, that they know the world. But I'm guessing they don't know about the little tree planted in Babylon. Buried in the snow beneath the heavy boughs of old pines, that sapling won't ever grow.

Somehow chosen, these men stand on Sunday mornings in their best jeans and flannels to pass the collection and communion plates. From my place in church, I've watched them hunkered in their pews. I've watched their hands paring dirty fingernails or digging out black slivers with hunting knives. I've watched their eyes struggling against sleep after a late night delivering calves or harvesting crops. But I've never watched them show themselves so; I watch them close now.

'She's bad as he is, if you ask me.'

'No worse, no better.'

Naomi won't open her eyes; her head is pushed down against the worn wood beneath us.

'If the law finds out, the boy won't be able to hunt. That ain't no life.'

Naomi never got to hunt; that don't bother them none.

'He's just a boy.'

We do not speak.

'How they all act these days.'

Naomi's eyes stay shut; she won't look. I won't close my eyes.

Ingwald will not hear any more of it. He is his son, but she is his daughter. The pastor's hands stay up; they are flailing and swinging with his screaming. He casts the elders out of the church; he commands them to leave him with his boy. Samuel sits on the front pew and does not move.

Quick, the men walk: on their way out, they file silent past our pew. I smell their sweat and hear their steps, and I look up to see their true faces. I want them to see me now. None will catch my eye. None until Mr Turgeson; he has not lifted his voice in this sanctuary. As he passes, though, he tilts his chin and stares me plain in the face. In those eyes, I see his hurting; with his blinking and chewed lip, he's asking me to say it is done. He wants me up on that cross looking down with *my son* and then *forgive* and finally *my Father* and for it to be over.

But I can't, or I won't, so I shut my mouth and my eyes. I shut them and wait. Turgeson can remember his daughter forever, laying bleeding on his lawn. I just wait until his breath leaving tells me he's gone.

And when I open my eyes, it is time. At the altar, there is a miraculous transformation.

Ingwald unfurls his wings, and his wings are tipped with claws. He grabs Samuel by the shoulders and heaves him against the communion table. 'Tell me! Tell the Lord!' Powerful and mighty, he is revealed.

All this time, all this time, I never knew: my uncle is the Seventh Angel. With one foot on the land and one on the sea, he straddles the world. He commands time to cease; he brings down heaven to earth.

He screams at both God and man. He screams 'Jesus!' and then he screams 'Samuel'. He screams and screams. The sound is a torment: wailing and gnashing of teeth. I can feel it burning on my tongue. I believe I am screaming too.

'I didn't do nothing.' And this time he spits. Samuel spits a gob of snot onto the carpet of the sanctuary, and it stains deep down into the floor. His spit sizzles and rises like smoke, like a spirit coming straight from hell. It rises like steam from the backs of sweaty horses gone out into the snow.

He is a demon, Samuel is, or there is one in him. He stains us all.

But the hand of the Lord is upon us; he brings us out by the Spirit and puts us in a valley of bones. Dry bones cannot live; we, the sons of men, speak now. In the Bible, the prophet says that the sovereign Lord alone can know, but we know. Even if we prophesy to the bones, foretell the breath of the Lord entering them and their coming to life, we will not see it happen.

He is the Lord, but there will be no rattling sound, no noise of the bones knitting together, bone to bone, with tendons and flesh appearing and skin covering. There will be no bodies, so there is no need for breath. There will be no breath prophesied; the sons of man will not call the four winds to come and breathe into the slain, that they will live. No wind will come and none will arise to his feet. There will be no vast army of the Lord. We are alone here, the living. Alone amongst only the awake; we will not call those already asleep. We are waiting to die.

Almost collapsed, Ingwald kneels beneath the picture of Christ. 'I am dead. I am dry. I am old, dry bones.'

Samuel just walks; he don't look right or left. He sure don't look at her or me. He sees us lying on the pews and he whispers as he passes. 'I didn't do nothing.' Three times he's denied us now, and he walks out of the church.

And as Samuel leaves, Mom catches the door and comes in; quiet in the pews, she holds me and rocks me. I am on her lap and she questions another time. I'm still and saying nothing even though Reuben was 'yes' to the men, and again Naomi is 'yes' to our mommas, and those liars are 'yes, yes' to everything ever asked. Naomi cries and they listen to her cries. Everything I gave — everything I now am — is for nothing. My wounds, on my hands and feet and heart, are only scars.

Now Gloria is here too and she has Naomi, and they are both crying; the momma hurting so with, 'Samuel, Naomi, my babies,' over and over. We are covered in our mothers and their coats. We are wrapped like the little Amish infants, swathed both summer and winter: too hot in warm but barely thawed in cold. Tiny faces peek out beneath black wool bonnets with cloaks hanging down, held in their black wool mommas' arms. In winter, the wool smells wet always, even on pink babies with still-closed eyes.

My momma is too pretty, skin too soft and hair too shiny. There are maps that show what grows, beef or wheat or corn; men see us the same. Our dresses are too thin and show what women have to give: mostly guilt, never-ending. A black cloak hanging down, like the Amish, could save us those stares.

We should've all stayed covered, just to be safe.

Gloria's talking and can't stop. 'Ingwald hasn't touched me since I was healed. Never. I've so missed being loved; my heart has withered away.'

My mom is crying now and reaches over to touch Gloria's face. Gloria grabs and holds Mom's outstretched hand; she pulls it to herself.

'My Glory, I get lonesome too.' My momma is trying to take some of the woman's pain.

But Gloria's face hardens. She straightens her back and stares. 'You know, Marie?' Anger coarsens her voice. 'All these years, watching those two men adore you almost killed me.'

Mom snatches back her hand, nearly hitting me in the face. 'I don't know what you mean.' She can't breathe. She straightens herself and pushes me off her lap, stern.

Gloria drops her head. 'My husband and I don't even share a bed. But you have more than enough love.'

The breath comes in and the breath pushes out. My mother loves Uncle Peter.

'I can't begin to know what you mean.' My mom's shoulders slump down and she puts her hand to her forehead.

Glory is weeping again; we can barely understand her words. 'But you do.'

'Sometimes it takes two men to make a whole.' And Mom

drops her head for a moment, a silent slump into sorrow. 'I could have never left Reuben behind, and then the Lord gave me Ruth as comfort. Glory, girls, we can't always choose who God gives us to love. His ways are not our own, and His timing is His.' She raises her head. Mom is no longer crying.

The lights in the sanctuary buzz, and the seats are hard and rough beneath us. Naomi is crying, but I am at peace for I already knew: it is well with my soul.

Keeping silent, my heart knows how I move inside the living things: I bring wholeness. And come spring, there is no matching the beauty of the trillium. Three white petals of sweet flower, they push up along the banks and in the meadow. Each petal is like clean milk in a pail: in some light it leans toward blue, but it smells pure and white and white alone. I look down deep inside where the three parts swirl into one: Mom, Daddy and Peter made me. My spirit is the very breath of God.

'We all have our sorrows, our brokenness.' Gloria is waving her tiny hands. 'Eric is a man of faith. Ingwald is a man of faith.' She breathes out. I can see her chest rise and fall. 'And Peter would never let harm come to us.' The light is pushing but fading against the windows of the sanctuary.

When Samuel sat here before, the elders weighing him down, he seemed to wear a halo. It shimmered about his head. But now, I slant my eyes and see it was just the angle of the light; it was just the dying light all along.

The change has come in her heart; Gloria is quivering and she takes ahold of Naomi's shoulders to still her hands. My aunt will bury her sin — Samuel — deep again. My momma will do the same. Each woman will breathe it in and keep it down in her bottomless soul.

'Our husbands' faith can overcome any unbelief.' Gloria stretches out one quaking hand to my momma. Their hands tie together.

Whatever happened before must remain unsaid: whoever has loved, whoever hasn't. Both babies — Gloria's and Naomi's — just confused the time. And my momma just found too much love. Even I can see as much: a man could give it to the Lord and that sin would be forgotten, struck from the mind; but if a woman told, she would be pressed down all the rest of her days. So she's got to hold it tight and hold it herself. Her burden is her own.

I'm sure that love was good once, what comfort or tenderness or plain slow-down rest there was. I believed them when they said so, even if I don't anymore.

And now we come together in prayer, and they say it again. We four, who are women and can still speak to heaven, make the sounds together. I say it for them. *My soul to take*, we still have the words. We are praying for the second coming: the sea will give up her dead and the land will follow likewise. We want the world to break open. It will. And when it does, we will fly away. We will fly away, swiftly home.

39

A SNOWSTORM IN THE MORNING CONTAINED ME, BUT THIS afternoon I couldn't stop walking. After all day yesterday in Grandma's house and all night in the church, I can't be trapped today. Once I could see my hand in front of my face, I was out the door, skirting the woods and up over the hill to Uncle Peter's place. The same trees and paths, the same snow. It wasn't blowing anymore, but I could hear the snow nonetheless: not falling, but swirling, closer to wings beating. Past the woods, with snow piled on the evergreens, coating each needle and clumping them fat. The branches hang heavy and low. The birds rest somewhere within the shadows, at least the ones that are left.

I slide open the door and Uncle Peter looks up; he is sitting on the base of an upturned ten-gallon bucket. And in his eyes, I see my eyes.

And I see — as if in a dream — a young man weeping behind the milk shed, building an altar, collecting the wood for a burnt offering. He asks the sky, 'Where is the offering? Where is the lamb?' There is no reply from the sky. Instead, inside Peter, the Lord's voice speaks in his blood: there is evil in this child — evil in Samuel. But as Peter stretches forth his hand and takes the knife to slay the child, an angel of the Lord calls unto him out of heaven. The angel of the Lord — Reuben — cries, 'Here am I. I am the sacrifice.'

And I see behind what is not a dream. When Peter took two babies behind the shed, he did so because he saw evil in one and love in the other: Samuel was destruction and Reuben was life. One boy would one day divide us and one boy would keep us together. When Peter chose not to slay Samuel, he also chose not to slay Reuben — even though it meant my mother would never be his. Peter's sacrifice was both evil and good. For the first time in my life, I believe I finally know what it means to love. And for the first time in my life, I know I am looking at my true father.

My dreaming and my awake, my time spent inside trees and fish: these are not burdens, they are gifts. And these are gifts straight from God through Grandma — straight from Grandma through Peter to me.

'Didn't see you there.' Peter gets back to sharpening the blade of his axe with the diamond stone he rubs slow and perfect along the edge.

Even from inside Peter's shed, I can smell the snow in the air — like the change between noon to midnight, or winter and summer, or wind from stillness — and I can feel it melt on my mittens, dripping. The man slides the stone along the arc, and then he burnishes the edge with his callused palm. As sharp as it is, the blade just bites his skin. And it is dead skin anyway, thick and unfeeling.

'What you need, Ruth?'

And I can tell it is time now, like when the bucks sniff the air. I'm afraid, with my mouth not making sounds. His old, rusty shotguns are laid out on the workbench, a butcher's block scarred by knives hacking bone or missing. A small pile of plastic shavings is gathered neat beneath the vice secured to the bench; he's already trimmed the shotgun shell.

The wind picks up outside the shed. The snow might have stopped or not. I can't hear it or smell it now; the weather goes on without me outside, and I have no say.

Sacks of birdseed are stacked by his knee, just enough to get the little ones through what remains of these cold seasons. He's remembered the oily black seed is their favourite. Peter remembers more than I know. But I do know that biting early into an apple discolours the white. It ruins both what is and what was to be. Things must wait to change natural; bite early into an apple — stain it with blood from the bite — and it browns.

Even still, I place my mitten on Peter's shoulder and then I bend down and put my lips on his crooked mouth. My eyes are shut, like a kitten's, but I feel his warmth in my mouth. My lips are soft, and his are hard, chapped from wind and snow. He smells of chewing tobacco and cider; I breathe deep. I feel his flat teeth. When it stops, I know it is my first one, the only time I've chosen a kiss. And it possesses me.

His arms push my shoulders back, but light, and he rises up still holding the axe.

'You're a beautiful woman, Ruth.' Big shoulders moving beneath his quilted flannel, he looks me square in the face. 'You look so much like your momma.'

There is a sway and a creak in the shed, and my blood pushes against my skin.

His finger traces the edge of the axe, feeling the smooth and feeling the sharp. Then he puts the leather cover on the blade, turns his back and walks out the door.

The Lord hears us when we talk to each other; He listens and hears. There is a scroll of remembrance that was written in the Lord's presence describing those who feared Him and honoured His name. The Lord speaks and calls us His: *they will be Mine.* We are His treasured possessions, His jewels. *I will spare them, just as in compassion a man spares his son who serves him.*

The shotguns are ready, and it is still snowing. Now is the time. Whatever birds remain will have seed. The door swings open and brings the weather inside.

Now Peter stands at the door. 'Fetch Samuel.'

I wrap my hands around the carved stock of the oldest shotgun; it was my Grampa's gun and will someday make a good companion for me. The gun feels warm and ready. My body can tell the time.

'Fetch Samuel.' Peter is done waiting.

So am I. And I will.

They are looking for him everywhere, in the woods and along the river, but I know where he is even without looking. Samuel is sulking, and he sulks in Grandma's barn. I heard the old tractor sputter to a start, and I can hear it running still. He is always poking around that damn tractor, always messing with what he don't understand. Quietly, I sneak across the farmyard toward the barn. Be sure, I'll find him out; he can't hide forever.

As I fling open the barn door, Samuel startles and looks up frightened from the back of the coughing tractor. But when he sees that it is only me, he smiles, but now I see those teeth as a sneer.

'Get, girl.' And his heart says *we got enough that's used and broken-down in here.* He jerks his head and sweeps his arm toward the door. He wants me gone.

With a roar, the tractor's power take-off grabs the dangling sleeve of his barn coat and wraps it around and around until Samuel's arm is tangled into the metal. He is screaming as the machine whirls him around and smashes him against the wall. He grabs at his entangled arm. In an instant, his left arm is torn off almost completely. The other stump is still being chewed. Both Samuel and the tractor are screaming, but the only sound I hear is the barn creaking in the wind. He is meat, bone and sinew; he is white fat and red membrane. He is stuck.

He looks up at me and begs me with his eyes, like a coyote with his foot caught in a trap; he wants mercy. 'Ruth. Ruth. Help me.'

I don't know if the Lord is saying yes or no, but I know He needs to start speaking louder now. Samuel must be bleeding heavy, because he is slumped in the midst of a dark, red stain on the oily floor. In the middle of the pain, he keeps saying that God hears him and He is answering his prayer. I know that He hears, and I believe that He answers; I just think I'm having a hard time hearing His voice over the sound of Samuel.

He's really panting now and keeping up a stream of prayer. 'Oh God, oh Lord, oh Lord.'

He is scared, and he is hurting. He is crying out. 'Oh God. Oh my God.'

And he sure ain't cursing; he is praying and praying hard. He is praying. 'Help me, Lord. Give me help.'

I guess that I'm the closest thing to an answer to prayer that he's going to get.

'I'm so cold. Oh Lord.'

I don't know what to do. Even though I want to leave, I feel like I can't just go and let him suffer so. I run out of the barn and look around the farmyard for anything that might help us through. I don't know if what I bring is better than what I leave behind; I can't even see clearly for the tears in my eyes. Following the fence lines, I run across the fields. I bring Peter.

By the time we make it back and into the barn, Samuel is laying flat on the floor, blood soaked through his shirt and pants. The boy must have slept for a while: a red snow angel is traced around his body. He sees us and barely raises his eyes; he cannot speak.

Peter moves quickly, dropping the first-aid kit between Samuel's legs and kneeling down before him. He pulls out the thick bandages and begins tying tight around the meat that used to be Samuel's right arm. 'Hold on, boy. Hold on.' He ties that rope hard.

Samuel is screaming again, but not aloud. I hear the screaming inside my head.

Peter reaches across to tie the left arm — less remains here. 'You'll live through this, Samuel.' The man keeps wrapping and tying. 'I've seen worse.'

And I see that Uncle Peter is saving this life. I see he never would have done it; he never did what needed to be done. He couldn't sacrifice a child that he knew was evil, and he couldn't sacrifice an infant that kept him from love. He has been out of the hunt too long.

I back away from the man and boy. Tangled together, from above, they must look like the stamen of a heart-red flower.

Samuel deserves to die. I know what to do. I run outside and into Grandma's house. I can see clearly; there are no tears in my eyes. I bring Ingwald.

We run across the farmyard and into the barn. When Ingwald sees his prodigal, Samuel's flesh tangled through and mixed with bloody metal, he cries out, 'Jesus!'

Peter scrambles up and raises his hands toward his brother. 'If we take him in, the boy will make it. He has more than a chance.'

Ingwald rushes toward Samuel and looks at Peter's face. Then, calmness enters the father's eyes, and his face goes white as Ingwald realises he has His answer. He speaks the Word: *'The axe is already at the root of the trees.'*

Samuel starts screaming again. Ingwald's cheek is mapped with scars.

I stand and watch. 'Pastor?'

Ingwald sways with his hands raised toward heaven. He closes his eyes and shakes his head.

Samuel is a voice above the wind.

Peter wipes a bloody smear across his forehead. 'Brother, I don't know if this is the answer.' He walks toward the door. 'But it's your God.'

'We already have His answer,' Ingwald is screaming over his son as his brother walks into the wind. He finishes, *'And every tree that does not produce good fruit will be cut down and thrown into the fire.'* Ingwald's knees clunk when they hit the floor.

He places his pale hand on Samuel's back and weeps and prays over him. He watches the life drain out of his only son as they sit, both tangled around the tractor, together on the bloody floor. As he holds Samuel's head like a jewel, Ingwald waits with one foot dangling in the manure gutter and one foot standing steady on the floor. It is cold, as it often is, even in this thawing time. There is ice and there is snow, and the wind blows constant outside the door.

While Samuel bleeds below, red seeping into the pitted concrete, I climb the ladder into the haymow once more. The light is fading, and I stumble and hardly recognise the place. I walk toward the hay chute and struggle to slide open the heavy door. It is windy and cold; snowflakes swirl around me as I stand high above the farmyard, looking out into the deepening night.

I look out toward the woods. *These are our trees.*

I look out toward the farmstead. *This is our home.*

I look out toward the river. *This is our water.*

Finally, I look out toward the heavens, to the snow and the dark; there is a glow from the farmyard light, glowing bigger than the moon. I hold myself against the chute. I keep holding tight.

Wrapped in Grandma's coat, still stained with Naomi's blood, I open her worn, leather Bible to the passage marked with a crimson ribbon. *Arise, my darling, my beautiful one, and come with me. See! The winter is past; the rains are over and gone. Flowers appear on the earth; the season of singing has come, the cooing of doves is heard in our land. The fig tree forms its early fruit; the blossoming vines spread their fragrance. Arise, come, my darling; my beautiful one, come with me.*

40

HE COMES, SNOWMOBILE SMEARING A BLACK STAIN ACROSS the white snow of the farmyard. He comes first — like I knew he would — Reuben. He moves big-boned and strong, quicker than he ought to be, pulling his long legs through the snow bank and galloping into the gaping barn door to see the end of it all. I hear the tractor cut off and then only the low moaning of the father. In my mind's eye I see Samuel, wet, being held tight. I know Reuben waits with Peter, apart from the dying, watching.

Now there is an angel who stands in the sun; he cries to the birds in mid-flight, he calls them to eat the flesh of the mighty and the small, all men and every living thing. Even the beast is slain and eaten. He is slain with the sword from the mouth of the rider, the angel that rides the horse. The angel stands in the sun and watches the birds gorge themselves on all flesh.

Next, Daddy comes, the rusty pick-up bringing dirty tyre tracks and boot marks. He stays inside those tracks.

And then the women come. That barn phone works, and the women come. Gloria and Naomi come quick, my momma driving the truck. Gloria runs to the barn and Mom is close behind her, pulling on her coat. Naomi stays in the truck, pressing her hand to melt the window frost.

Gloria almost makes the barn door when they catch her. Peter and Mom hold Glory's arms and block her way. The birds are swirling, making the air black with their wings. They swoop and cry with their high, screaming voices.

And now, up here in the haymow, there is no place to go, no fish or bird or animal to slip inside and slide away. There is nothing but my skin and my eyes, no coming time of fear or dread. Except that final reckoning, it comes still; I have no choice in that.

Dust and chaff and old, old dirt has been falling into my eyes. Outside, the clouds must have shifted; when I look up through the door again, shafts of sunlight stream down at me. Dust mites float in the air. As they turn and swirl, they are beautiful and glint in the light like tiny pieces of gold. There is beauty in this world too, even in this haymow — even, and at last, in this place.

My brother kneels before me. Reuben is wiping my face, wetting his hanky by pouring water from his hunting flask, rubbing blood and dirt from my cheeks. And Naomi is here too, holding out her hands like a cup. She's come to find me. Eyes blinking, she rests on a hay bale with empty hands.

I'm mostly tired and not yet scared, not yet at all. But it is still on my heart, and he is at rest in front of me. So I ask him, and he answers.

'She was ours, Ruth. I couldn't leave her there, out in the cold. I couldn't just leave her all alone.'

And this is why Reuben finally moved.

March

March will not die quietly. There is a blizzard coming —
even after the early thaw, the sky aims to snow again. All that
mud and muck lining the roadsides, sticking to our boots,
will soon be layered with sparkling icy white. The blood was
revealed, but the snow will cover. It will all be beautiful again.

41

We couldn't have an open casket; Samuel was too torn up. Daddy kept saying, 'He's in there alright; don't you worry.' But I wasn't worried; last time I saw Samuel, he was pale and empty on the floor. It'd take more than a miracle to live through that, and I don't think we get many miracles around here anymore.

It is amazing, though, what a body can live through. Reuben told me once about some scientists that froze a rat and then thawed him out fifty years later. After he was melted, that little Lazarus remembered things from before he was frozen. It is a wonder that the rat could come back alive from the icy dead; I guess he wasn't really dead after all, just waiting. Now, I've seen a yearling deer froze to a fence post and leftover apples iced onto a tree, but I don't suppose neither was much good after the thaw.

Samuel didn't end up going down amongst the trees of Babylon; he didn't fill another secret grave behind the church. He was laid next to Grandma in the plot Ingwald had planned for himself. I was surprised we were able to get him in the ground. Must be the machines they got now for digging can break right through the deep frozen earth. In old times, folks had to predict the number of graves they would need over winter and dig them before the frost set in hard. I do wonder how they decided who would die. I also wonder when the thaw will come again to Failing. Spring takes her time in coming here, but I am happy to be kept waiting for a while.

Whatever is buried is meant to be revealed; whatever is secret is meant to be known. *With the measure you use, it will be measured to you — and even more. Whoever has will be given more; whoever does not have, even what he has will be taken from him.*

So I wait; I wait listening to the sound of my breath coming in and going out of my body. At the funeral, I asked my momma if she could hear me breathing. She said she couldn't, but it sounded so loud to me, I still think she could; I think they all could hear the sound of my lungs working.

I understand: just because you think you don't hear something don't mean it's not there. Maybe you just didn't listen close enough or maybe you just can't remember if you even tried to listen. Mom and Daddy keep bringing me forth on Sunday mornings to be anointed with oil during the prayers for the sick; they're keeping a close watch on me. Holding hands they stand, nearest to one another, together with me in our lonely pew. Reuben spends his Sundays running that trap line with Peter. They've got miles of line crisscrossing both my uncle's and my grandma's land.

I will feel better soon; I keep telling them that I will be better soon. I just need to get more sleep and stop pondering all the time about frogs freezing in the mud and thawing in the spring. I need to stop thinking about breathing, sweet air coming in and going out. I need to stop praying about Samuel in the deep, dark hole, and what is buried with him in his frozen brain. I ponder on blame and babies and bathwater and such. I wonder what is worse: creating life that will just die or destroying life that should not ever live? Who is guilty, the gardener or the snake? And who will carry this weight for eternity, Samuel or me?

Naomi ain't helping. While her parents wait upon the Lord with fasting and prayer, she has been staying with us, sleeping in my bed.

She lays in the crook of my arm and whispers all night. 'Did she breathe? Did she fly?'

I can't answer her questions, because I can't hear the answers.

I've got enough questions of my own. When those who have fallen asleep rise again to meet Christ in the sky, will their memories thaw and fly with them? Will I fly up to meet Jesus in the sky? I don't think I'll be sleeping tonight, neither. But at least I'll have Naomi laying by my side. From the beginning, from the first breath God gave man, God gave Naomi to me.

After my momma named me Ruth, Gloria thought it only right to name her miracle Naomi. They knew we would be friends forever, and I would follow Naomi and protect her wherever she would go. I have done my best to keep their promise to each other; I have done my best to keep Naomi safe.

My love for her burns within me like a flame; she is the child I carry within my heart. I am the lover of her soul; she will not be taken from me. I will be with Naomi, should the Lord tarry, until we lay down together and die. Even then, we will hold each other in death, breathless and asleep underneath the ice and snow and mud. We will hold each other and together never be alone.

AND HERE WE ARE AGAIN. NIGHTCRAWLER BABIES SLIDE UP through the mud, sniffing to see if they can smell spring on the air. This old birch, with her slippery new skin, has shot out three coiled tendrils, green infant branches spreading wide and swaying in the wind. Now I know which one is the innocent fawn and which one is the guilty thief. I wonder still why God didn't take the momma this time.

It sure ain't amazing grace, but it is sufficient, near enough.

My grace is sufficient for you,
for my power is made perfect in weakness.
2 Corinthians 12:9

Acknowledgements

Due to the highly allusive nature of *Sufficient Grace*, I am deeply indebted to the biblical, Norse and Ojibway stories and traditions represented. The work of the great hymn writers has had a profound effect on my life and my ear. Curriculum available from the School Violence Prevention Program under the auspice of the Native American Initiative of the Center for Civic Education is an excellent source for legends such as 'The Forsaken Brother'.

As this book began under the auspices of the Creative Writing MA program at the University of Melbourne, I would like to recognise the unwavering support of my supervisor, Marion May Campbell. Tony Birch, my Creative Writing PhD supervisor, was also instrumental in the development and extension of my work. The encouragement provided to me by the students, friends and mentors I met through the program was — and continues to be — invaluable. I owe special thanks to Josiane Behmoiras, Claire Thomas, Victoria Reeve, Kate Middleton, Olivia Fitzgibbon, and the Friday night gang. Also, I wish to recognise the members of Men's Group, including Michael Farrell, Julian Novitz, Kent MacCarter, Aaron Mannion and Emmett Stinson. Many other friends and colleagues have contributed to the manuscript, including

Michelle Walter, Penelope Goodes, Ali Lemer and Stefan Laszczuk.

Sections of *Sufficient Grace* were previously published in altered form; I appreciate the contribution of the editors of *Postgraduate Review*, *Strange*, *antiTHESIS* and *Wet Ink*.

My dear friends Michele Halvorson Michaels and Mike Kramer passed away during the writing of this book; I honour their memory. For those I have forgotten or cannot mention, I very much value your help.

Thanks also to the Felix Meyer Scholarship for Literature 2007, which granted funds for me to revise the manuscript. The Unpublished Manuscript Prize for an Emerging Victorian Writer in the 2009 Victorian Premier's Literary Awards also provided many opportunities for me, including meeting a dear friend, Catherine Harris; and my encouraging and expert agent, Clare Forster of Curtis Brown. I'm grateful for the entire team at Scribe Publications, including the graciously meticulous Ian See. The guidance, insistence and understanding of my editor and publisher, Aviva Tuffield, have remained steady throughout a very difficult time. Without her belief in me and the manuscript, I may have never finished the book. My gratitude is permanent.

I wish to acknowledge the steadfast support of my family, especially my siblings Ryan, Lori and May, their families, and my parents Byron and Judith. My father taught me to hunt and fish, and my mother taught me to read and love; all of these skills were necessary to write this book. The love and care of my family in Australia, especially Brad Turner and Aaron Mannion, carried me throughout the creation of *Sufficient Grace*. Brad, you brought me here. Aaron, you kept me here; you are my favourite writer and my best friend.

Finally, I appreciate that although this is a work of fiction, people close to me — now or in the past — may read this novel as a betrayal of both the family and church in which I was raised. I have not intended to cause any hurt. I wrote what I was given to write.